SONG OF SERENITY

What Reviewers Say
About Brey Willows's Work

Changing Course

"Comsos dust and prowler balls, this was good. The romance is exactly what a good love story should be like. ...This was an exciting adventure with a satisfying romance. A quick read that kept me turning pages. A story with a lot of heart."—*Bookvark*

"*Changing Course* is a wonderful book about intergalactic love between two people who were never supposed to meet and how a once chance meeting changed the course of both their lives forever."—*Les Rêveur*

Spinning Tales

"This was a charming read! I liked the main character and the way the fairy tale realm works. I also found some of the problems and solutions to be quite funny and fun to read. This is a good read for those who like fairy tales and retellings."—*Fierce Female Reads*

Fury's Bridge

"[*Fury's Bridge*] is a paranormal read that's not like any other. The premise is unique with some intriguing ideas. The main character is witty, strong and interesting."—Melina Bickard, Librarian (Waterloo Library, London)

Fury's Death

"This series has been getting steadily better as it's progressed."
—*The Good, the Bad, and the Unread*

Fury's Choice

"As with the first in the series, this book is part romance, part paranormal adventure, with a lot of humor and thought-provoking words on religion, belief, and self-determination thrown in. ...It is real page-turning stuff."—*Rainbow Reading Room*

"*Fury's Choice* is a refreshing and creative endeavor. The story is populated with flawed and retired gods, vengeful Furies, delightful and thought-provoking characters who give our perspective of religion a little tweak. As tension builds, the story becomes an action-packed adventure. The love affair between Tis and Kera is enchanting. The bad guys are rotten to the core as one might expect. Willows uses well placed wit and humor to enhance the story and break the tension, which masterfully increases as the story progresses."—*Lambda Literary*

Chosen

"If I had a checklist with all the elements that I want to see in a book, *Chosen* could satisfy each item. The characters are so completely relatable, the action scenes are cinematic, the plot kept me on my toes, the dystopian theme is entirely relevant, and the romance is sweet and sexy."—*Lesbian Review*

"This is an absolutely excellent example of speculative dystopian fiction. ...The main characters are both excellent; sympathetic, interesting, intelligent, well rounded within the context of their situation. Their physical chemistry is great, the slow burn romance which follows behind is a wonderful read, and a great cliff-hanger to match the will they/won't they of the Chosen. Whether you like fantasy or not you should give this book a go. The romance is spot-on, the world building excellent and the whole is just speculative fiction at its best."—*Curve*

The Fury Trilogy

"The whole is an intriguing concept, light and playfully done but well researched and constructed, with enough ancient and mythological detail to make it work without ever becoming a theology lesson. …Brey Willows has created an amusing cast from Fates and Furies to the gods of old. The gods are extremely well done, literally personifying the characteristics we associate with them, drawn with wit and humour, they are exactly who we would expect them to be. …Thoroughly enjoyed these; romances with a difference, fantasy set in the here and now with an interesting twist."—*Lesbian Reading Room*

Visit us at www.boldstrokesbooks.com

By the Author

SONG OF SERENITY

by
Brey Willows

2021

ISBN 13: 978-1-63679-015-2

This Trade Paperback Original Is Published By
Bold Strokes Books, Inc.
P.O. Box 249
Valley Falls, NY 12185

First Edition: December 2021

Credits
Editor: Cindy Cresap
Production Design: Susan Ramundo
Cover Design By Tammy Seidick

Acknowledgments

Thank you, as always, to the Bold Strokes team for all you do. To my editor, Cindy, who always makes my books better and sends insanely encouraging emails that help keep my impostor syndrome at bay. To Sandy, for never telling me off when I ask about dates and about pitching a nine-book series. And to every reader who likes a bit of fantasy in their lives, thank you.

Dedication

To my buddy of all things, my best friend,
my reason for getting up every day.
You are my muse.

"We have mistaken the common livery of the age for the vesture of the Muses and spend our days in the sordid streets and hideous suburbs of our vile cities when we should be out on the hillside with Apollo. Certainly we are a degraded race, and have sold our birth right for a mess of facts."

Oscar Wilde, *Beautiful and Impossible Things*

Chapter One

Calliope Ardalides walked up to her house on the far side of the Afterlife, Inc. campus and straight past the god munching a candy bar on her porch. He watched her, wiping crumbs from his frizzy white beard, but she ignored him.

"Calliope—"

"No. I've already told you. Find someone else to pester." She opened the door and didn't bother to close it behind her. He'd come in anyway, and this way he didn't break it, the way he did the last time she slammed it in his face.

"You muses are the most stubborn creatures ever created." He trundled in after her, opening yet another bar of chocolate.

"Zeus, if you were human, you'd be fat as a winter pig and twice as unhealthy." She grimaced as he shoved the wrapper in the pocket of his sweatshirt. "And must you go around looking like a homeless god who hasn't showered this eon? Don't you have an image to uphold?"

He tugged at the wrinkled sweatshirt and brushed some smudge from the thigh of his worn jeans. "I'm off duty. And as head of Afterlife and your father, I'm ordering you to listen to me."

She shifted a load of files from one section of her desk to another, making way for yet more. "I'm three thousand years old. I have to listen to all of you squabble all day long, thanks to a fury deciding that the muse of justice should be an arbitrator once again. I no longer have to take orders from my father."

"Ha!" Zeus pointed at her. "But you do have to take orders from your boss."

"I have to listen to you. I don't have to take orders from you."

He started to spark, tiny lightning bolts zapping between his fingers. "All I want—"

"I know what you want. You want me to tilt the scales a little, allow your followers more leeway so you gain more followers than your brothers. Because you've been in competition since the day the Titans vomited you forth."

"Yes! It's not too much to ask, is it?"

She sighed and reminded herself to be calm. His zapping temper tantrums could set fire to paperwork, and she didn't have time for that. "You know full well it's too much to ask. If I do it for you, and the other gods found out, I'd have to do it for them too. And then you'd need more, and the circle would continue. Or, if I didn't do it for them, I'd lose all credibility and be unable to arbitrate the way I need to." She held up a sheet of paper. "Now, unless you'd like to sit with me and go through the complaints I've received recently about the way you've been answering prayers…"

He held up his hands and backed toward the door. "Keep those to yourself. I'll come on my day, and not a day sooner. You're an unfaithful daughter." His smile took the sting from his words.

She waved him away and slid into her office chair as soon as he was gone. The piece of paper was actually a list of things she wanted to take on vacation with her next week and had nothing to do with his complaint forms, although there were plenty of those. Pushing herself up from her desk, she wondered when she'd ever felt so tired. Surely when she was working as a muse in ancient Greece it hadn't been this hard.

She was on her way to the kitchen for a strong cup of coffee when someone knocked, so she turned aside to get the door.

"Themis!" Calliope went to stand back so she could come in, but it didn't work. Themis, the goddess of justice, pulled her into a strong embrace. She knew full well that Calliope wasn't big on physical affection, but she insisted it was a necessary part of existence.

Wriggling away, Calliope shook her head at Themis's laughter and led the way to the living room, where Themis flung herself on the couch and got comfortable as Calliope made coffee.

"Are you excited?" Themis asked.

"Excited?"

"About going away. How long has it been?"

Calliope thought about it. "Only about twenty years, I think. And it was mostly normal work until the furies brought about all the changes." The last five years had been full of transformation. The three fury sisters, Alec, Meg, and Tisera, had brought about the biggest changes in human history. Namely, they'd brought the gods out of the heavens and onto the soil, and now they moved among people as they'd once done in ancient Greece, but even more so now. It had dramatically and not terribly creatively been deemed the Merge, as the immortal realms and human realms came together. From that time forward new laws were constantly being enacted and Themis had definitively turned down the role Calliope had taken as a challenge. Little had she known how great the challenge would be.

"Only twenty years? Two decades since you took a vacation?" Themis accepted her cup of coffee and sniffed appreciatively. "I took two in the last six months. Hell, the new contract states every employee at Afterlife gets at least three a year. Why doesn't that apply to you?"

Calliope began separating the folders she had piled on the coffee table. "It does apply to me. I simply don't have the time to get away. I really appreciate you stepping in to cover my role while I'm gone. I lost my patience with a few newbie gods the other day and told them to work it out themselves. Not terribly professional of me and a good indication it's time for a break." She held up a small stack of files with purple labels. "These are the god-to-god complaints. There are the usual ones involving Zeus, Hades, and Poseidon. Ignore them, and don't let them bully you into making changes while I'm gone. The more serious ones are coming from the Hindu and Muslim sections, which are having some teething problems with the new system. You might have to deal with those." She held up another, much fatter stack. "These are the human-to-god complaints. Prayers not answered or answered in such a way the human isn't pleased."

"When are humans ever pleased?" Themis pulled a sheet out of the top file and scanned it, then began to laugh. "Ganesh turned someone into a platypus?"

Calliope frowned, not really seeing the humor in it. "The human prayed to be a better swimmer, like water would just flow off them, and so they could beat their opponents like they'd been drugged, they'd fall so far behind." She put a red circle around the number at the top. "So Ganesh thought it would be funny to turn them into an animal that swims extraordinarily well and can also deliver venom from a hind leg."

Themis continued to laugh. "You can't fault his creativity."

"You can if the poor creature lives in the desert and meant they wanted to swim in swimming pools." She pointed to the red circle. "I mark them according to level of guilt. Red for most definitely, orange for uncertain, and green for not at fault. There are very few green circles."

Themis eyed the piles of folders over her coffee cup. "And then?"

"Each god has a monthly appointment with me to go over their complaint forms. If they're guilty, they have to make amends. If I'm uncertain, we'll discuss it, and I'll usually let them off with a warning." She sat back and tapped a pile with her toe. "The god-to-god complaints I save for the last Wednesday of the month. I call in the complainers, listen to each side, and give a verdict. They have to abide by it thanks to my new role here. If they contest it, they have to take it up with Tisera, and that fury is less flexible than I am."

"And if it's more serious?"

Calliope motioned vaguely toward the main building. "That goes to all three of the fury sisters or the fates. I don't need to handle the huge stuff, just the daily things."

Themis tucked her legs under her. "And your music?"

Calliope glanced at the harp in the corner and felt the loss of it. "I don't have time."

"That's a travesty. I've never heard a more beautiful voice."

She waved the words away like the nonsense they were. "You know my sister Poly's voice is more beautiful than mine. And the sirens are stunning, too."

"Poly's voice is beautiful but it's always sad. She never sings anything fun, just songs about being good and faithful and praying. Such a bore." She grinned. "And the sirens sing so they can kill people, which is a downer too. You sing because you love to sing, and whatever it is brings a sense of peace."

"I'm the muse of justice and serenity. I should hope it brings people peace." She closed her eyes and rested her head on the sofa. "I've never been so weary. I don't think peace is part of this world."

Themis reached over to squeeze her hand. "And that, my dear, is why we need vacations." She set down her coffee cup and stood. "I'll be here before you leave in the morning, but write down any more instructions you think of. Then go, and don't come back for at least two weeks. I promise I'll call if things get out of hand, but you're leaving your work in the hands of the goddess of justice. I promise I'm capable."

Calliope finally smiled. "I know full well, and remember that if you ever decide you want to come down from Olympus and take over my job, I'll gladly hand it over."

Themis pulled her in for another strong hug. "Not on your life, sweet one."

Calliope closed the door behind her and leaned against it. She moved quickly to her bedroom and set her suitcase on the bed. It was only half packed, as she hadn't been certain she'd actually go. But Themis was right. It was time to find her song again, to find peace and serenity in her own being. She'd become her job, and that was something humans were supposed to do, not immortals. At the Temple of the Muses, she'd once again remember who, and what, she was.

Chapter Two

"Why do I let you talk me into this shit?"
Jordan James raised her face to the warmth of the sun. There was nothing like it this high in the Swiss Alps. "Because you adore me and would do anything to see me smile."

"Fuck off." Austin tightened the nylon straps around her legs. "I get nothing from our friendship except terror and killer doses of your ego. I'm officially retiring as your best friend. If I don't die first."

"You won't die. You'll be harnessed to the cable all the way across. And if you do, then I'll accept your resignation." Jordan looked over the edge. They'd already been climbing the Via Ferrata, the highest and longest adventure climb in Switzerland, for the last two and a half hours. She'd been looking forward to this part the most. The steel cable stretched across the gorge, nearly a mile above the raging river below, which from this height looked like a piece of string. They'd hold onto one cable at shoulder height while stepping on another, and then inch their way across the mile-long gorge. They'd almost be walking on air.

Austin rested her hands on her thighs, breathing deeply. "I'm going to have a panic attack. I can't do this."

Jordan patted her shoulder. "Well, you can't go backward. It's a one-way system, and you wouldn't be able to go down those ladders or step out onto those steel pegs in the rock face from this direction. So, forward you go!" She moved to the edge of the cables and tugged on her carabiner to make sure it was clipped in. Her heart raced as she took the first step onto the cable and felt it thrum under her boots. She lived for this feeling, this rush of adrenaline brought on by her constant battle with nature to see who would win out. She hadn't walked away from a challenge yet. "Look, I'm going first. Just follow along, and we'll be on the other side headed toward that cave with the waterfall in no time."

In truth, Austin did look ghostly. "I swear to God I'm not doing this with you ever again. Next time, we're going to the spa where the only thing I'm in danger of is picking the wrong wine."

Jordan filtered her out as she crept along the steel cables. She looked down, and there was nothing between her and a mile drop except a piece of cable not much bigger than her wrist. A breeze swept over her, moving the hair at the base of her neck, and she shivered happily. She felt the cable shift slightly when Austin stepped out, but she kept looking forward, and sometimes down because she liked the way it made her heart race, and her knees buckle slightly. It was the body's natural flight reaction, one she'd learned to ignore as she raced down mountains, jumped out of helicopters, and flung herself from cliffs with a big kite strapped to her back. It was over too soon, and she was back on solid granite once again, making her way around the cliff face to the next ladder. There wasn't time to stop and chat, since there were other climbers spread out behind them.

They made it to the cave with the waterfall, and Jordan stopped to take a couple of selfies and photos of the beautiful space. Tall granite walls played with shadows as crystal clear water sluiced from a gash in the rock above them, seeming to come from nowhere, disappearing over the edge into a waterfall that couldn't be seen from the cave itself, though the crashing of the water was clear and loud. She posted the pics right away. If something did go wrong, and accidents happened on these kinds of adventures, then at least her photos would remain out in the world as opposed to on an obliterated phone at the bottom of a canyon. Beauty like this should be shared.

Five and a half hours after they'd begun the climb, they made it to the top. A group already there shared their champagne, and Austin flung herself dramatically in the snow, to everyone's amusement. Jordan threw a snowball at her, which was mostly ice thanks to the fact that they were on top of a glacier. Austin sat up and half-heartedly flung one back, which led to a lazy snowball fight among all those who'd made it to the top.

Jordan loved moments like these. Sitting on a mountaintop with other people who pushed themselves physically just for the simple joy of it. Adventurers who loved nature and seeing what their bodies were capable of in the face of its unforgiving beauty. Soon, it was deemed time to get going so they wouldn't be up there after dark, and she gave Austin a hand up.

"I feel like my thigh muscles have steel rods in them." Austin limped forward.

"It's awesome, isn't it? I love when my body hurts like this." Jordan twisted and stretched as they made their way down the glacier, an easy walk through thin snow and tumbled stone.

"There's something fundamentally wrong with you. You need a shrink." Austin kicked at a stone.

"C'mon, you have to admit that was fun." Jordan turned and looked up. "Look how high we were!"

Austin glanced over her shoulder and then stopped to really look. "All right. You're right. It was incredible, and I can't believe I made it."

Jordan raised her arms in victory. "I knew it!"

Austin pushed her forward. "Jordan James, always right. What I'm most excited about right now is that thermal spa at the end of this walk."

"Me too."

They traipsed on, silent as good friends can be, and made their way to the hotel and spa that catered to people who were doing the Via Ferrata. It was another reason Jordan liked this particular adventure choice. Not only did she get to do the physically punishing climb with other people who were like her, but after, she got to talk about the climb, reliving it and hearing other people's experiences of it. She liked to do that with any extreme adventure she took on, and the hotel made it that much easier. And Austin was right, the thermal spa was a huge bonus. Austin joined a group of women who were drinking wine and laughing, but Jordan wandered off to the pools in the shadows where it was quiet.

She sank into the hot water and stared at the night sky full of stars. Although she knew it was rare for it to happen this far south, she'd hoped to see the northern lights while she was here. But not tonight. Just a clear sky, laughter echoing around her, and nowhere to be for the next two days. She closed her eyes and let her body float until she sensed someone else getting in.

"Do you mind? The other pools are a little loud."

The world was full of gods and goddesses now, and Jordan had a minute to wonder if the beauty who'd just gotten into the pool with her was one of them. The little white string bikini was barely worth wearing, except that it highlighted the woman's caramel brown skin perfectly. Jordan pulled her body into a sitting position and winced when bubbles floated up from her swim trunks. "By all means. Please."

The woman's smile was flirty and sexy, and Jordan's nipples grew hard under her sports bra.

"You were ahead of me on the trail today." The woman leaned back, the lights from the pool highlighting that the bikini was see-through.

"Was I?" Concentrating on word-things was going to be difficult.

"You were fearless." She held out her hand. "I'm Rosa."

"Jordan." She shook her hand and grinned slightly when Rosa didn't pull it away.

"You moved like a mountain goat, and you didn't even hesitate when you stepped out over the gorge." Rosa floated closer, until her thigh rested against Jordan's.

"Good to know you liked what you saw." This trip was getting infinitely better.

"I do."

There seemed little enough left to say that wasn't being said with body language. Jordan lifted herself from the pool and held out her hand, which Rosa quickly accepted. They draped towels around themselves and headed to Jordan's room.

The next two days were a blur of sex, relaxing with massages and in the thermal pools, and a quick hike up the glacier at dawn to get some photos. She checked her email a few times to make sure her next trip was in place, and then she and Austin headed for the shuttle that would take them to the airport.

"Are you going to call her when we get back?" Austin asked.

Jordan took a bite of her granola bar and shrugged. "She gave me a kiss that would have melted the last glacier on earth and said it had been fun. She didn't give me her number, and I didn't give her mine."

Austin took out a packet of crackers and offered one to Jordan. "I don't know how you do it. You have hot sex, and you never get attached. I want to marry them by our second cup of coffee."

"Maybe that's the problem. Stop going for coffee first."

Austin threw a cracker at her, and they were quiet for the rest of the ride to the airport. Jordan loved her life. She was free to do whatever she wanted, whenever she wanted. No one told her things were too dangerous or made any demands on her time. And if, sometimes, it got a little lonely, she just made plans for the next trip.

CHAPTER THREE

Calliope closed her eyes and listened to the trill of the birds in the trees and the rushing of the River Tweed. Her cottage was at the far end of a single-track road bordered by thick hedges and tall pine trees. The last house on the lane, it had an unimpeded view of the river, the green pedestrian suspension bridge, the temple, and was pretty much perfect in every way.

She sat in her Adirondack deck chair, the book she'd brought forgotten on her lap. It had taken a couple of days to leave work behind, and now she couldn't fathom why it had taken so long to get here. Afterlife seemed a million worlds away, as did the rivalries, human foibles, and mountains of paperwork. She rolled her neck and caught sight of a deer staring at her from the trees.

"Hello, lovely."

It left the trees and was followed by two babies. It came to her and snuffed her hair and she laughed softly. "I'll see what I can find." She rose and went inside, where she cut an apple into pieces. She sat down again and let the mother and babies take the apple from her palms. The simplicity of the moment brought tears to her eyes. She couldn't remember the last time she'd seen anything other than seagulls, crows, or pigeons. LA wasn't a haven for wildlife, and she wasn't fond of skunks.

Done with their apples, the trio wandered off to graze, but didn't go far. Sunlight filtered through the trees, lighting a path along the river that brought back memories of simpler, quieter times. When the gods had begun to move among humans five years ago, it had brought enormous changes. Many were good, some were difficult. Others were awful, like when people couldn't handle the immortals and questions of existence and it slowly drove them crazy. She used to walk among humans as a muse, inspiring them to greater beauty and a deeper sense of justice. Now she shifted complaint forms from one pile to the next.

"Ms. Calli, how are you today, lovey?"

She looked up, welcoming the move from her morose thoughts, and smiled at the farmer who owned the cottage next door, as well as the land above them that covered the old earl's property. "Duncan, how are you?"

He tipped his tweed cap and poked his walking stick at the ground. "Well now, I've come with a wee bit of news."

She motioned to the chair next to hers. No one ever used it, but buying only one had seemed sad, somehow. Now she was glad she had it. He settled into it with a sigh and pulled off his cap, then took his pipe from his coat pocket. He motioned with it, his question clear, and she nodded.

He lit the match and held it to the tobacco. "Word has it," he said, and puffed, "that the Bemersyde Estate has sold."

She frowned. "I didn't know it was for sale."

"It wasn't." He puffed again, looking at the river. "But some corporation from America came and made an offer. You know the farmland has been untended since the big food corps made farming out here so hard. And what with Brexit, well, Bemersyde decided it was a good deal. Didn't talk to any of us, of course. Just went on ahead, as folks are wont to do these days."

"They bought all of it? All twelve hundred acres? What are they going to do with it?"

He shook his head, still puffing on his pipe. "Haven't heard." He smiled at the trio of deer watching them from the shadows of the pine tree. "You've got friends."

She smiled. "Let's hope whoever bought the land appreciates them the way we do." If the land had only just sold, it would likely be years before the new company did anything with it. She'd have her sanctuary undisturbed. Why then, did she have a sense of foreboding?

She and Duncan talked about local doings and who had moved in and who had left. The village changed like the banks of a river; slowly and surely, but not always noticeably. In the hundred years she'd had the cottage, the village hadn't changed all that much. Soon, he stood and stretched, leaning on his walking stick.

"I'm off. Good to have you back. You staying for a bit?"

"A few weeks, at most."

He tilted his head toward the hill. "Going to see about the temple?"

He rarely mentioned the temple. It was another fact she loved about being here. They knew who and what she was, thanks to a special edition news report the demigod Selene had done on the muses, but no one seemed to care all that much. They'd known her before the news report, and so after, they simply knew what her real job was. They treated her much the same as they did the other villagers. "Is there something I should know?"

He relit his pipe and puffed, the lines in his face deepening like creases in a paper bag. "Nothing untoward, don't think." He gave her a wink. "You've brought a bit of something special, that's all."

She raised her eyebrows but didn't ask anything and returned his wave as he ambled off down the road toward his place. The sun had set and turned the sky into an artist's palette of sherbet pastels. It was a good time for a walk. She went into the cottage and got a scarf and light jacket, then headed across the street and up the dirt path that led to the temple. She'd allowed herself the time to settle her soul before going to the temple, as she wanted to arrive at it with a more open heart than she'd had when she arrived.

On top of Bass Hill was the Temple of the Muses, built in the eighteen hundreds. The nine marble pillars on the circular plinth had originally surrounded statues of her and her sisters, and Apollo, their boss. She'd been friends with the poet who had inspired the earl to build the temple, and she and the earl had spent many nights discussing his poetry. He'd built the temple not only as a tribute to the poet, but to her and her sisters who inspired the creation of beautiful art. That was also when the earl had sold her the little cottage on the edge of his property, excited at the prospect of a muse living so close.

But then, in a time of economic need many years after the earl's death, the statues had been stolen, leaving the temple bare and forgotten. To her knowledge, they'd still never turned up.

The village had eventually restored it with personification statues of the four seasons, a poor substitute, in Calliope's opinion. The women of the seasons were ephemeral and hard to pin down, prone to tantrums and inconsistency. At least the muses were constant. Once the gods at Afterlife had come out into the open, the village had decided that the temple should be restored to its former glory and used as an actual temple instead of simply a sculpture dedicated to a poet in a tiny village few people came across. The four seasons hadn't even known of its existence, probably saving the village from freak storms and flooding. Statues representing the nine muses had once again been put in place between the pillars, and the four seasons sculpture had been moved to the Museum of Weather's forecourt in Edinburgh.

Even in the dusk light, she could see how different it looked from the last time she'd been there. Incense drifted on the breeze and candlelight sent shadows skittering over the statues, making them seem almost lifelike. The grounds around the temple had been cleared of weeds and planted with flowers of all kinds. The haphazard path, once made up of stone and tree roots, had been smoothed and refitted with steps. She bent to sniff a particularly beautiful rose and then made her way into the small open space.

Gifts were piled around the feet of the statues, much like those that had been left for the gods in their temples over the years. Bunches of flowers, symbolic instruments, letters, and even some food, had been left as people knelt to ask the muses to guide them in their creative endeavors. Thankfully, no one was there now, and Calliope could read some of the pleas in peace.

They were touching, many of them. People who wanted to sing with passion, who wanted to write with their souls, who wanted to paint so the world could feel more deeply. Those were things she understood, and she piled those letters at the side. Others made her wince, and she left them where they were. The ones pleading for fame, who wanted to be pop stars and celebrities everyone knew, the ones who wanted to make millions from whatever it was they wanted to create—those she left where they were.

A branch breaking made her look up. A young woman, probably not much more than seventeen, stood staring at her, as though trying to decide whether or not to say anything.

"Hello." Calliope stood and picked up her pile of letters.

"Those aren't yours." The girl motioned toward the letters. "They were left by people asking for stuff."

Calliope smiled, sensing the fire in the girl, and pleased that someone cared enough to speak up. "Ordinarily, you'd be right." She turned slightly and looked over the statues. "But that one there? That's me." She grimaced slightly. "Not much resemblance, I don't think, but you can always tell because in all my statues I'm holding a writing tablet. To this day I don't know why."

The girl took a step back, her pale blue eyes wide. "You're the Dryburgh muse."

That was a new one, but she didn't mind it. "I am, I suppose. My name's Calliope. What's yours?"

The girl stared at her for a moment before answering. "Iona."

"Well, Iona, I think it's wonderful you look out for the temple."

She tilted her head, still looking like she might bolt. "Do you answer?" She nodded again to the letters in Calliope's hand. "When people ask?"

It was a thorny question, but the truth was always better than a lie. A lie found its way to the light every time. "Not in the way the gods do, no. We can't hear prayers."

She looked utterly let down. "There's no point to all this, then?"

Calliope lifted the letters. "Oh, but there is. I'll take these and give them to my sisters, whichever one the request applies to. And maybe my sisters can find these people and help them. You see, to help people, to be their muse, we have to be near them. The gods can answer prayers from anywhere. But a muse…" How odd, to be standing in a temple explaining to a teenager what she was, what she did.

"But you haven't been here in a long time." Her tone was almost accusatory.

"No, I haven't. But my sisters come by, sometimes, to check in. Although, come to think of it, they probably haven't been in a long time either. And recently, someone has been sending the letters in a package to Afterlife every few months." She smiled. "Is that you, who sends them?"

Iona shrugged, a teenage shrug of embarrassment at having been caught doing something good. "Seemed only right."

The letters were warm and sweet in her hand, like carrying a batch of spring tulips. "I didn't see your name on any of these. And I don't remember seeing your name on them at the office, either." Something about Iona, about the girl's wild, copper hair and light eyes, the way her spirit almost seemed like a wild thing wanting to blow through the forest, called to Calliope. The girl needed a muse to let out the passion threatening to burst from her, even if she didn't know it.

"I have to go. Night." And with that, she turned and loped down the path toward the suspension bridge that led over the river to the village of St. Boswells.

Bemused, Calliope watched her go, and noticed the slight shadow attached to her left side. There was something amiss, something that had damaged her spirit. That kind of thing could spread, taking over a person's soul until there was nothing creative or passionate left, just a bleak desert of gray existence.

She had two weeks, and she had a feeling she'd see more of Iona. She breathed in the incense and stretched to touch the domed roof of the temple. It had taken on new life and the stone hummed with the words and desires of the people who left a part of themselves there.

As she made her way back to the cottage in the dim twilight, she began to hum. By the time she got to the cottage, she was singing, something she hadn't done in far, far too long.

Chapter Four

Back home in Northern California, Jordan rolled out her plans and stood looking over them with her architect and sister, Ramona, at her side. "What do you think?"

"I think you're a nutcase for wanting to do it in Scotland. It's rainy and gray for most of the year. I went in June once and I was wearing a ski jacket. I've never been so cold, and I've been dog sledding in the Arctic." Romana's sharp gaze followed the lines of the plans. "But as far as the park itself goes, I think you're ready to go. We've got surveyors there waiting to go over the cave systems with you, and an architect and land planner who will work with your teams on the other parts."

"Excellent." Jordan couldn't wait to get there and get things running.

"But remember you need to meet with their government official as soon as you get there. They insisted on meeting you and discussing your plans from an environmental position in person. They haven't issued their planning permission yet, and until you have the permits, you have a lot of land and nothing to do with it. But if that's the case, you've got thirty days to pull out. You'll need to turn on all that butch charm people seem to like."

Jordan carefully rolled up the plans and put them back in the tube, then placed it on her luggage. "I've been to Scotland several times. The people are really friendly, but I'm not sure if they like me or if they just find me entertaining as some kind of American oddity. Either way, I'll win them over. I want this so bad."

Ramona kissed her cheek before she picked up her handbag and headed toward the door. "I know you do, and you always get what you want. Aunt Sue would be proud, you know. Be sure you call me when you get there and let me know how things are going. I can video in if you want me to talk to your Scottish contacts about anything." She opened the door and stopped for a second. "Don't forget to come home, okay?"

Jordan stopped what she was doing and looked up at the vulnerable tone in Ramona's voice. She also understood the reason for it. "You know I'll be back. And you can come out any time you want to. Say the word."

Ramona smiled, but she looked sad. "I'm going to miss you, big sister. You only just got back from your climbing trip and now you're off again. One day maybe you'll stay home long enough to visit the family."

Jordan winced but put a smile in place so it didn't show. "Get out of here. Tell Dad I said hi and I'll see everyone when I get back."

Ramona blew her a kiss and left, closing the door softly behind her.

It wasn't that she didn't want to visit her family. It was just that since the gods had come out, family squabbles over belief systems had become an extra dinner companion that Jordan didn't care for. And since her mother had died, she couldn't bear to think about where she'd gone once she'd left them. Jordan wasn't at all interested in the afterlife; it was this one that mattered. Focusing on the next one meant missing out on the only one she might have, and that wasn't about to happen.

Jordan checked her passport and documents one last time. She had everything she needed, and she'd set off in plenty of time in the morning. She never minded sitting at airports. She liked walking around, people watching, munching whatever bad food she could get her hands on, and buying novelty things she didn't need as well as magazines she probably wouldn't read. Even the transfer flights didn't bother her. It gave her a chance to get another glimpse of the earth from thirty thousand feet, and she was always in awe at the beauty below her. It was an overnight flight, so she'd sleep through a chunk of it anyway. But even the airport was part of the adventure.

She threw a couple more thermal shirts in her suitcase, as well as a waterproof pair of hiking boots. Once she was packed and everything was by the door, she stood in her living room, at a loss as to what to do next. There wasn't any point in looking over the plans again. There wasn't anyone to call and talk to except her family, and she couldn't handle that right now.

She wandered into the kitchen and opened a few cupboards, trying to decide if she wanted something to eat, but nothing sounded good, and all she had was canned food. She'd already cleaned out the fridge and sent the few things she had with Ramona so they didn't go to waste.

Irritated at the creeping loneliness, she grabbed her keys and headed out. She'd get back in plenty of time to get some sleep before her trip, but there wasn't any reason she couldn't have some good old-fashioned San Francisco fun before she left.

She kept the top down on the two-seater convertible that was totally impractical but something she couldn't part with. She loved the speed and the wind in her hair, especially as she drove along the bay. Subtle colored lights lit the stone and glass walls of the two-story building that looked out onto the Pacific Ocean, and she relaxed as she pulled up in front of the valet. The woman took her keys and gave her a sexy little smile.

She loved San Francisco for a variety of reasons, and the excess of hot lesbian women was definitely top of the list. The bouncer opened the door for her, and the grumble from the people waiting in line was shut out when he closed the door behind her.

"Well, Jordan James. Be still my black heart." The bartender leaned over the bar and kissed Jordan's cheek. "What brings you slumming?"

Jordan looked around. "You've really let this place go, Lynda. I mean, how can you pick up a seedy woman in a place so clean you can see your reflection in the floor?"

Floor to ceiling windows provided a perfect view of the bay and the huge glass bottom deck allowed for a view of the water as it crashed and pushed its way around the thick steel pillars below. Black, white, and steel would have made the ultra-modern interior cold, but the colored lights against the walls along with the sexy colorful paintings of women in different positions throughout made it enticing and sensual. Jordan loved it so much she'd decorated her apartment similarly. It was a place that suggested sex, not marriage.

Lynda slid a glass of whisky in front of her. "You sticking around for a while this time?"

Jordan relished the burn of whisky in her throat and couldn't wait to taste the real thing when she got to Scotland. "Nah. You know me. I'm off to the UK tomorrow."

Lynda shook her head and wiped at a nonexistent spot on the bar. "You're one of the most rootless people I know."

"Rootless?"

"You go wherever the wind takes you. You could live anywhere, go anywhere. No one and nothing will ever tie you down."

"Here's willing." She raised her glass in a toast, but the words had tiny spikes, like the thorns on a rose, that pricked at that sense of loneliness that had been niggling at her soul.

No matter. Her life was awesome. Who needed roots when you had the world at your fingertips?

Lynda moved on to another patron and Jordan turned to survey the bar. Women chatted quietly at tables, laughter occasionally filtering through the ocean scented air. She considered heading upstairs to the dance floor where she could lose herself in the thumping bass, but it wasn't exactly what she wanted tonight. Like opening her kitchen cupboards, she simply couldn't decide on what it was she was craving. Instead, she took her drink and headed outside.

She leaned on the railing of the deck. The moon laid a path along the water, like a yellow brick road leading her somewhere far away. The thing was, she was always walking that path, but there was never a wizard at the end to tell her where home was. Lynda was right. Although Jordan's family was here and she loved them, this wasn't her home. But what was home, anyway? A place to sleep. A place to keep your stuff. A place to have sex. Those things could be anywhere, and the less stuff you had, the freer you were to have your run of the planet.

She sensed someone beside her and smiled when another glass of whisky was placed on the railing in front of her.

"You look like you could use a friend."

She looked over the woman wearing a dress that might actually be painted on, since her nipples were rock hard and extremely visible. Jordan looked away from them and smiled over the rim of her glass. "I think you're right."

Chapter Five

The Mainstreet Trading Book Shop was one of the handful of shops on the main street in St. Boswells. Fortunately, it was attached at the back to the Mainstreet Deli, which made for a good combination. Calliope walked the mile footpath from her cottage to the bookshop, where she browsed for at least an hour. The owner, who had likely owned the shop since it was built in the eighteen hundreds, if the wrinkled clothing and ink-stained fingers were anything to go by, was polite but quiet, which suited Calliope well. Like librarians, real bookshop owners seemed to understand the inherent link between quiet and books that was necessary to properly traverse other worlds via the pages of someone's imagination.

She bought one romance novel, one travel book, and one book on ancient philosophy, which she then took with her into the deli section attached at the back, an open mishmash of wood tables and odd chairs. The bookseller handled this area, too, explaining that his wife usually took on that side, as she was more of a people person, but their daughter needed help with the sheep and so his wife was in a field nearby. He gave all this information with succinct vowels and no hesitations, and then promptly moved into the bookshop after he'd delivered her piece of Guinness cake and her beautifully smelling latte. Created, he said, from the finest local coffee beans.

Coffee beans didn't grow in Scotland. But she decided not to tell him that.

She slid into the pages of the philosophy text first, a combination of old philosophers and modern, and it brought tears to her eyes. How she'd loved listening to Plato quiz Socrates. It had been a time of questions and searching for truth, and she'd been proud to be the muse involved in their questions on justice and equality. Of course, equality didn't mean what it did now. But it had been the beginning of something special. She'd forgotten those days sitting under the hot Greek sun in the open spaces where men would gather to listen. Women weren't allowed, technically, but no one chased them away, either. It made for wonderful discussions among the women once they were home and gathered in the gynaikon, the courtyard just for women.

With a deep, satisfied sigh, she leaned back in the creaky wood chair and finished the last of her latte. She picked up her books, sure to place the romance novel in the middle where it was less conspicuous, and made her way through the bookstore once more, intending to head home and watch the sunset paint the river. The door opened, the little bell announcing someone's entrance, and she looked up.

Her heart stuttered and she nearly tripped over a pile of glossy books waiting to be shelved. The woman who had walked in was something straight out of a lesbian romance novel, which were all the rage now. She'd lost herself in one or two when she'd needed a bit of escapism over the last year. Tall and muscular, the stranger had short brown hair was cut tight on the sides and back but left a little long on top so it fell over one eye in a rakish style that reminded Calliope of the pirates she'd once sailed with in the fifteen hundreds.

She stayed where she was, tucked between the cookbooks and automotive guides.

"Hi." The woman was clearly American. "I was wondering if you have a Starbucks in the area?"

The bookshop owner looked at her a little blankly. "Edinburgh, I suppose."

The woman winced. "Okay. Is there anywhere to get coffee? The bakery has already closed."

He tilted his head toward the back. "Aye."

She waited for more, but when none was forthcoming, she shoved her hands in her pockets. "Okay. Thanks." Hands still in her pockets, she ambled past Calliope, who sank into the shadows of pork tacos and mustangs.

There was something about the woman. Something important. She didn't know what it was yet, and in truth, she didn't want to. She was here on vacation, and anything more complex was an irritation she didn't need. But her senses, honed from thousands of years of inspiring people to be the best at what they did, the part of her immersed in creativity and creation, knew that this woman was crossing her path for a reason.

The bookshop keeper glanced at her as he passed and gave her a little shake of his head. Tourists in St. Boswells were rare. Well, they used to be. Now that people were visiting the Temple of the Muses more often, perhaps that was changing. Although, given the dearth of shops or cafés, it wasn't changing much. Was that why the woman was here? To go to the temple? It was an interesting thought, but it didn't feel right.

She peeked around the shelves and saw that the woman had seated herself at the same table Calliope had been at minutes before. Her gaze was open and curious, and though she tried to engage the shopkeeper in conversation, he gave quick, polite answers, and the woman finally gave up.

Calliope shook herself from her trance. If she were due to meet this woman, it would happen at the right time. One thing she could always count on was things happening when they were supposed to. The fates were quite precise about such things. She clutched her books to her chest and slipped from the cookbooks and motor maintenance to the front door. Once outside she breathed deeply. The sky had turned to slate, and the air was already damp, though it hadn't begun to rain. She set off quickly down the path that would take her past the red brick homes to the bridge that led across the river and then to her cottage.

She made it inside just as the sky opened and sheets of rain fell in torrents, pounding against her windows. She placed the books on her side table and lit a fire to take away the damp, then turned on the stereo to listen to classical music while she made herself a cup of tea. All the while, she couldn't stop thinking about the woman in the bookshop. It had been years since someone had made her stop and stare. It was never about looks. If that's all it was, she'd have had her fill when they relocated to LA. Although Greece certainly had its share of beauties as well. No, for her it was about something deeper. The sense of someone's spirit, the way they experienced the world. The last two centuries had been difficult as people concentrated on building concrete structures and pollution spewing towers, and she'd pulled away. The new position at Afterlife had given her even more reason to insulate herself from the rest of the world.

And now, just when she thought she was done with humans overall, that absurdly sexy woman walked into her bookshop in the middle of nowhere. She curled into the couch, tucked her feet under her, and sipped her tea. Picking up her book, she decided to stop thinking about what might happen. She'd find out soon enough if they were on the same path.

In the morning, Calliope sat watching the sunrise while sipping coffee as the steam created patterns in the cool morning air. She loved this time of day, even back home. The beginning of the day spoke of promises. Things were bright and crisp in the morning, and anything at all could happen. She rested her head against the chair and began to sing an old lullaby she'd learned in ancient Greece, letting the tune be carried on the morning breeze, twisting and flowing through the leaves and across the water.

While she was singing, Duncan came along, his cane tapping, his pipe smoke wafting through the air. He settled into the chair beside her and closed his eyes as she sang. When the last note drifted away, he tapped his pipe and relit it.

"I don't know the language, but that was beautiful. Don't need to understand the words to ken the meaning, eh?"

She continued to sip her coffee. "It was a lullaby mothers sang to their children when I was young."

His laugh was hardly more than a soft wheeze. "When a muse was young. That's something to puzzle over in the wee hours of the morning." He tapped his pipe. "Heard tell the new owner of the estate's come in."

"Have you met them?"

He pointed his pipe toward the river. "Thought you might want to go over with me. Big meeting over at the center."

The Tweed conference center was less than a mile away, more toward New Boswells than St. Boswells. "I'd be happy to. Now?"

He nodded and puffed.

"I'll get my jacket." She rose and went inside. After rinsing her coffee cup, she pulled on a light jacket and her hiking boots, since the path was likely to be muddy after last night's rain. Anticipation made her shiver. The meeting was important. But why?

She kept to Duncan's pace as they made their way along the muddy path. He was a little more unsteady than he'd been the last time she'd seen him, and the thought made her sad. Human lives were so fleeting, and they left so much undone. Had Duncan left things undone? Had he enjoyed what he could? It would be unseemly to ask, since it sounded like an end-of-life question and she didn't want to worry him, as though she knew something he didn't.

Other people were walking the path too and welcomed Calliope like an old friend. One or two were a little more reticent, but even after five years, people were still coming to grips with the immortals among them. By the time they made it to the conference center there was a large group of locals from all the neighboring villages who wanted to hear what would be happening with such a massive piece of land.

"Better not be Amazon," one woman said. "Have you seen their centers? Soulless concrete monsters with drivers going all day and night. We'd never have any peace again."

"I heard it was one of those big food corporations. You know, the ones who buy up all the farmland so they can sell their modified oranges and fancy grapes," a man replied to her.

Calliope wasn't sure what a fancy grape was, but surely if there was such a thing, she would have seen it in LA by now. Rumors in villages like these were often baseless and brought about by clickbait articles on the internet. But it provided things to talk about, and as long as it stayed harmless, it wasn't a problem. Rumors had been around for thousands of years. Now they just spread faster.

Duncan linked his arm through hers, surprising her a little until she saw the slight weariness in his expression. How old was he? He'd seemed to walk along fine when he passed her cottage. Maybe she needed to keep a closer eye on him. As far as she was aware, he had no local family. They made their way to some seats in the middle of a row so he wouldn't have to get up to let people past.

She took a moment to look around. On stage was a pop-up banner with a photo of a snow-capped mountain with the words Alpine Entertainment splashed over it. Below it was a photo of a smiling child with its hands in the air, as though on a ride. A buffet table ran along the side of the room, filled with giant urns of coffee and hot water as well as pastries of all kinds. A small sign had the logo of a bakery in Montrose as the provider.

The lights flickered and people took their seats, happily munching on cherry scones and cheese twists. Duncan was talking to a man in front of them, laughing about something. It was good to see he had friends.

A tall man with silver hair, excessively shiny black shoes, and a severe looking black suit with an incongruous purple tie tapped the microphone and the room went silent.

"Thank you for coming. My name is Marcus, and I run the Tweed center. What is being discussed today greatly affects us as well, so believe me when I say I understand your concern." He glanced toward the back of the room. "The sale of the estate was a surprise to us too, but I'm happy to say that I think we're about to see some great changes around here. To tell you about them is the head of Alpine Entertainment, Jordan James."

He stepped back and there was polite applause, but no one joined him on stage. Calliope could practically see the worry radiating off him. Shuffling and murmurs began when still no one came forward. And then a sudden burst of thunder vibrated through the room and the room went dark, making people jump.

The huge screen lit up, showing an aerial view of rivers, treetops, and snowcapped mountains. Eagles soared almost on a level with the camera, and skiers slid past far below. The world in all its beauty was seen from above, and then the lights came on and someone stepped on stage, a mic in her hand.

It was the woman from the bookshop.

In dark jeans and a blue flannel shirt, she was absurdly attractive. Humans weren't generally so good-looking. Perhaps she had some divine blood in her background. Otherwise, Calliope was at a loss as to why her mouth went dry and her stomach flipped.

"Hi there." Jordan James stood at ease in front of the mic. "As Marcus said, my name is Jordan, and I own Alpine Entertainment." The large screen behind her changed to the start of a presentation. "Alpine is all about environmental fun. Too many people have lost touch with nature, with what it means to be a part of this amazing world."

There were nods from the audience, even as a few recorded the session on their phones.

"So we remind people how incredible it is to be outside. To challenge themselves, each other, and to truly be in the moment." The screen changed to show a family laughing together. "We try to keep electronic engagement to a minimum. We don't provide Wi-Fi, and the areas where we base our operations are all pretty remote, which means that people are almost forced to engage with the world around them and with each other. Families remember what it is to talk, to laugh, to look beyond a screen."

The expressions of interest in the audience were obvious. Jordan was making a good pitch. The confident tone and timbre of her voice was one Calliope would have listened to without hesitation. She'd even stop working just to listen to her.

"When we approached Bemersyde Estates, it was because we had a vision for the area." The screen changed to show a variety of locations. "From our base in Denali, Alaska, to our operation in Playa del Carmen, to our simpler one in London, to our most extreme in the French Dolomites, we've got the experience to know how to make the best of every environment, enriching the local life while enriching the experiences of everyone who enjoys what we offer."

The next screen brought on the murmurs and uneasy shuffling once again. This one showed zip lines, rope bridges, and roller coasters.

Jordan held up her hands. "I know what you're thinking. I've fielded the same concerns from all the places I've mentioned. Our base in Alaska is on the edge of a national park. It's pristine and perfect, and the locals were worried about the impact we'd have." She took the mic from the stand and moved to the edge of the raised dais. "And that's why I'm here. We could go ahead with our plans without consulting the community, but we wouldn't do that. We want your input. We want to know your worries, what you think would be best—"

"What would be best is for you to give the land up and head on back to your fancy flying wires in Alaska." A man with a large, frizzy red beard stood up, his arms crossed.

Jordan nodded like she'd been expecting this. "I understand—"

"No, you don't." A woman stood on the other side of the room. "How many people do you get visiting your operations?"

Jordan sat down on the edge of the stage, showing she wasn't going anywhere and really was prepared to answer their questions. Calliope admired her calm reserve in the face of hostility, even if she wasn't sure herself how she felt about Jordan's business venture.

"At the park in Alaska, which is only open from May to September, we see approximately six thousand. In Mexico, we see almost half a million."

Angry muttering erupted, and the woman who'd stood raised her hands. "And you think we want half a million tourists traipsing through our villages? Destroying the fields and trees?"

Jordan shook her head. "No. Obviously, you don't want things destroyed. But tourism keeps villages alive. It gives them opportunities. How many hotels and bed and breakfasts have gone empty in the last year? How many people have been worried about paying rent? We're looking to hire nearly five hundred people once we're up and running. Those jobs come with optional housing on the grounds."

The room quieted. Jordan was right. Businesses had suffered greatly after a virus had forced the world to shut down for nearly two years, and recovery had been slow. Trading a quiet village life where not much changed for prosperity wasn't going to be a hard sell. Calliope took in Jordan's easy posture, her open expression. No wonder she'd been so relaxed. She knew full well that what she was offering was something hard to turn down.

Calliope stood and caught Jordan's eye. She smiled slightly when Jordan leaned forward and had to catch herself to keep from falling off the stage. "Can you show us the specifics and boundaries of your proposal, please?"

Jordan looked transfixed and then seemed to shake it off. She gracefully got to her feet and the screen shifted to a layout of the park.

She started talking, but all Calliope could see was that the parking lot butted up against the bottom of Bass Hill. The Temple of the Muses would overlook a parking lot. The entrance to it would be less than half a mile from the back of her cottage. She tucked her shaking hands between her knees. Over her immortal dead body would that happen.

Chapter Six

Jordan stared at the ceiling in her room, trying to figure out what the damp patch most resembled. An angry potato, perhaps. Or maybe a disapproving sloth. The bed let out an equally disapproving groan as she shifted. It was enough to propel her out of bed and into a heavy sweatshirt. The locals kept telling her how great the weather was, but she couldn't figure out how fifty degrees was any kind of great. Not at the end of May, when it was already in the balmy seventies in California. Still, she'd chosen this location and she wasn't about to leave it just because it wasn't as warm.

She moved silently through the musty hallways with their worn red patterned carpet, hoping not to wake anyone. There were only six rooms in the Queen's Swan Inn, and as far as she could tell hers was the only one in use. The restaurant and little café were often busy, but as soon as she left the main room, she had the place to herself. Narrow hallways with a few steps going up here and down there led to quirky alcoves with resident spiders or to chairs that looked like they'd been stolen long ago from a manor house that preferred garish to comfort.

She hated it.

But there'd been little choice in accommodation in this area, something she'd definitely have to change once her park was up and running. There were a handful of B&Bs here in Melrose, and at five miles away, it wasn't a hardship to get to her location at Bemersyde. The Dryburgh Hotel had looked impressive, spreading out like a river of brick, but when she'd inquired about staying, the manager had been abrupt and rude, which made the decision for her. Similarly, the reviews spoke of rude staff and a general feeling of being unwelcome. The hotel was just outside the boundaries of the land she'd bought, and she wouldn't be sending any business their way if she could help it. There were several large brick buildings that had appeared abandoned, and they'd be perfect to renovate for hotels like the one she'd just been at in Switzerland. Spas, good food, and both family-friendly as well as adult-only places would make the resort even better.

Out on the road, she took a deep breath of chill night air and tugged her sweatshirt hood up. It was utterly silent except for the call and return of owls, a sound she'd always loved. She shoved her hands in her pockets and stared at a sky so full of stars it almost hurt to try to imagine the vastness of the universe that held them. She began to walk, wandering past little cafés and tea shops, places that promised the best shortbread or the best bitter. Though how something could be good and bitter she wasn't sure.

Her thoughts wandered as she did, down corridors of doubt to walkways of excitement, to rooms full of plans. The meeting at the center had gone pretty well, overall. She'd come up against groups who weren't sure about having her kind of entertainment venue around, but they all fell under her spell eventually. However, she'd never tried to do something in a village this small before, and never in one steeped in so much history. That had seemed to be one of the main concerns, that she'd overrun the history of the place. When she'd asked what history Bemersyde, specifically, held, no one could give her an answer except to say it had been in that family for a long time. They cited the Dryburgh suspension bridge, which was just a basic bridge, and the Dryburgh Abbey, which was a pile of ruined stone with a big window that overlooked the ruins of itself. Someone had mumbled about a temple, but she hadn't caught it. If there were a real temple here, she'd have known about it from her research.

There seemed little question she'd have her hands full, but if she could get the city council to stamp the paperwork, she could deal with anything else. They'd put off seeing her, saying they wanted to wait until after the announcement, making it clear they wanted village consensus before giving in to her. Really, though, it wasn't about them. Bemersyde wanted to sell, and she wanted to buy. What she did with the land was up to her, for the most part. And she was going to do fantastic things with it.

The bushes beside her rustled and the wind gusted, making the trees creak and sway. A large white owl landed on the hedge in front of her, its wings outstretched as it settled. She froze, staring, and it stared back. Should she walk on? Bypass it? She took a step forward and it jerked, its wings ruffling, making her stop once again.

She had the eerie feeling it was trying to tell her something, but what it was she couldn't fathom. Another owl called through the silent night, and the one in front of her twitched, its head swiveling to the right, only to turn back to her once again.

"I'm not sure what you want," she whispered. Something about it reminded her of the woman at the center, the one who had asked to see the plans. The woman, tall, with olive skin and hazel eyes, had taken Jordan by surprise. There was something magnetic about her, something that made Jordan swallow hard. She'd nearly fallen off the stage in a weird desire to be closer to her. For a moment, she'd been unable to move. A lot like right now.

The owl blinked at her.

She sighed and took a step back. "Okay, well, if you're not going to transform into some hot woman or something, I'm going to take off." She kept backing away and it kept staring at her. When she was about ten feet away, it launched itself from the hedge, right toward her, its wings flapping hard. She ducked as it screeched and slapped her with one heavy wing before it flew off into the night, a ghostly shadow that melted into the dark night sky.

The sidewalk was cold under her butt as she plopped onto the ground and hugged her knees to her, trying to stop the ringing in her ear. The wind had dropped and there wasn't a bird call, or anything else, to be heard. Something tickled her cheek and she reached up to find a large white feather tangled in her short hair. Grimacing, she pulled it free.

"Fucking gods." She sighed and stood, rubbing at her cold butt. There was a chance, of course, that this wasn't anything supernatural. It was just a curious, unafraid owl who wasn't used to seeing people out in the dead of night in its territory. It had challenged her and won, and then left. She twirled the feather between her fingers and pictured it staring at her, then set off quickly back to her hotel. At least her ceiling art wouldn't scare the shit out of her.

Calliope stroked the barn owl's head and it closed its eyes under her touch. She could sense what it had seen, and petty satisfaction rolled through her. Scaring a human was too easy and it probably wasn't fair, but she didn't care. In truth, she'd been surprised to know that Jordan was out walking at such a strange time of night, but maybe she hadn't adjusted to the time difference yet.

The owl nudged her with its beak and then flew off into the trees. She'd been unable to sleep, the thoughts of the adventure park ruining her sanctuary crowding her mind like ants on a decaying apple. She had to do something.

After dumping the dregs of her chamomile tea, she went back to bed and snuggled under the thick comforter. The call of the owls lulled her to sleep, but for some reason she kept seeing the light blue eyes and sexy, lazy smile of the woman trying to take away her place of peace.

She woke tired and cranky. Her duvet was tangled around her legs, and she kicked at it until it fell in a heap onto the floor. Her slippers were cold, and she huffed as she pulled on her thick bathrobe and flipped on the heat. Soon, fresh coffee sent an aroma of calm through the cottage, and after a hot shower, she felt much better. It was raining and chill outside, which made it a perfect day to fall into a book and lose herself in another world. She curled up in her favorite chair by the large bay window that overlooked the river, tucked her feet under her, and began to read.

She looked up, bleary eyed and bemused, when a knock at her door startled her out of the lush sex scene in the romance novel. She set it aside, then stretched and went to the door.

Duncan stood under a large floral print umbrella with little waterfalls coming off it in a circle around him. He held up a brown paper sack. "Maud's muffins from t'bakery."

She smiled and took the bag, then stepped back so he could come in. He shook the umbrella off and then dropped it in the umbrella stand beside the door before he hung up his wool coat and plaid Balmoral cap. He smoothed back the little gray hair he had left and trundled over to her table, where she'd set up a pot of tea and laid out the muffins.

He slid into the seat with a sigh. "Figured you wouldn't go out in this, being from La-La Land and all."

She dropped a sugar cube in his tea. "You know full well I love the weather here. But you're right, I hadn't gone out. I lost myself in a book."

He sipped his tea and made a sound of approval. "Books are good things to get lost in."

They sat in silence for a while. He clearly wanted to chat, but she wouldn't rush him. True words were often spoken best when least hurried.

"The lass that's going to build on Bemersyde," he said, picking at the top of his muffin.

"Yes?"

"She's staying in Melrose. Thought maybe you'd like to know." He didn't make eye contact.

"I have a feeling we'll see her around here, don't you?" She didn't feel the need to admit the owls had already told her where Jordan was.

He shook his head and frowned at his empty teacup, which she then refilled. "Not in Dryburgh. No reason to come this low." He finally looked at her with that canny look he got when he was trying to say something he didn't want to say plainly. "Less, of course, she came directly to see the temple."

Just the thought of the park plans made tension pull at her shoulders again. "You were silent after the meeting, Duncan. How do you feel about the plans?"

"Don't rightly know, Calli." He sipped his tea, blowing on it though it didn't need it. "Change happens, don't it? You'd know best, being older than the dinosaurs and all."

She threw a sugar cube at him. "Not quite." She got up and put more wood on the fire. "Change happens, yes. But it doesn't hurt to make sure it happens for the good when it does happen. This change..." She poked at the fire, fueling the flames. "There are a million other places she could go."

Duncan finished his tea and headed toward the door. Pulling on his coat and hat, he finally turned and looked at her as he opened the door. "Mayhap she hasn't thought of that. Mayhap you should tell her." He touched his cap, took his umbrella, and headed out.

Calliope went into her room to put on something warmer, as well as her rain boots. No sense in getting her nice shoes muddy. She set off along the path to Melrose, readying her argument. Few stood a chance against a muse who'd argued with Aristotle.

Chapter Seven

If a goddess had a smell, it would be the way the pastry in front of her smelled. Jordan inhaled deeply and took a sip of strong coffee. The tiny café boasted that it had been in the family for five generations, and it looked like at least three of them were still behind the counter together. She'd ordered the Ecclefechan Tart simply because it sounded funny, but it tasted like she imagined something from one of the heavens would taste. They had plenty of pastries she'd be back to try, and she'd even taken a black bun to go, though she had no idea what it was.

She brushed the crumbs from her shirt, lifted her coffee in thanks, and made her way out. Whispers that weren't nearly whisper enough followed her out, and it was clear she was the talk of the town. Melrose was five miles away but would still be heavily affected by her business venture. They only stood to gain.

She smiled at people who had come out after the rain had stopped and the sun had broken through the clouds in thin orange slices. The giant metal clock on the side of an old church suggested she get a move on if she wanted to be on time to her meeting with the local politicians. According to her phone GPS, their office was in the market square, which she'd learned was just a big open space with a lot of shops around it. Yet another ornate clock above the office door told her she was right on time. Just as she was about to push it open, she sensed someone behind her.

"Excuse me, Ms. James? I wonder if I might have a word."

She looked over her shoulder and promptly dropped her coffee cup. The lid popped off and caramel liquid splashed over the bottoms of her jeans. Fortunately, the woman who had caused her sudden clumsiness jumped back in time to avoid being splashed.

"Damn, I'm so sorry." Jordan looked from her shoes to the woman like she'd lost her ability to speak coherently.

"No harm done. At least, not to me." She looked at Jordan's shoes and jeans.

"I've been covered in worse." She scooped up the coffee cup and turned to throw it in the nearby bin. The clock chimed the hour. "I'm really sorry, but I've got a meeting inside." She tilted her head toward the office. "Could we talk after?"

The woman gave a small smile. "I have business inside as well. After you."

The same strange sensation she'd had with the owl washed over her, and she began to wonder if this woman was one of the irksome immortal set wandering the planet these days. She certainly had the beauty and poise. Jordan held the door open for her and gave her a quick smile as she passed. The scent of summer apples wafted over her, and her knees grew weak. Damn, how she loved when a woman smelled nice.

She followed her in and allowed the sight of the muddy yellow rain boots to ground her. Those weren't godly. Or sexy.

"Calli!"

She looked up when a man called out. He strode toward them with his arms open wide. He looked a little like one of the gnomes from a recent Disney film she'd seen. Short and squat, he wore a pointed little beard and plaid trousers. All he needed was a pointed hat to complete the look.

"Lass, it's been an age since you've been here. I've got three more grandchildren since I saw you last." He looked beyond her and spotted Jordan, and his smile faltered. "I was going to ask what brought you here, but I think I know."

The woman gave that small smile and stepped aside, and he held his hand out. "Stephen McKay. Ms. James?"

She shook his hand, liking the firm handshake and that he met her gaze easily. "Please, just call me Jordan."

He nodded. "Aye. Will do." He looked at the woman and then back at Jordan. "Would you like to be part of this meeting, Calli?"

What? Why would he invite this woman to their business meeting? She went to speak but was cut off when the woman looked at her. There was a warning in her eyes, and Jordan hesitated.

"I'd like that, Stephen, thank you."

In a back room, there was a long conference table set up with a simple kettle and coffee cups. Three other men sat around the table, and they all rose when they saw Calli. There was no question they were all genuinely happy to see her, but she didn't say much.

Jordan shook their hands as they introduced themselves and then they all sat down.

"Thank you for understanding that we wanted to do this in person, Jordan," Stephen said. "As I'm sure you've seen, this is a very big issue for our little area."

If it weren't for the woman seated opposite her, staring at her much the same way the owl had, she would have been in her element. As it was, she couldn't seem to find her footing. "Of course. I wouldn't expect it to be otherwise. Can I assume the paperwork is ready?"

To her bemusement, they looked at the woman, who continued to look at Jordan.

"My name is Calliope Ardalides. I live in Dryburgh, just across the river." She waited until Jordan nodded, as though to make certain she could follow the simple statement. "Have you been to Dryburgh, Jordan?"

It was a simple question. So why did it feel loaded? "No, Ms. Ardalides, I haven't. It's just beyond the borders of my park if I'm not mistaken."

Calliope's eyebrow twitched, the only change in her expression. She turned to the men. "I'd like to ask Jordan to take a walk with me. Perhaps we can resume discussion tomorrow?"

Jordan didn't try to hide her irritation. Who was this woman, to highjack her meeting? "Excuse me—"

"Of course, Calli. Let's say tomorrow at the same time, shall we?" Stephen stood up, and the meeting was clearly over.

Jordan turned toward Calliope, ready to tell her off. But then she smiled, and Jordan became an awkward teenager standing in front of her first crush.

"Jordan, would you walk with me? I'd like to show you something special. Something you may not know about."

If her life had depended on it, she wouldn't have been able to say no. Or anything else offensive or otherwise negative. She just wanted to see that smile again. "Sure."

They set off and when Jordan saw they were headed down a somewhat muddy walking path, reached out to touch Calliope's arm. The moment she made contact, electricity slammed into her fingertips, making her yank her hand back and cradle it to her chest. "What was that?"

"Maybe you were dragging your feet." Calliope's head was tilted, the look in her eyes indecipherable. "Did you want something?"

Jordan finally stopped cradling her hand. It hadn't hurt, and she hadn't been dragging her feet. "I was going to suggest driving to wherever you want to go, if it's very far?" She looked beyond Calliope at the path.

"It's only about five miles, give or take." She looked appraisingly at Jordan's leather boots. "But I suppose you don't want to get those filthy."

It was strange, how she suddenly felt the urge to hide her feet behind a bush or something. There was no judgment at all in Calliope's tone, nor in her eyes. If anything, she looked a little amused. Somehow, that was worse. She motioned over her shoulder with her thumb. "I rented a car. It's about the size of a matchbox, but it works on these itty-bitty roads."

Calliope motioned for her to lead the way, and she did so, her hands stuffed in her pockets, her tongue firmly tied. She couldn't think of a thing to say that wouldn't sound trite. Or prying. Small talk was never this hard. They got into the little red car, and she pulled out. Calliope gave directions but didn't say anything else. It was impossible to tell how old she was, though Jordan searched for any of the telltale signs. There were no lines at all around her eyes or on her forehead, but she didn't look young, per se. "You said you live in Dryburgh? You don't sound like a local." Jordan slowed as some sheep wandered across the road, stopping to look at them before sloping onward.

"I have a home here, yes. But I live in California most of the year."

Jordan brightened at the idea of common ground. "Hey, that's great! So do I. Northern or Southern?"

Calliope smiled as a lamb clambered past. "Southern. I'd prefer Northern, but my work requires that I stay near LA."

"I think all of California is awesome. The big cities, the ocean, the beaches, the trees huge enough to drive through. It has everything a person could want." Jordan turned down the next road, and the next, as Calliope guided her. "I live up north, myself."

"Pull over here." Calliope motioned to a section of the road that was no more than a patch of dirt.

"Okay. I suppose we could just lift the car out if it gets stuck." Jordan glanced at Calliope who gave her that small smile once more before she got out.

"This way." Calliope stopped at the base of a small hill. "This is Base Hill."

Jordan didn't see anything particularly impressive about it. "What's that sculpture thing at the top?"

Calliope's eyebrow quirked, and instead of answering she set off, and Jordan only barely managed to keep pace with her as she moved quickly to the top.

"Oh." It was some kind of shrine. It was round and set on a stone pedestal, with nine thick columns topped by a stone dome and statues of women between each column. Jordan took in the altar in the center, the candles burning, the offerings on the altar and all around the base. A young woman was cleaning up, clearly caring for the area. When she saw them, she bowed her head and then moved away.

"Thank you, Iona." Calliope smiled at the girl, who ducked her head even lower and allowed her red hair to cover her freckled face.

"Tell me about it," Jordan said, leaning against a pillar.

"It's the Temple of the Muses." Calliope lifted a letter and read it, before setting it back down gently. "Not that old, as temples go. Built in the late eighteen hundreds in honor of a local poet. But once the Merge happened—"

Jordan harrumphed. She couldn't help herself. It was as instinctual as breathing whenever someone mentioned the Merge, the combining of the human and immortal worlds thanks to the gods coming out of their hidey-holes five years ago.

Calliope's eyes narrowed slightly, but she continued. "Once the Merge happened, the shrine took on new meaning for people. Rather than just a strange folly left on top of a hill, it became a pilgrimage site. People leave things here to ask the muses for help, for guidance and gifts."

The pieces clicked into place and Jordan couldn't help but sigh right down to her soul. "You're one of them, aren't you? An immortal."

Calliope held her hand over the flame of a candle, moving it back and forth. "In a way, yes. I'm one of the nine muses. The muse of justice and serenity, specifically."

"And the people around here, they know that? They seem to like you."

"You say that as though they shouldn't, if they really know who I am." Calliope mirrored Jordan's pose against a pillar, but her arms were crossed.

This time, there was something in her tone. What could Jordan say to that without being utterly insulting? "Well, you know, people can be pretty split on whether life is better now, with your kind in it."

Calliope's eyebrow went higher and there was no smile on her lips. "My kind?"

Jordan pointed toward the altar. "Things like this don't get set up for my kind, that's for sure."

"I wanted to show you this so you understand. What you're proposing to build goes against everything this area is about." She held up a letter. "People come here for hope. They make their way to this tiny village totally focused on what they want to ask for. And the ones who come to us are asking for gifts to do with beauty. With making the world a better place."

"And you think they can't do that just because there's a place nearby where they can hang out and have fun, too?" Jordan pushed away from the pillar to look Calliope in the eye. "They can still come here. No one is stopping them."

"But your adventure park didn't take this into account. You're planning on putting a parking lot right there." Calliope pointed to the base of the hill like she was pointing at a pile of dog poo. "You're going to turn the area around this temple where people ask for wonderful things into a land of concrete and screaming children."

"That says more about you and your relationship to children than you might think." Jordan pinched the bridge of her nose. Why did the most beautiful woman she'd seen in years have to be one of them? "And I did take this into account, by the way."

"You did?" Calliope frowned. "Then how could you go ahead?"

"I saw that there was a hill here, and it had something built on it. But the Wiki page said it was basically not much more than a sculpture. Still, the edge of my purchase goes to the base of the hill. It doesn't include it. So, you keep your temple and I get my park." This wasn't going to be the end of it, no question. She could feel the arguments radiating off Calliope without her having spoken. Like the words were seeping from her skin, about to fly off like knives.

"No. That's not how this works. As I said, you can't change an area of natural beauty as well as worship into an adrenaline junkie's trampoline. I won't allow it."

If there was anything Jordan despised, it was being told what she could and couldn't do. Especially by someone who had no idea what it was like to be human. She straightened and worked to keep her tone civil. "You don't have an option. I've bought the land. The permits are just waiting on signatures. My crews are on standby to begin the groundbreaking. I'm sorry it might interfere with how pretty your little temple looks, but if people want your help bad enough, I'm sure they'll still plod up here. Heck, maybe you'll even get more footfall from people who want to hang out with us both."

The last time Jordan had seen a woman this visibly angry, she'd had to run from the house with literal pottery flying past her head. That was when she realized that she needed to have at least some idea of the language if she was going to bed a woman. One-night stands weren't a given in some countries, apparently. If Calliope had any dishes to hand, Jordan would bet money she'd be running down the hill dodging bowls and mugs. She backed away. "I think I should go."

Calliope didn't say anything. Not with words, anyway. Her eyes were blazing, her hands were on her hips, and her jaw was clenched. "You don't want a fight with me, Jordan. The muse of justice doesn't lose."

"If I'm right, a muse inspires other people to be awesome. They're not awesome themselves. You don't scare me, princess."

Calliope took a step toward her, and she took a step back, misjudging the hill and promptly landing on her ass in the mud. Calliope stood looking down at her.

"You have no idea what I can and can't do, and your ignorance is showing. If you insist on taking this forward, I will fight you every step of the way."

Looking up at her from where she sat with mud oozing into the back of her jeans, Jordan had to admit to being at least a little scared. Backlit by the sun, Calliope looked like the immortal she was. Jordan struggled to her feet and wiped her muddy hands on her jeans. "I love a good challenge. I'm ready when you are." Attempting to look dignified, she stomped down the hill and back to her car. Calliope didn't follow, for which Jordan was grateful.

She squelched into her seat and closed her eyes as she rested her head on the steering wheel. Her hands were shaking, and her stomach turned. Of all the fucking obstacles, this wasn't one she'd foreseen. It was true, fighting the immortal set could damn well be a losing battle. She lifted her head and stared at the bit of the dome she could see over the trees. No matter what, she wouldn't back down. They'd taken enough from her, and now was her chance to take something back.

Chapter Eight

Calliope sat on the porch, a cup of tea in one hand and a pen in the other. As thoughts came to her, she neatly wrote them in the notebook balanced on her knee. She would begin researching local laws and environmental cases later. For now, she let her mind wander, much as she taught her mentees to do when they were under her tutelage. It freed up the thinking, allowing for options and possibilities that might not otherwise come to the forefront of the mind, bogged down as the mind could be in practicalities and worry about outcomes.

She checked the time and decided it was late enough in California. The phone rang four times before someone answered.

"Please don't tell me you're not even awake yet? How are you getting things done if you sleep in?" Hopefully, she didn't sound as judgmental as she felt.

"You're on vacation, which means you get no say in what time I take on the day." Themis yawned loudly. "And seven in the morning is the middle of the night, as far as I'm concerned."

Calliope decided to let it go. It was nice of Themis to take over at all. "Okay, I'm sorry. I could use your help with something, and I can't get into the database from here. Something about ISP addresses or some such thing. Apparently, even the gods are restricted in cyberspace."

There was a moment of silence. "Why do you need access to the database when you're on vacation?"

Calliope smiled at the suspicion in Themis's tone. "I'm not working on Afterlife things, if that's what you're thinking. I've come up against a legal issue here I need to deal with."

There were rustling sounds and then the sound of Themis walking through the house, her slippers sliding along the hardwood floors. "Again, what possible issue could you have while on vacation?"

Calliope gave her a brief overview. "So you see, I need to find out what legal options I have around sacred sites, as well as any environmental impact studies that might be useful."

"I assume you've tried talking to this person, before you start all the legal wrangling?"

Calliope pictured Jordan leaning up against the pillar. "Of course. I brought her to the temple, showed her how important it is. She basically said it doesn't matter that it will overlook a parking lot."

Themis scoffed, the sound of a tea kettle whistling in the background. "Clearly, she doesn't understand what a muse is. Did you threaten her with godly interference? That usually works."

"The thought occurred to me, but I don't want to use it unless I have to. She's not a believer, I don't think, so it wouldn't hold much sway. She's stubborn and clever and clearly ambitious."

Themis's laugh was like a clear brook under a summer sun. "So she's attractive as well?"

"I didn't say any such thing. Why would you infer that?"

"Because I know you. And I know what you like in a woman, and those three things are at the top of your list. What does she look like?"

"Irrelevant." She rolled her eyes when Themis laughed again. "She's almost as tall as I am. She has sky blue eyes, short hair, muscles, and a grin that can make you furious in a millisecond."

"Sounds edible." Themis stopped to swallow whatever she was drinking. "That means you'll have fun while you're driving her to the brink of madness by capsizing her dreams. Good for you."

Calliope blanched. "She can take her particular dream elsewhere. There's no reason to have it here."

"Do you know that for sure? That the area isn't important to her for some reason?"

Calliope couldn't respond. It wasn't like they'd had that much time to chat about their deeper reasons for doing what they did. And ultimately, it didn't matter. She wouldn't have her special space encroached on that way.

"I didn't think so. Anyway, I'll do some digging on Scottish law, and I'll get in touch with a few of the Celtic gods to see if they've set up any zoning specifics. But maybe you should talk to her some more. You can be quite persuasive." Themis lowered her voice. "And if words don't work, try dusting off that hot body of yours. Wipe away the cobwebs from between your legs and try that kind of persuasion instead."

Calliope nearly choked on her tea. "I'm not trading my body for…for…"

"Calm down, old lady. I'm teasing. And if it's okay with you, I must go. We've got a couple of gods in a dispute over naming rights to a temple in a border town."

Calliope's first instinct was to ask which gods, what border town, and then dig into the logistics. But that wasn't her concern right now. "Thanks again for helping me out. You're the best."

"Don't forget it. And next time I invite you to Olympus for dinner, I expect you to come," Themis said.

"Deal." They hung up and Calliope continued to make notes, but her heart was a little lighter. She spent far too little time with friends, and that needed to change. Muses fed on creativity, specifically the creativity of others. Without that, she'd be nothing more than…well, human. She rose and stretched and went inside to dress. The afternoon had been warm, but once the sun was down it had become chilly. She often wondered why she and her sisters experienced things like cold and hunger when so many of the other gods didn't, but she'd never found an answer.

She set off down the woodland path, past the temple, and headed to the Bemersyde house. The Haigs were locals but didn't act like it. Generations of wealth meant they had everything they needed, and the local villages were far too pedestrian for their tastes. They had a driver who took them to their second home in Bruntside, Edinburgh, any time they got the desire for more than hills and rivers. There, they could do their shopping on George Street, where high-end specialty shops sold things most people didn't need or even like but would buy anyway. Calliope had spent plenty of time traveling all over Scotland, but she still preferred the little villages like Dryburgh to any of the larger cities.

She got to Bemersyde and slowed as she approached the old stone home. Parts of it originated in the fifteen hundreds, and in the eighteen hundreds, Sir Walter Scott had spent much of his time there. Places like this, with history built into the foundations and emotions dripping from the ancient stones, made her heart sing. So much had been created here. So much love given and so many fights endured. It was a place of depth and meaning, and soon it would be a hotel for people who wanted to swing from ropes.

She went to the west wing, where the family still resided. The rest of the house was already a bed and breakfast, a sure way to continue to get the income to keep the old place from crumbling like the nearby abbey had, although the bed and breakfast had been shut since the pandemic several years ago.

A butler opened the door and waved her in without saying a word. He showed her to the drawing room. It hurt the eyes and every one of her creative senses to look at the mishmash of things considered good taste. Red chairs of one era clashed with tables of another, an ornate chandelier far too big for the room hung low enough to look like it was sagging to the floor in need of rest, and various gaudy knickknacks from different eras covered most available surfaces.

The current Mrs. Haig entered wearing velour sweatpants with *Honey* written down the leg in gold print. A blindingly white sweatshirt complemented the sweatpants with a gold design that wrapped around her, making her look a little like a flower being strangled by a golden snake. She was only about twenty-two and had married the current Mr. Haig, who was fifty-seven, two years ago. It was a constant source of amusement in all the surrounding villages.

"I'm just about to start my Pilates session. What did you need?" she asked.

Calliope squeezed her eyes shut for a moment before opening them again and putting forth her best smile. "Good morning, Mrs. Haig. Lovely to see you. I was wondering if you had a moment to discuss the sale of Bemersyde to Jordan James."

She huffed and started to turn away. "That's not my thing. That's Mathew's thing, and he's away."

"Do you know when he'll be back?" She tried to keep her irritation from surfacing.

"He's supposed to come back tomorrow night, and then we'll be here for a few days before we leave for our cruise." She looked around almost disdainfully. "Then I won't have to come back to this burial ground."

"I'll come back tomorrow evening, then. Enjoy your class."

The woman turned away and Calliope was clearly dismissed. She didn't leave right away, though. She moved through the room, looking at the various items. Garish as the setup was, she recognized some fine pieces of sculpture and ceramics. On the wall, half covered by an ugly tapestry, was a painting. She moved the tapestry aside, coughing as dust floated over her like a mist, and then stared at the painting. It was an original David Wilkie, one depicting small town village life.

She heard a sound behind her. The butler stood there, also looking at the painting.

"It's such a shame the house has come to this," he said softly, not looking away from the painting. "It used to be so grand."

She turned back to the painting. "I remember well. I came here many times over the years, usually when singers were here. But this..." She smiled at the memory. "I was there when he painted this one."

"I thought I recognized you." He leaned forward and motioned to the shadowed form at the back of the painting.

It had been a good day. She'd sung, and then used her powers as a muse to help the young woman put all her love into her voice when she sang next, ensuring that the man listening understood what she was saying with her heart. They'd married the next summer. She turned at the warmth in the butler's voice, and he motioned for her to follow him. When they were in the large kitchen he motioned toward a chair and she sat. While the kitchen retained the spirit of the old house, the appliances were all new. The butler, however, looked like he might have been born at the same time as the house. He moved slowly, a slight bend to his back that he clearly tried to fight, and his face was a map of the life he'd led here.

"I'm sorry, I don't remember you. Have we met?" she asked, gratefully taking the cup of tea.

He placed a plate of shortbread in front of her and then sat down with his own cup of tea. "My name's Jacob. You haven't been here in a long, long time. I was a young man the last time you came." His eyes, rheumy and tired, looked at her, taking her in. "One of us has fared better than the other, I'd say."

She never knew what to say in the face of a human's awareness of their mortality. "I use good skin cream."

He took a piece of shortbread. "I'm sure you do."

They sat in companionable silence for a little while. "How do you feel about the sale of the estate?" she finally asked.

His sigh spoke of many things, chief among them the kind of depletion one has when there's little left to look forward to day after day. "All things pass, and I suppose the house was bound to go the way of all things. And the Mrs.…well, she doesn't belong here, does she? Not one of us. At least the house will still be used, and maybe new folks will come to love it too."

"You're not staying on with the new owner?" She couldn't imagine him dealing with families and people excited about ziplining through the treetops.

"She offered. Told me in person, mind. Not through the computer or some flunky. Shows something about her, doesn't it?" He wiped crumbs from his shirt into his age-spotted hand and daintily dropped them onto the plate. "I live in the keeper's cottage, away back on the grounds. She's said I can stay, long as I like." He nodded slowly, thoughtfully. "Leastways, I don't have to leave my home. Been there for forty years, wasn't sure where I was going to go when I heard about the sale. Now I can retire. Drink tea, watch the sunset."

Drink tea and watch the sunset. The simplicity of his final time on this earth brought tears to her eyes. "I think that sounds like a lovely idea."

He looked at her cannily. "You're going to try to stop it."

It wasn't a question, and she wouldn't insult him by pretending not to know what he meant. "It seems so wrong, to turn this place into a theme park." She motioned vaguely around them. "To take history, and beauty, and quiet, and turn it into something to be paid for and exploited."

Silently, he poured them another cup of tea. "But change is part of it all, isn't it?" he asked eventually.

What a tiresome thing, the concept of change. "Things do. But this change doesn't have to happen. We can keep it from happening. We can keep things the way they are."

Mrs. Haig swept into the kitchen, her face blotchy and sweaty, her hair stringy. "I've been calling you! You're not retired yet, you know. I need water. You don't want me to die of dehydration, do you?" She glanced at Calliope, frowned slightly, then dismissed her continued presence in the house as unworthy of commenting on. She made a hurry-up motion with her manicured hand, then swept out again.

He pushed to his feet and patted Calliope's hand. "Sometimes the ways things are isn't the way they should stay. They've become something that needs to change to get better."

He went to the fridge and pulled out two bottles of water, then gave her a quick wink as he left the kitchen. She tidied up the mugs and shortbread, taking a piece for her walk back, and let herself out the back door.

She pondered what he said about change, and what she'd seen of the house. Was he right? Should she step back and allow the adventure park to take over as a part of the natural evolution of the place? The thought made her breath catch. She simply couldn't. It was hers, in so much as it was anyone's, and she couldn't let it go without a fight.

She stopped by the council office in the market square. Stephen told her Jordan had already been and gone, and she wasn't happy when he explained that they wanted to wait to speak with Calliope before moving further. It was excellent to know she had the council on her side, but she couldn't take advantage of her station as a muse. She recommended they allow the matter to sit with the community for a few days, giving people a chance to mull over their concerns and hopes. Then she could get involved once more after they had a better sense of things. Throughout her walk home she considered the various things she knew and didn't, and returned to her research by the fireplace for the remainder of the afternoon.

She looked up Jordan James and couldn't help but be impressed by all she'd accomplished. A university graduate in business and environmental studies, she'd gone on to create her adventure parks that also gave a portion of their profits back to charity organizations. She'd been photographed with various celebrities at big charity events and that sexy, lazy smile was always present. Calliope slammed the laptop shut and picked up a book, determined to put Jordan out of her mind.

The following day brought slate gray skies filled with never-ending raindrops that threw themselves against the windows like they'd discovered it was their sole purpose and they were determined to be the best at what they did. Calliope resisted calling Themis to see if she had found anything, though she kept checking her email just in case. She scrolled through the internet looking for specific laws and guidelines and was happy to find plenty of rules regarding the sale of land, as well as some obscure laws about what could be built on property in Scotland. Whether or not she could make the case that those laws applied to this situation was a bigger question.

Come evening, she got in her car and made her way slowly to Bemersyde. The windshield was a constant waterfall, and she didn't want to end up in a ditch, or worse, hitting an animal. But it was far too stormy to walk. The butler once again let her in, but this time took her to a smaller, less cluttered study. A roaring fire welcomed her, and when Mr. Haig turned from it, his smile was equally warm.

"Thank you, Jacob." The butler inclined his head slightly and left the room. "I'm honored that you've come…" He stopped and tilted his head apologetically. "I'm sorry, we've never been introduced. I'm Mathew Haig." He held out his hand.

She took it, liking his firm handshake and unwavering gaze. "Calliope Ardalides. But please, call me Calli."

He indicated a chair. "Please." Once they were seated, he crossed his legs. "My wife said you came by to talk about the sale. I have to admit, having one of the gods want to talk to me about business is a little intimidating."

She smiled, liking his straightforward manner. "First of all, I'm not a god. I'm a muse, which is far less volatile and far less demanding."

He shook his head. "I disagree. Being creative can be far more demanding than getting on your knees and praying for forgiveness for something you've already done."

Delighted that he understood, at least a little, of what she was about, she engaged. "That can be true. But no muse has ever required the sacrifice of a child or the killing of a goat."

"Ah, but you require the sacrifice of self, do you not?" He looked at the painting above the mantlepiece. "You require that the artist put themselves into their work, that they give themselves to the creative nature you help them develop. Anything less isn't acceptable."

She studied the painting that flickered in the firelight, almost making it seem like the people in it were moving. "You're an artist."

He shrugged slightly. "A mediocre one at best. Because I couldn't let go of my ego, of my fear of failure. That painting is the only one I kept."

"It's very good." And it was. But he was right. The emotional element, the part of himself that needed to be in it, was missing.

"Let's move on from my list of regrets, shall we? Talk to me about your concerns regarding the sale." He poured amber liquor into a glass and offered her some, but she shook her head.

"I'm wondering if it's too late to stop the sale. Or to put conditions on it." She leaned forward slightly. "You understand what I am. You understand what the temple means to people, now more than ever. To go through with this sale would destroy that."

He steepled his fingers under his chin. "I'm sorry. The paperwork has been filed. One of the conditions was that neither the temple nor the area of Bemersyde where the Wallace statue is were part of the deal. She hasn't said otherwise, has she?"

Calliope sighed, frustrated. "No, she made it clear it will continue to stand. But it will also be at the edge of her parking lot, overrun by people who want a place to eat in the shade, who will then leave their trash behind. The sanctity of it will be destroyed."

The crackle and flick of the fire was the only sound. She waited for him to say more, because if she had to, she was going to be rude.

"I should have come to see you before I signed the papers. You're the muse of justice and serenity, aren't you?" At her nod, he sighed. "You don't just approach the immortal set, though. And I admit it didn't occur to me as you'd been gone so long, and I'm deeply sorry for that. But the sale is signed, and we'll be leaving in a few days." He glanced over her shoulder as though to make sure the door was closed. "My wife isn't interested in country life, and I admit to liking the availability of everything in the city as I get older. I wasn't fortunate enough to have children or siblings, and so the Haig line finally dies out."

"You could still have children." There didn't seem to be a valid argument now.

"No, that time is past. I no longer want them, you see."

"And the history of the house? All the beautiful things in it?" She swallowed against the lump in her throat.

He brightened. "I was going to have most of it moved into a storage unit until I figured out what to do with it. Would you, I wonder, be willing to help? You understand the worth of things, and there's no one I would trust more than the muse of justice to see to it that the right things go to the right people. I'll even donate fifty percent of whatever gets sold to a charity of your choice."

It was a nice thought, and there was no question it would raise a large sum. Perhaps large enough to pay for legal fees to fight the advancement of the adventure park. "I'd be happy to."

He settled back in his chair as though a weight had been taken from his shoulders. "Now, as far as the sale goes, like I said, that paperwork has been filed, although it won't be finalized for thirty days, as is common with this type of thing to protect both the seller and the buyer. It's my intention to sell, and I can't be talked out of that, and I'd rather you not talk Ms. James out of buying during that grace period. However, as I'm sure you know, planning permission for her adventure park has been withheld for the moment."

Calliope smiled at the thought of the councilors who had greeted her when she'd arrived. "Yes, I believe that may have thrown Ms. James a bit. I get the feeling she isn't used to things not going her way."

"Someone with enough knowledge and fortitude could keep that planning permission in purgatory for years and years, I would think. Certainly long enough that the person who wants to build here would give up and look elsewhere."

He looked so satisfied with his seeming solution she hated to burst his bubble, but if there was a thirty-day grace period, then she had a chance to put a stop to this within that time frame. "It's true, but as the muse of justice it would be rather disingenuous of me to use the legal system to create mountains of paperwork to stall what would otherwise go through." She would find another way. She had thirty days, and she'd done far bigger things in far less time. "In the meantime, I understand you're leaving tomorrow?"

He clipped the end off a fat cigar and lit and puffed so his cheeks looked like the billows of a bagpipe, red and lined. "On a cruise. Never fancied one myself, but the Mrs. is looking forward to it." He dipped the cigar in his whiskey and tapped off the excess. "I'll let Jacob know you'll come by in due course to take care of the house. Charge me whatever you feel is fair, to take care of it."

She couldn't imagine allowing a stranger to sell off her family home. "And there isn't anything you want to keep?"

He looked at her squarely, and in the firelight she could see the intelligence and sadness in his eyes. "I think sometimes you immortals forget what it is to die. Maybe the muses understand a bit better than others, though. Creativity is about life, isn't it? And life often requires the fear of death, although that too is changing thanks to the work the gods are doing among us. What purpose would it serve for me to take material things with me to my other home, which already has plenty in it?" He dipped and puffed. "I've only got about six months left, you see. Some disease where the only word you need to know is cancer. And so I'll spend my time drinking and watching my absurdly beautiful young wife run around on a beach, and when the end comes, I'll be ready." Dip, puff. "And none of this stuff will go with me. At the end, it's just you, and all the things you've accumulated are meaningless colors painted on different surfaces. What you leave behind only matters to the living, and sometimes, not even to them."

Tears welled in her eyes, and she couldn't think of a single thing to say. They watched the fire together in companionable silence until she finally got to her feet. "Thank you for seeing me. I hope you enjoy your cruise, and I promise to be a good steward to your belongings."

He stood and took her hand in his. "I hope you find a way to get what you want, Calli. I'm just a man, and I need to find my way out of this life in a way that feels good to me. But I appreciate the muses perhaps more than the gods, though I probably shouldn't say that this close to the Pearly Gates. Good luck."

He leaned forward and kissed her cheek, and she saw the shadow of the next life lurking in his yellowing eyes. Death, or at least one of her subordinates, would be coming for him soon. Possibly sooner than he thought. Her heart ached for him, because as frustrated as she was with his determination not to budge, she understood his desire to control his leaving.

"Thank you. I'll keep you informed about the sale of things. I assume Jacob can put me in touch with your solicitor for all the details I'll need?"

He walked her to the door, which Jacob opened, fading into the shadows behind it as he was wont to do. "I'll get everything in place tonight so it's ready when you are. You've got a month, so there should be plenty of time to do what needs to be done, but I'll speak with my solicitor tonight to make sure the papers are drawn up, so you don't have to worry about the legalities." He looked at the property being soaked through in a deluge of rain. "I didn't think I'd miss the rain, but you know, I might."

It was clear he wasn't talking about the rain in Scotland, but rather, whatever the weather held in the afterlife. She gave him a last quick smile and ran through the downpour to her car. On the way back she considered humanity and death, something she'd not had to think about since her new position at Afterlife meant she dealt with facts and figures rather than emotions. As she neared her house, the dome of the temple came into view, lit from below with candles flickering in the wind, throwing shadows like spirits sent up from the prayers of the people who had left offerings. Even in a storm like this, the temple was a beacon, a place of comfort and hope.

Mr. Haig might have his agenda, and she respected that to some degree. But she had one too. And hers meant more to humanity than the opportunity to take a cruise or to ride a roller coaster through the trees.

CHAPTER NINE

Jordan's heart raced as she dropped thirty feet into the pitch-dark, her headlamp highlighting slick, sharp walls lined with moss and run through with a silver network of veins. She landed lightly, bending her knees for impact, and relaxed the rope attaching her to the land above. Turning slowly, she took in the magnificent cave system.

"Nice to be down here with a woman who knows what she's about."

Jordan grinned at Leith, who was releasing from her own rope. "Can't say I haven't heard that before."

Leith's big laugh echoed off the walls around them and into the cave system beyond. "I've no doubt of that." She tugged on the line and some of the slack was taken up by her crew above, and then another section of rope was lowered. Leith removed the new coil and slung it over her shoulder. "Henceforth, I'll call you nothing but Romeo. C'mon, let's go."

Leith moved to the metal rigging already in place and flipped on the floodlights. Jordan squatted, excitement making her knees weak. She loved this feeling. When things were coming together and her vision was in process, it was like the world was making itself ready for her.

The floodlights showed metal bridges and walkways that led through the middle and along the sides of the cave. "Are we in the largest one?" she asked.

Leith led the way down the metal walkway in the middle. "Nope. This is the second largest in this section of the system. We figure your people will enter back there," she pointed with her thumb behind them, "where the cave slopes upward toward the surface. We'll build steps so they don't have to rappel in. Then they'll come in here, where you'll have your zip lines running from platform to platform on each side, until they reach the main cave." She hooked into a zip line at the edge of the platform. "We don't have full walkways yet, so we'll need to zip over."

She pushed off and was quickly lost in the darkness except for the sound of her metal clip moving along the metal wire. Jordan counted to ten and then followed suit. Flying through the damp, dark cave air, unable to see more than ten feet in front of her, made her want to shout like she was on a roller coaster. The line slowed as the incline decreased and she got ready to dismount. Her heavy boots thunked onto the metal platform, sending a booming echo beyond them. Leith was already moving toward another batch of floodlights. When they came on, Jordan swallowed hard at the immense beauty around her. "Jesus. I saw pictures, but nothing does this justice."

Leith looked as though she totally understood Jordan's reverence. "This one is nearly two hundred feet long, one hundred and thirty across, and fifty feet high. Perfect for zip-lining from side to side." She turned and motioned Jordan to follow. "You can see how it descends slowly, so the rides will be nice and easy. They'll go to that final platform there," she pointed to a thick metal platform built into the left side of the cave, "and then you'll have stairs leading to the surface."

Jordan leaned on the railing, taking it all in. Then she got down on the floor and lay on the metal, looking up at the curved, damp ceiling. "This is incredible."

Leith lay down beside her, her hands clasped over her stomach. "Aye."

"Have you run into any problems?"

"Nothing unusual. Working with cave systems is always tricky until you know how strong they are. You've got a good one here.

Not crumbling, plenty of room. The platforms went in nice and snug, like they're part of the system already."

"Wildlife?" Jordan asked, listening for any sign of bats.

"Not up here. Wait till you see what we found lower down, though."

Jordan turned to look at her. "What? You didn't tell me there was more."

Leith jumped to her feet and yanked Jordan to hers. "Wanted it to be a surprise. C'mon." Once again, she hooked into a zip line, and then looked back at Jordan. "Once you're airborne, count to twelve, and then aim your headlight at the ground." With a grin, she pushed off into the darkness.

Jordan waited a few seconds in order to give Leith plenty of room ahead of her and then launched off. The air was cooler and damper, and when she counted to twelve and looked down, she yelled out, ecstatic. A luminescent limestone river ran below, winding through the cave, appearing and disappearing as it tunneled its way through rock and fell into pools like some magical elixir in a fairy tale. Jordan slowed her line as much as she could so she could take it in. Iridescent shimmers slid brightly along the walls, and as she moved, she heard the unmistakable sound of a waterfall.

The line slowed and she leapt onto the much smaller metal platform. She crossed to where Leith was waiting, leaning against the platform rail. Falling from high above was a waterfall, at least ten feet wide, that fell in a long noisy curtain to the bottom of the cave, where it splashed into a pool and created a mist that swirled and eddied like the wind before it moved off along the river she'd flown over.

"Where does it go?" she asked, going to the other side of the platform, but all she could see was the river heading into the darkness.

"Deeper underground. It disappears about forty feet before it gets to your main cavern."

"And beyond this?" Jordan went back to the cascade and tried to peer around it.

"Haven't had a chance to check it out yet. We only got this platform in a few days ago, but I figured you'd ask. The water is raging too hard right now thanks to that last storm, but in the next few days we should be able to rappel down to the pool and then slide along the walls to see what's beyond the fall." She grinned and crossed her arms. "If you want to, that is."

Jordan raised her arms, wishing she could touch the cave ceiling. "This is insane. It's perfect."

Leith's expression grew serious. "This is going to take some serious geological work before we do much more to it. I wasn't even fully sure about this platform, but it held. With water coming in that hard and fast, we'll need to make sure the ground around it is totally solid. We'll be putting a lot of vibration through this system, so we need to be sure we're not going to mess it up down here."

The possibility that it might not be safe enough to use was disappointing, but she would live with it if that was the case. "No problem. I appreciate you doing all this." She winced slightly and looked sideways at Leith. "Especially without my permits totally in place."

Leith laughed again, making Jordan smile. "Not totally in place? I don't think there's an in between there, mate. You have them or you don't. And since this is your land, you have the right to put in zip lines down here, even if you have to wait for your permits to put other people on them." She shoulder bumped Jordan. "But I've seen your other places, and after watching you free climb that bitch of a mountain in the Alps, I figured I could count on you coming through. And you know how much I love this kind of thing."

Jordan knew full well how much Leith loved a challenge, which was why she'd chosen her for the project in the first place. She was the best adventure guide and environmentalist in her field. She knew every technique, every option, and she was always calm. In all the years she'd been throwing herself off cliffs, into caves, under the sea, and out of airplanes, she'd never had an accident. She was conscientious and bold, a combination Jordan loved. Too bad she was more like Jordan in the butchy department and elicited zero physical attraction. But it was good to have her as a friend, and now, colleague. "Because the caves are on my land and no one has mineral rights, the caves are mine to do with as I please, no permits needed. But when it comes to making it a public place, that I need to have permits for. See? Not totally in place, but kind of. If they don't give me the permits, then I'll just have the coolest private zip line park in the world."

"Lucky you." Leith tapped her watch, which lit up in the dark. "We'd better head back. Don't want to get caught down here at night, at least not yet."

Quickly and quietly, they made their way off the platform and began the sweat-inducing journey along the cliff wall back to the last cavern, where they jumped onto the platform and then climbed the makeshift stairwell to the surface. They made it above ground just as the last of the light was giving way to the gentle grasp of purple dusk.

They sat around a campfire constructed by the crew, and Jordan ate the strange mixture of baked beans, sausage, and mashed potatoes from the tin bowl. They discussed the different issues they needed to check, the types of materials and lighting they needed to bring in, and where the parking lot and various buildings would be. The crew were laid-back and fun, and Jordan embraced the feeling of being right where she needed to be.

The sun set and it grew cold, but they bundled up and watched as a meteor shower began. She lay back with her hands under her head and sighed deeply. This time of year, it didn't really get fully dark this far north, something she liked enormously. Sleep was such a waste of time, and she resented that her body needed it. There was so much to do in life.

Leith lay beside her once again. "I've heard people talking in town."

Jordan's high began to subside. "Yeah."

"Sounds like you've split the community. Some up in arms, some thinking you've been sent by the gods."

Jordan scoffed. "The gods and I have nothing to do with each other. And there are always some people who don't like things to change. But they get over it. Or they don't, and they move." She shrugged and pointed out a particularly brilliant meteor trail.

"Thing is, Jordan, your usual style of running into something like a horny bull in mating season may not work so well here. You may need to try being more subtle."

Jordan turned to look at her. "A horny bull? That's how you think of me?"

Leith looked almost earnest. "I've seen you in action in all kinds of ways. But seriously, you have to consider the way of life here. Some families have been here for generations. I come from a village a lot like this, and people would be well bent out of shape if you tried to force them to accept your way or nothing at all."

"Do you think I should pull my project?" She wouldn't, but she was curious as to Leith's perception.

"Nah, mate. I've seen the great things you do, and how you treat the environment and give back to the world. I'm just saying, a tender touch is sometimes better than a whip."

"Why does everything you say sound sexual?" Subtle and gentle weren't Jordan's forte.

"Because you're a horny bull, like I said."

A few guys from the crew got up, saying it was too cold to stay out, and Jordan agreed. The ground was damp and even through her caving coveralls she was getting chilled. As she stood, she had a thought.

"Where is that river? The one that drops into the cave?"

Leith turned so she was facing the hills behind them. "It doesn't look like much up here. It's over that way, about half a mile or so. Looks like a big creek, but the fall makes it seem bigger."

Jordan wished she could make it out, but light pollution definitely wasn't an issue here. Beyond their lights and the campfire, the hills were shadows, although she could hear the bleating of sheep and the calls of owls. At the thought of the owls, she shivered and began picking up her things.

They made their way down to the cars and then back to the village. She was mentally making lists of the people she needed to call and the shipments she needed to check on. She'd been so certain the permits and licenses would come through with no problem she already had the materials on the way. But what if the people opposed made a difference? The thought brought the image of Calliope.

"Have you had any experiences with the gods? Or any of the immortals?" she asked Leith.

"I have." Leith tapped the steering wheel. "Went to an info session about the Christian sector. Weird, isn't it, that we call them sectors now instead of religions? Anyway, Jesus was there, along with Mary and a couple of others. They said the big guy himself doesn't meet with people, and that rubbed a lot of folks wrong, what with the gods from the other religions being accessible. Why do you ask?"

"I haven't bothered with them. But one of the people opposed to my operation is a muse."

Leith whistled. "Not good to have them against you, buddy. Can you talk her around?"

"No idea." She grinned and slicked her hair back dramatically. "But if anyone can, it's me, right?"

Leith's big laugh filled the car. "Aye, mate. If anyone can woo an immortal around to their way of thinking, it would be you."

They pulled up outside Jordan's hotel. The cave system was only five miles beyond the primary proposed adventure park area, but with the tiny unlit roads here it felt like about twenty. She'd have to do something about that if she planned on staying open after dark.

Leith leaned over. "I'll call you in a few days when the water settles so we can see what's beyond the fall."

Jordan gave her a thumbs up and watched her drive away. The foyer was empty, as were the rooms. There was no sound coming from the restaurant. If she didn't know better, she'd think she was the only person in this old place. She hurried to her room, and then went in and leaned against the door behind her. She was being silly. But there was something about this village that felt different from the others. Or was that just her imagination, thanks to Calliope and the owl? Shaking her head, she pushed away from the door and stripped down, leaving her damp clothes in a pile. They wouldn't smell any different than the hotel.

A hot shower made her feel better and the physical exertion had tired her out. She fell into the lumpy bed and began to drift off.

Just as she was falling asleep something hit the window. She sat up and was confronted with the ghostly specter of a white owl looking in at her. Her heart jumped to her throat, and she backed up in the bed. "Shoo," she hissed at it. "Take your weirdness back to your friend."

It tapped the window with its beak and then leapt into the air and was gone.

She slipped back under the covers, her pulse racing and goose bumps running along her arms. "Intimidation by owl is a new one." The need to speak out loud was overwhelming. She'd never wished for someone else in the room with her quite so badly. "You're not going to scare me away." She pulled the covers tighter around her, right up to her chin.

Sleep didn't come easily. And when it did, she was busy chasing a woman who kept looking over her shoulder and laughing, a sweet, musical sound that fueled Jordan's need to be near her, to catch up. But no matter how close she got, the woman was always out of reach.

Chapter Ten

Y ou need to stop doing that," Calliope said, stroking the owl's head. "She'll think I'm sending you."

The owl blinked at her, swiveling its head around and back again.

"Yes, I know she's going to upset your quiet. And I'm working on that. But you're going to make her even more stubborn."

It hooted and received a return call from the distance. Ruffling its feathers, it hopped forward on the table and then launched silently into the air. She appreciated its concern, and its help. But Jordan wouldn't understand what it was trying to say, and Calliope didn't want to make it even harder to get Jordan to understand why it was so important she change her plans. Few people realized how much birds, particularly owls, given as they were to being the pets of the gods, understood the human language. Sadly, humans weren't as adept at understanding them in return.

The phone rang and she glanced at the time. It was far too late for a call that wasn't an emergency. She answered the number that came up as unrecognized.

"Thank goodness you get reception. I don't know how you can stand it out there."

Calliope relaxed into her chair. Not an emergency, just drama. "What's wrong, Clio?"

"Our sisters are refusing to come to my annual gala. Like, as a group, flat-out refusing. It's one thing for you not to show up, because everyone knows you're, well, you. But the other seven of my sisters? It would totally ruin the party, as well as my reputation."

For a muse dedicated to history, Clio was quite possibly the shallowest of Calliope's sisters. She hadn't always been that way, though. It was the Industrial Age that had started it, with all their marketing about how good things were going to be. And then the Electronic Age had come and swept her into hyper cyberspace, where she'd disappeared into an often-smarmy pool of vanity.

"I'm going to skip right over what you mean about my personality and go to the larger issue at hand, which is why they should show up to make you look good."

She huffed. "You know the gala is a huge thing for us. It brings together so many creative people, and then we inspire them, and the world goes crazy in all the best ways. Thanks to us, the arts are back on the rise and artists are starving a lot less." She said something to someone that Calliope couldn't make out. "C'mon, please talk to them."

"Do you have company?" It was a simple question but loaded nonetheless. They'd had several conversations about the amount of people Clio entertained in her bed. Calliope couldn't help but find it unseemly for a muse to be so rampant with her pleasures. Erato, certainly, but that was part of her power.

"Don't start. Just because you're an iceberg of celibacy doesn't mean the rest of us have to be. Please, Calli?" Her tone softened. "I really believe in this event, and it raises a ton of money for our designated charities. The music center took on another hundred students last year. A hundred!"

Much as she hated to admit it, what Clio was saying was true. The ACA had done incredible good for all areas of the arts, and the fact that it was run by a muse made it the preeminent arts college in the world. "I know, Clio. It is a really good event for a good cause. I'll talk to the others when I get back and see what they say, okay?"

"Thank you, thank you, thank you. I don't suppose I can get you to come this year?" The question was less hopeful than simply polite.

"You know how I feel about gatherings like that. But you never know." Between Jordan's assertion that she didn't know how to have fun and her sister calling her an iceberg, she was starting to feel the sting a little.

"I won't hold you to it, and thank you for helping me." Once again, she murmured something unintelligible to someone else. "Okay, I have to run. Call me when you get back from cow town?"

"Will do." She hung up and closed her eyes, allowing the soft creak and sway of the trees to ease the stress in her shoulders. She should have left her phone in LA.

The next morning, she walked across the river to town and was surprised to see the occasional sign in people's front yards.

Say no *to noise!* In one yard.

Say yes *to jobs!* In another.

Say no *to commercial land grabbing!* In yet another.

She ordered a coffee at the bookshop café and sat across from Duncan, who had his cap pushed back and his reading glasses perched on his nose. He slid a piece of paper toward her.

Town hall meeting Thursday evening at Tweed to discuss the permits applied for by Alpine Adventure Parks, Inc. Please come and give your opinion on the matter for the councilors to consider. 7 p.m.

"I wondered about the signs in people's yards." She stirred sugar into her coffee thoughtfully. "I'm glad they're taking the step to include the villages."

"You should speak."

She was already mentally formulating what she'd say. "I'll be sure to."

"Do muses date?" he asked, looking over his spectacles at her.

"Are you asking me out?" she said, slightly taken aback. He'd never asked her anything personal in all the years she'd known him.

"Oh, if I were three decades younger, I'd try my hand, don't you doubt. But no. My great-niece, though, I think you and she would get along merrily." He set his spectacles on the table like he was getting ready for a debate.

"First of all, if age is the issue, then I've got you beat by a few thousand years. Second, yes, muses date, but I don't have time. Thank you for thinking I'm good enough for her, though."

"Ha!" He shook his head and took a bite of carrot cake. "I bet no immortal has ever said those words before."

No, they probably hadn't been uttered by an immortal, ever. But working among the gods while not really being part of that distinguished group allowed her a view of them most wouldn't get to see. "Well, it's true."

He let the topic drop, and they watched a few people come and go until Jordan walked in and headed straight for the café. She gave them a cheerful good morning and ordered from the bookstore owner, who was far less friendly with her than he'd been with them.

Jordan stopped at their table, her steaming coffee in hand. "Will you be at the meeting on Thursday?"

"We will." Something about Jordan made her heart beat a little too quickly. That come-get-me smile, that insouciant way she cocked her hip, the way her eyes crinkled at the corner… Calliope looked down at her coffee. "I assume you will be as well?"

"Definitely. Now that everyone has had a chance to think, I'll be there to answer any questions people may have." She lightly touched Calliope's shoulder. "Maybe we could have coffee before? Or after? Or dinner?"

Calliope looked up, surprised and not a little suspicious. "Trying to win me over, Ms. James?"

"Absolutely. And I'd like to get to know you better."

Calliope jerked when Duncan lightly kicked her shin. She frowned at him and turned back to Jordan. "Very well. The Pit and Pendulum has good food, but it's in Jedburgh. You could meet me at my house, and we could drive together. Unless you prefer to meet me there?"

Jordan held up her hands, nearly spilling her coffee. "I'd rather ride a horse than drive anywhere around here. I'm used to much bigger roads. I nearly had a heart attack when a tractor was coming at me the other day. What you consider a two-lane road here is barely a single lane in California."

"Hence one of the concerns about your business." She couldn't help but smile a little at Jordan's slight flinch. "Six at my place, tomorrow? Obviously, I'll drive."

Jordan's smile went right to her eyes. Her pretty, happy eyes. "Excellent."

"Cross the suspension bridge I took you over the other night. Turn right at the temple and my house is the first one you come to."

"I love the way directions work here." Once again, there was that smile. "See you tomorrow."

She left and Calliope couldn't keep from watching her saunter out, looking utterly self-assured and sexy in her low-slung jeans and designer sweatshirt. Duncan cleared his throat and she looked at him, having nearly forgotten he was there.

"I thought you didn't date?" he said.

"If I said no, you might have kicked me harder."

He grinned. "Aye, well, it's your chance to work on convincing her, is it not? Get inside her head, work your muse magic. And maybe have some fun, too."

"Fun is overrated." She nearly winced as the words came out. Who had she become, that fun was something to be dismissed? "You're right. It might be enjoyable. Just because she's insufferably confident and wants to ruin our beautiful haven doesn't mean I can't enjoy her company."

"That's the spirit. Doesn't hurt that she's not hard on the eyes, either, does it?" He raised his eyebrows.

"I hadn't noticed." She'd definitely noticed.

He gave her a disbelieving look before he went and ordered another coffee, and when the bookstore owner looked over to her, she nodded for another. "Take away, please."

"Somewhere to go?" Duncan asked.

"I went and saw Mathew Haig yesterday. He asked me to oversee the auction of the contents of the house. I was going to start making a list today and then get in touch with an auctioneer."

Duncan whistled. "That'll make a pretty penny. Mind if I tag along? Nothing to do in the house today."

There was the underlying sadness in his eyes she'd noticed earlier, and it bothered her deeply. "Of course. I'd love your input and you can help me catalogue things."

They walked over to Bemersyde since the day was crisp and bright. She told him about her conversation with Mathew and he followed along in that thoughtful way of his.

"He's right, you know. The gods are among us now, so we know there's an afterlife. Took the mystery away, but also brought death closer, in a way. Now it's something you have to think about, plan for. You can't just wait and see because then where will you end up? In that place Death has set up, for the people who believe but don't?" He swatted at a piece of fern sticking out in their path. "Nay. You have to know before you go."

"And do you have a preference?" she asked, curious.

"I was raised in the Kirk, of course. Most of my generation were. So that's probably where I'll end up."

Calliope was familiar with the Presbyterian version practiced in Scotland. "It's a popular one. Plenty of room."

He looked at her as though to see if she was kidding, and then sighed when it was clear she was. "You joke, but this is my soul we're talking about. What if I don't like it there? What if there's no bagpipes?"

"You could ask. There are plenty of information sessions."

He simply shook his head and she understood why. For so many, faith in the divine had been part of who they were. Faith being the operative word. They had no proof and had to simply believe, to trust that the person they were praying to was listening. But since the Merge, where gods had made themselves not only seen, but now walked among humans more freely, they had their proof, often coming to them from a chat show or live announcement or news segment, and for many believers it was disquieting. Faith and business had clashed, with believers having a choice just like they had a choice of cereals or restaurants. The only magic that remained was that the afterlife remained a mystery the gods didn't share. You didn't know until you got there what it would be like. Except for Hell and the Deadlands, both of whom advertised freely what might be available. Although Hell always used an asterisk since they wouldn't guarantee anything.

They arrived at Bemersyde House, and Jacob opened the door. He greeted Duncan warmly, and it turned out they'd gone to school together and had known one another most of their lives, though their paths didn't often cross because Jacob spent most of his time at the house.

"Have they gone, Jacob?" she asked, draping her jacket over a chair.

"They have, Calli. What can I get you?"

She looked around and the enormity of the job hit her. "I've just realized I can't do this myself. I'll need to hire in a company. Give me a minute."

The two old men took seats in the kitchen and began a conversation she couldn't follow, given the speed and depth of the dialect. She went to the front room and sat in the window seat, where she scrolled through her contacts. Happy to find she still had the number of an auction house she'd worked with once long ago, she called them, and they agreed to come out soon to help.

In the meantime, she took out a notebook and fountain pen and began writing, based just on what she could see in the room. It wasn't long before she had to turn the page, and the one after that. Jacob and Duncan came in, and Duncan handed her a steaming mug of tea.

"How's it going?" he asked, sinking into a worn chair.

"I've got a team coming to help. But I've made a small start." She held up the notebook and then turned to Jacob. "Is there anything here you're particularly attached to?"

He took his time to answer, looking around and then studying his mug. "There's a painting upstairs. I don't know much about art, but I've loved it for years. I probably couldn't afford it no matter the cost, but it's the only thing in the house I'll miss."

Calliope stood, intrigued. "Show me."

They followed him up a wide staircase to a room on the left. He said it was a guest room that he couldn't remember ever being used, but it was kept clean and ready anyway. She knew the painting he meant right away. Hung above a fireplace, it was of a woman on a beach. She stood staring at the painter, her hand just barely touching her face, her long skirt brushing the sand except where her bare toes peeked out. There was something hauntingly beautiful about the woman.

"I used to see her in my dreams," Jacob said softly.

"I can see why," Calliope said. "And I think it should go to someone who appreciates her. I'll see what I can do."

He glanced at her and then led the way back downstairs. She picked up her coat. "Is there anything else I can help with? Anything you need?"

The breeze blew the thin curtain at the open window, and Jacob shivered visibly. "It's strange. All these years I've cared for the place, knowing people would be back eventually. But now there's no one coming back, and soon I won't know what to do with myself."

He seemed less at ease with the simplicity of life he'd mentioned only the day before, but she wasn't sure what to say. "Perhaps you could take up a craft?"

Duncan laughed and clapped Jacob on the back. "You'll take up chess! And day drinking with me."

Jacob brightened. "That sounds like a good solution."

A craft might have been better, but not everyone was so inclined. "Well, you know where I am if you need anything, and I'll come back to meet the auction house people in a few days."

Duncan joined her on the walk back to her place and commented only on the flowers and blue sky. But he seemed far more chipper than he had earlier. Had he been lonely and in need of a friend, much as Jacob had? It seemed so, and she was glad they'd been brought together once again. Companionship was so important when it came to the richness of life. Not that she would really know, having no time for such things.

She was lost in thoughts of her dark office piled with files, and her home that although lovely, often felt empty, when Duncan patted her shoulder.

"Deep thoughts like that aren't for afternoons like this one." He continued down the lane toward his house, whistling a happy tune as he went.

Once inside, she lit a fire and checked her email. There were several from Clio asking if she had any news yet, so with long practiced patience, she called Thalia. Of all her sisters, Thalia was the most level-headed but also the most optimistic.

"I thought you were on vacation," she said when she answered.

"I am. But Clio is up in arms, and I promised I'd find out what was going on." She curled up in her favorite chair, glad to be home.

"Of course she called you. Did she tell you why we're not going?" There was the sound of machinery in the background.

"She said all of you are refusing to attend, but she didn't say why. I assumed she didn't know." Assuming was something Calliope didn't do. Why had she done so this time?

"We're refusing to go because she wants to stage a play. Like, a full-on directed thing where we essentially play ourselves using our old Greek wardrobes. She wants to turn the charity gala we agreed to into some kind of show where she can shine. It's tawdry, and we won't do it."

Calliope squeezed her eyes shut and tried to keep her tone level, though she was fed up. "Obviously. She neglected to tell me that. I'm sorry I've bothered you."

The sounds of construction dimmed, and the sound of a door closing meant she could hear better. "Sis, it's been way too long since we caught up. I'm glad you called. I miss you."

Tears, unexpected and unwelcome, welled in Calliope's eyes. "Ever since I took the job at Afterlife, I don't seem to have any kind of life of my own, after or otherwise."

"You've never been one for running around with your skirt hiked up around your waist, so to speak, but you did enjoy lots of cultural things. Maybe when you get back, we can go to the theater?"

"I would love that. When do you get back from your current project?" She felt bad not specifying, but she couldn't quite remember what architectural project Thalia was working on, or where.

"We finished the meditation room, and now we're working on the cow pastures where people can feed and pet them. Ganesh has put his trunk in constantly, so we're running behind. Shiva thought it would be funny to turn some of our timber back into trees, just for the destruction it caused, and then he and Ganesh got into it. You know how it goes. But we should be back in LA by mid-month."

Now she remembered. The new Hindu temple was being built in Colorado, where there was plenty of space for the sacred cows to roam. "That would be perfect. I might be a little delayed getting back."

The sound of shouting and an elephant trumpeting made her hold the phone away from her ear.

"Sorry, gotta run. Sounds like they're at it again. Love you."

Calliope put the phone down and picked up her laptop. She sent a somewhat pissy email to Clio telling her that if she wanted help in the future, she'd better provide all the information. And she let her know that she agreed with their sisters. A theater production of them as muses was in poor taste. Should she scrap that absurd idea and return to the original concept of raising money for charity and the arts in a purist way, then maybe she'd see if their sisters would reconsider.

She shut it down and spent the rest of the afternoon reading. Or, she tried to. But thoughts of Jordan kept straying from the box she'd put them in, distracting her from the written word. What should she wear tomorrow? Did it matter? It wasn't like she'd be trying to impress her. They were far too different, and Calliope knew full well that loving a mortal led only to heartbreak. But still, there was no question Jordan was incredibly attractive, and a night out with an attractive woman wasn't something she came by often.

A knock on the door startled her out of her reverie and she was surprised to find Iona there, looking like she might bolt any second. "Come in, Iona."

She stepped just inside the doorway, looking around nervously. "I'm sorry to bother you. It's just…" She thrust out a piece of paper. "I saw this, and it seemed important."

Calliope took the damp piece of paper and held it to the light.

If I can't sing, I may as well be dead. If you exist, if you can help, please, please help me. Without music, I don't know who I am anymore. I can't see a reason to keep going. Please help me. Nova Stokes

"That name sounds familiar," Calliope said, gently tracing the scrawled handwriting full of fear and desperation in every tight letter.

Iona shuffled slightly, her eyes wide and still darting around like she was waiting for a god or imp to leap from behind the sofa. "She's the singer who was attacked by some crazy fan a few months back. He messed up her vocal cords."

She remembered the story now. The poor young woman had been a rising star, passionate and well liked. After her attack, she'd gone into seclusion. "Thank you for bringing me this, Iona. You're right, it's important and I'll see that she gets attention."

Iona looked right at her this time. "You'll help her? Personally?"

"We help as many people personally as we can, and if we can't get to them, we send others from our team."

"There's a team of muses? Like, more than just you and your sisters?" Her eyes went impossibly wide.

"There didn't used to be, but when the gods came out people started needing us more, and we felt it was better to train more muses than to only be able to get to certain people. One of my sisters handles the trainees." How odd, she thought, to explain the beauty of what they did in such base terms.

Iona stepped back, opening the door without looking. "I hope you can help her."

"Me too." She watched as Iona darted back into the night like a hare worried about being caught by a fox. The girl was special, there was no doubt about it. She had a creative soul, but Calliope wasn't sure what her gift was yet. At some point before she left, she'd be sure to find out and help in whatever way she could. Someone so dedicated to the temple should be rewarded. At least, that's what the gods always said.

In theory, Nova should be in the area, since people didn't usually send flunkies to deliver temple prayers for them and she could feel the desperation attached to the letter. If so, maybe she could meet with her and find a way to give her hope. When creative people had their gift torn away, it was like losing a fundamental part of themselves, a piece of soul that couldn't ever heal over, and Calliope had seen it often enough over the thousands of years to know it was a reason many of those bereft decided not to live anymore.

Information on Nova Stokes wasn't difficult to find, and she left a message with her manager. Within the hour, she had a message asking if she'd be free to meet with Nova the next day, and she arranged it for the morning. Mornings were always better for heavy conversations, when the day felt like it still had plenty to offer, and the heaviness of night didn't weigh someone down with looping thoughts that only served to take them further into darkness.

As she lay in bed, she considered her trip so far. She'd gotten involved in a land dispute, become an executor of a place she didn't have any ties to, met a woman who was both captivating and irritating in equal measure, and was now about to try to help a young woman distraught at the loss of her gift. Not exactly vacation material, but she felt more a part of the world than she had for a long time.

Chapter Eleven

Jordan was bored. Nearly to death. There was so little to do, and the public footpaths were nothing more than vague paths through fields, sometimes into groves of trees, and then through more fields. Walking here meant…walking. Not for a purpose or to a place. But just wandering to enjoy the fields and fields and fields. Nature was great, and she adored and respected it. But walking for the sake of walking the way they did in this country was baffling.

The only high point had been when she'd roamed the ruins of Dryburgh Abbey, which must have been an impressive place in its day. She didn't really understand the point of ruins, though, of which this country seemed to have its share. Why not repair and rebuild them instead of letting them litter the countryside as big piles of stone with an occasional intact window or wall? It was good to see them, sure, but they could be so much better. The cemetery around the abbey had bothered her. All those moss-covered gravestones with names no one remembered. They, too, amounted to little more than littered stone with a bit of scribbling on them. Thankfully, Aunt Sue had been cremated. She couldn't imagine her being in an empty, forgotten place like this.

On her way back, she detoured around the empty Dryburgh Hotel and headed down a steep hill toward the temple Calliope had taken her to. She wasn't sure why, but she wanted to see it again. After walking along a massive stone wall enclosing an enormous field that must have belonged to some important person, she came to a pretty little fairy-tale cottage, the last one before the hill. Made of stone, it looked almost light pink in this light, and green-blue gables offset the doors. Skylights were the most modern thing about it, and she could picture Calli sitting in a patch of sunlight.

Singing and the sound of a harp slipped out the open window. It was so beautiful, so sweet and pure, her heart fluttered in her chest. She leaned against the tall cedar tree across from the cottage and closed her eyes to listen. The melody was like liquid gold floating through the air, touching her and moving on to touch everything else. It nearly made her want to sing herself, even though she had the range of a brick and sounded as good as tin hit with a hammer.

She opened her eyes when a car pulled up in front of the house and a young woman got out of the back. Even in sunglasses and a ball cap, Jordan recognized the young singer who had been all over the news a few months back. She knocked on Calliope's door and the singing stopped. Jordan moved into the shadow beside the tree but didn't look away. Calliope opened the door, and Jordan got tingly all over. She was in a long, flowing skirt and a simple tight tank top that hugged her breasts too perfectly. Jordan swallowed hard, and then was touched at the way Calliope reached out and pulled the girl to her and held her as the girl's body shook with sobs.

She took her inside and closed the door behind them, and Jordan couldn't help but feel like she'd intruded on something important, something not meant for anyone else to see. Walking quickly away, she saw that the driver of the car had already put the seat back, pulled his cap down over his eyes, and was probably fast asleep. She took the path uphill toward the temple and stopped when she got there.

Sunshine streamed over it, painting it pale pink much like the color of Calli's house. Incense wafted into the air around it, and several people knelt quietly, lost in their own thoughts and prayers. It was serene, and Jordan suddenly understood what Calliope was worried about. But there wasn't anything she could do. The plans had been drawn and the permits were based on those plans. Surely this place would adapt.

As she walked across the suspension bridge, she stopped to look at the wide, slowly flowing river below that was so clear she could see the rocks on the bottom. There'd been a time she'd been as lost as that young singer. When her body, too, had felt like it would break apart from the sobs that tore through her. But no one had been there to hold her, to tell her things would be okay. What she would have given for someone like Calliope to take her in her arms and tell her that the world wasn't as dark as it seemed.

She shook away the maudlin thoughts. The girl she'd been was long gone. In her place was someone who knew what she wanted and how to get it, someone who took care of people and the environment and made the world fun at the same time.

Her phone rang and she answered, grateful for the interruption to her thoughts. "Hey, Leith. What's up?"

"The crew is here. Thought maybe you'd want to come chat?"

That would be a perfect distraction, and a good way to reinforce her excitement about why she was here. As she headed toward the hotel and her car, she thought about Calliope in that outfit that suited her so perfectly. She really couldn't wait to learn more about her, and although it was a shame they were on different sides of the fence when it came to Jordan's business, there was something about her that pulled at Jordan's soul. Few people ever interested her so deeply, and it irked a little that the first person to do so in a long time had to be one of the immortals. Still, that too could be an adventure of sorts, and she wasn't one to turn down adventure.

When she arrived at the edge of the Bemersyde land, she found several vehicles lined up on the long driveway and followed the big rig tracks onto the grassy area. A large number of crew were standing around chatting, and Leith waved and jogged over before she'd even put the car in park.

"Heads up that we've got some folks not happy we're here," she said, motioning toward a group standing on the Bemersyde House steps.

"I thought we might have some more time before that happened, but in a place like this it's not surprising word got around." Jordan waved at the small group, but no one waved back.

She and Leith walked over to the crew, and she introduced Jordan. There was plenty of banter and lightheartedness right from the start, which eased Jordan's mind somewhat. Until she considered what she had to tell them.

"As you know, I bought the land and all the plans have been drawn up. Any materials that didn't arrive in that rig will be here in the next few days. I specifically asked for local contractors like yourselves because you'll know best about the type of land we're working on and any problems we may come across." She smiled at their satisfied nods. "My intention is to go ahead with the planning. Get things staked out, look at the geological surveys again, that kind of thing. But as you can see, we have some opposition," once again she waved at the sour group on the stairs, "and they're holding up my final permits."

There was some general grumbling. "Is it like to fall through, then?" one crew member asked.

"No way. Like I said, we're moving ahead like I've already got the permits. There's a big meeting on Thursday to discuss it, and I have no doubt at all that I'll win people over and we can dig in."

That seemed to pacify the crew, and they rolled out the plans and began studying them on the hood of the nearest Jeep. Jordan stood back and let them talk, only adding information when it was asked for or to clarify what she wanted. Being an overzealous manager never made for a good work environment. She watched and waited and helped, but she'd learned early on that she had to trust the people she worked with. Micromanaging was something she left up to the gods.

Someone behind her cleared their throat and she turned around, already having an idea of what was going to be said.

A woman in a tweed skirt, rain boots, and a tight jacket buttoned up to her throat looked at Jordan with such a pinched expression she almost looked pained. Her hair, pulled into an impossibly tight bun, looked like it might be holding her face in place. "You're the new owner, right?"

Jordan held out her hand and received the barest touch of a handshake in return. "I am. How can I help you?"

The woman's jaw clenched as she looked around. "Your permits haven't been approved yet. You can't be doing work until they're approved."

"You're absolutely right." Jordan smirked a little at the woman's surprised expression. "And I wouldn't dream of beginning to build without my permits in place. But my crew here is getting ready. They're checking over the grounds, making sure we won't have any issues, and that we're doing all we can to incorporate the environment into what we're going to do."

"But...but that's starting work, isn't it? And you're not supposed to be starting work."

Jordan turned slightly and motioned toward the Jeep. "I wonder if you and the others with you would like to look at the plans? We can have a chat right now, if you like?"

Once again, the woman looked surprised, and not a little suspicious, but then she looked over her shoulder and waved the others over. Jordan led her over to the plans and the small group gathered round. The rest of the crew gave them space, but Jordan motioned to Leith to stand by.

She pointed to different parts of the plans and explained what they were, and then the group began to ask questions, which she answered honestly and without hesitation. Their worries weren't anything she hadn't come across in some form before, so she was prepared and happy to explain in detail. When someone raised environmental concerns, Leith stepped in and answered.

She also managed to slip in that she'd been to Jordan's other places, and how they'd done things there. When someone asked who her people were and she told them about her village in the Highlands, the camaraderie and friendliness changed dramatically. She explained the way she'd seen it work, and how she saw it working in this village with an air of understanding that Jordan couldn't replicate by virtue of the fact that she was an outsider. But Leith was a native, also from a small Scottish village, and it made a huge difference. By the time the group had finished, each of them shook Jordan's hand firmly and said they were looking forward to the meeting on Thursday. The group walked off, talking about the prospect of jobs and adventures they'd always wanted to experience.

Jordan leaned against the Jeep next to Leith. The crew had moved off to the steps, where they were sitting talking and laughing. This was going to be fun.

"You're welcome," Leith said, looking rather smug.

"For what? Explaining your job?" She stumbled dramatically as Leith bumped her hard with her shoulder. "Thank you. Seriously, I think you may have just won over this village for me. I hate to admit I was getting worried."

Leith tilted her head thoughtfully. "I think it will have helped, yeah, because they'll go and tell everyone else. But the one thing you can't deny is that their solitude will be crushed. And for some around here, that's enough to challenge you right to the end." She grinned slyly. "Like that pretty muse in the cottage by the temple."

"Word gets around, doesn't it?" Jordan missed living in a city where rumor didn't fly as fast as an eagle diving for prey. "What have you heard?"

"That you had the balls to ask the muse to dinner. That she's never been to dinner with anyone in all the time she's lived here, but you come along with your big boots and let-me-do-you smile and suddenly she's making a date."

Jordan laughed so loud the crew glanced their way. "That is not what you've heard."

Leith shook her head. "Part of it is. I'll let you figure out which part." Her smile dimmed. "Really, though, be careful with that one. You and I have talked about the immortals and how capricious they can be. I don't think the muses fall into that category, but who knows? And the people here respect her. She's become their very own immortal, you know? If she stands against you, plenty of people here will too."

"Hence, me asking her to dinner." Jordan hoped that Leith didn't see how her words created a gully of doubt in her mountain of confidence.

"Well, remember what she is. The muse of justice is going to want things to be fair. Better give that some thought before you try to win her over with that smile of yours."

Jordan pushed away from the Jeep and punched Leith lightly in the shoulder. "If I didn't know that you went for the same type of woman I do, I'd almost think you were interested in me."

Leith held her stomach and made a gagging sound. "Now I'll have nightmares. Thanks for that."

Laughing, they headed toward the crew. And although plans were set in motion so that the crew weren't just sitting around day after day waiting, Jordan couldn't help but worry about what was to come.

CHAPTER TWELVE

Calliope smoothed her hand down her skirt for the millionth time. The last time she'd been this nervous she'd been beside Catherine the Great, helping her write out the terms of the king's surrender of the throne. She hadn't even been this nervous when she'd watched Pavarotti get on stage after she'd helped him with a serious case of stage fright. And she'd certainly never been this way over a woman.

When the knock on the door came, she stood quickly but then counted to ten so she didn't appear too eager. Her heart struck up an indecent rhythm when she opened the door to see Jordan there in black jeans, a black silk button-down shirt, and rough looking black boots. It was only when Jordan's smirk deepened that she realized she was staring.

"Off we go, then," Calliope said, moving forward so that Jordan had to back up or be knocked over.

"I brought you these," Jordan said, pulling a bouquet of freshly picked white daffodils from behind her back.

Calliope swallowed hard at the sudden emotion it brought on. She couldn't remember the last time she'd received flowers. "Thank you, they're beautiful." She went back into the house and placed them in a glass with water, then went back to Jordan, who'd remained in the doorway. "Now, to dinner."

Jordan moved aside and followed her to the car. Once they were on their way, Jordan turned to her. "You look beautiful. That top makes your eyes look like a summer sky."

Heat suffused her cheeks. "Thank you."

Jordan's eyebrows twitched. "How refreshing not to compliment a woman and have her self-deprecate the compliment away."

Calliope glanced at Jordan. "I don't think you ever have to worry about a muse not knowing her worth."

Jordan laughed, a deep, unhindered sound that made Calliope smile in return.

"No, I guess not. Tell me what you're the muse of, exactly? Because you're all in charge of something, right?"

"So you don't think we're simply there to inspire others but don't have any talent ourselves?" She grinned as she threw Jordan's words back at her and then slowed to let some silly pheasants wander across the road. "In charge of sounds rather...hmm. Not quite that. We've been given gifts ourselves, and we help others develop those gifts that are like our own. I'm the muse of justice and serenity. All of us have music as part of our beings, and I love to sing. But my main calling has always been to help humans be just, and to help them find peace. That peace often comes through music, but not always."

From the corner of her eye, she saw Jordan's brief frown and wondered what she'd said had struck a nerve.

"And you have eight sisters, all of whom have their own gifts." Her tone was still light and playful.

"Correct. I have eight sisters who are a pain in my proverbial bottom. I'm the eldest, and so I'm in charge. They've been quite a handful over the years." The thought of her sisters made her smile. "And your family?"

Jordan hesitated for a moment. "My mom died when I was young. Cancer. But my dad and I have always been really close, and we still are. I see him whenever I'm in Colorado. And I have a sister and brother as well."

"That's where you're from?" Calliope registered the sadness still there in Jordan's tone when she spoke of her mother.

"I am. That's where I got my sense of adventure, I guess. My mom and dad loved to ski, and we used to go all the time. Then after my mom passed, my dad would take me skiing, snowboarding, whatever I wanted to try, and he'd always do it with me."

"What a lovely memory." Calliope turned into the parking lot of the restaurant, and they didn't say anything more until they were seated.

"I have to admit, I googled the muses to learn more," Jordan said, not looking up from her menu.

"Wikipedia is fairly accurate, though it leaves a lot out." She looked over her options and found herself skipping over some choices because they might make her breath stink. Not that a kiss was part of the night, but she didn't need to be offensive if they were close to each other, either.

"Yeah, well, there's a few years to cover, isn't there?" Jordan looked over her menu. "Can I ask how old you are?"

"You shouldn't if you want to impress me. But you have, so you've already lost out. I'm three thousand three hundred and two years old, to be reasonably precise, although to say we came into being on a certain date is somewhat ludicrous given that we didn't even use calendars back then. But age doesn't matter to us. It's a human thing, really."

Jordan frowned slightly. "Yeah, well, when you have a paltry eighty or so in comparison, it's hard not to get hung up on it."

Calliope winced slightly, having forgotten how sensitive humans were to talk of aging. "Of course. Sorry."

They placed their orders and Jordan sat back, looking more relaxed. "Thank you for coming out with me tonight."

"Thank you for asking me. Even if it is only to discuss business type things."

Jordan quickly shook her head. "It isn't. I meant what I said. I'd like to get to know you. Are you close to your sisters? Who are your parents? What's your favorite flower? Who is your favorite person in history?"

Calliope held up her hand. "Give me a chance to answer!" She waited until the server had set their drinks down before continuing. "Yes, I'm close to my sisters, but I'm especially close to Thalia, as she's most like me. I work a lot, and I miss them." She took a sip of her drink, aware how the next bit might sound. "My father is Zeus, who you've probably heard of."

Jordan snorted and choked slightly on her drink.

"My mother is Memnosyne, literally the goddess of memory. Zeus and my mother had a brief fling when Hera was in one of her fits of temper, and that led to my mother giving birth to us."

"To nine girls? That had to have been a surprise."

Calliope tilted her head thoughtfully. "I've never asked her, actually. She's considered a minor goddess, even though she's crucial to the human experience, and she keeps to herself. We're not close to our parents, overall, though I have to work with my father quite often. I work at Afterlife, you see, in their justice department."

"LA isn't far from San Francisco." Jordan's eyes lit up. "I could see you when we got back."

The thought of continuing to see Jordan beyond whatever happened here between them in Scotland made her pulse race. "Yes, perhaps so. Anyway, my favorite flower is the white foxglove, and my favorite person in history is an impossible question to answer." Being the center of Jordan's attention was intoxicating in a way she hadn't experienced in an awfully long time. She liked it. Very much.

"Surely you've come across someone who lit a fire in you." Jordan smiled at the server who put her food down in front of her.

Calliope allowed various memories to come to her and chose one that felt safe to divulge to a stranger. "Marion Carstairs was a lover of mine for some time, although she went by Joe to anyone who really knew her. And I got to know her *very* well. When I think of someone who lit a fire in me, aside from the obvious people like Plato and Darwin, it would be her." She dipped her bread in sauce and smiled at how she could still see the way Joe's eyes sparkled. "She was a British speed boat racer. I met her in 1930, when she was beyond words. She had tattoos, she dressed in men's clothing, and she gave absolutely no cares whatsoever about what anyone thought. It made her extremely popular at a time when women were pushing against the boundaries placed on them."

Jordan looked at her over her glass. "Sounds like someone you know now. Not to sound egotistical or anything."

Calliope laughed, realizing it was true. "Yes, I suppose she was a bit like you. Adventurous, daring, will do what she has to in order to get what she wants."

"But also wants to make people happy." Jordan's expression turned serious. "That's important too."

Calliope didn't respond, and they ate in silence for a while. She wasn't sure what to say that wasn't prying or wouldn't lead to a heated discussion, and the notion that Jordan resembled a woman she'd been passionate about was a little unsettling. But soon the tension began to turn her food bitter, so she broke it. "Can I ask why it's so important to you to build your adventure park in this little village? When you could build it anywhere at all?"

It looked like she'd struck a nerve when Jordan flinched and set her fork down. She sat still for a moment, looking lost in thought.

"Maybe save that one for later. Instead, are you with anyone special?" Calliope was mortified at the non sequitur as well as the personal question she didn't really have a right to ask.

Jordan's eyebrow twitched slightly, and her smirk went a little deeper. "Happily single, actually."

"A free spirit in every way." Was that a good thing or a bad thing? She couldn't decide.

"In every way." Jordan pushed her plate away, having scraped it clean. "I love being able to up and go at a moment's notice. Someone calls and asks me to go rock climbing in Switzerland? I'm in. A woman wants to join me in bed when I'm kayaking in Thailand? There's no reason not to enjoy her. I can do anything I want, whenever I want, with whomever I want."

Despite the carefree words coming out of Jordan's mouth, Calliope sensed a vacancy in them, a distinct lack of emotion. "And do you ever get lonely?"

Jordan appeared to consider the question. "Sometimes it would be nice to come home to someone, to share special moments. But those times don't balance with the freedom I get from not having someone depending on me. I like being unattached without someone making demands on my time." She looked around. "Want to get dessert here? Or maybe find somewhere else?"

What a relief that the night wasn't over yet. "You say that like there are a million options. But I believe I know a place not far away."

Jordan paid the bill, though Calliope offered to split it with her. "I'm old-fashioned this way. Indulge me."

Calliope accepted, more than a little charmed at Jordan's easy, innate chivalry. They went back to the car, and she shivered as she felt Jordan's hand skim her lower back. It was familiar, and perhaps a little forward, but it felt so nice she found that she leaned into the touch and was sad to lose it when they got in the car.

"Why are you really so opposed to my park?" Jordan asked as they drove down the dark lanes toward the next village.

Was there a deeper motivation she hadn't examined? Something she hadn't said? She considered it and Jordan allowed her the time to answer. "The reasons I've given you already are real. It's a quiet place and you're going to diminish, if not extinguish altogether, the peace of the temple." She drummed her fingers on the steering wheel. "But it's also personal, Jordan. This place is my sanctuary. It's my place away from the world. It's been dedicated to the muses, and there's only one other temple to us in all the world. I come here not just to get away, but to reconnect to who I am. I come here to hear the song of serenity, the one I used to sing before I became embroiled in the world of gods among people. When being a muse meant making the world beautiful, one person at a time."

It was as honest as she could be, and Jordan leaned her head against the passenger window, silent, as she considered what Calliope had said. When they pulled up in front of More Moolicious, Jordan brightened.

"I have no idea what this is, but I love it on principle." Jordan quickly got out of the car.

"Honestly, I'm not sure either. I heard someone in the village talking about it, but I've never been here." Pictures of milkshakes in a million unnatural colors adorned the walls, along with glossy images of brownies and cookies covered in various toppings.

"I want one of everything," Jordan said, eyeing the menu intently.

"That might get a bit sickly. I think I'll have the peanut butter shake." Calliope had found the invention of peanut butter one of the best things humans had created.

"I'm going to have the triple brownie stack with chocolate ice cream and fudge sauce. With marshmallows."

Talk about sickly. It made Calliope's teeth hurt just thinking about it. "You know that's a two-person dessert?"

Jordan scoffed and held up a bright pink plastic spoon. "Who are they kidding? I bet I can finish mine before you finish yours."

Calliope picked up her shake from the counter. "I'd take you up on that except that I'd be afraid I'd send you into a sugar coma before you finished."

They sat at a sticky table near the window. Fluorescent lighting and children yammering in the corner did away with any intimate vibe that might have been present, for which Calliope was grateful. She didn't need a romantic entanglement, especially with someone so enticing.

They spoke of surface things and allowed the heavier issue that lay between them to simmer. Calliope laughed at Jordan's story of getting caught up in a street parade honoring death while she was in Mexico, and she made Jordan laugh in turn as she shared a few anecdotes about disagreements between the gods. Soon, however, it was time to go, and Calliope was sad the evening was at an end. She hadn't had a night out like this one in the last decade.

The roads were pitch-black on the way back and Calliope drove carefully. There was a strange electricity between them, an air of expectation and uncertainty. Did Jordan feel it too? Or was she alone in this?

"Calliope, I'm sorry. I understand what you've said about your serenity. I really do. And I wish it was different because I feel like we've got a connection." Jordan's expression was hard to gauge in the dark car, but her tone was genuine. "But it matters to me, this place. I want it to be a legacy for reasons you don't understand, and I can't back down from that."

Calliope sighed, weary with the fight and sad that this was where they were at. "And I can't give up and allow the temple to become the background for people who wouldn't revere it and who would wreck the peace people desire when they come to a temple to ask for guidance."

"And the bit I said about our connection?" Jordan asked.

Calliope contemplated her answer, needing to be honest but not wanting to hurt Jordan's feelings, either. Blunt was best. "I don't have relationships with humans, Jordan. They're too painful and too brief."

Jordan rested her head against the headrest and didn't say anything until they pulled up in front of her hotel, where she turned to look at Calliope in the dim streetlight. "So you think we have a connection too."

Calliope shook her head and smiled, and Jordan grinned back at her.

"Look, I can't compete with gods for a woman's attention. I'm human, and flawed, and definitely going to die one day. Honestly, I don't do relationships either. And I respect that you don't want to put your heart on the line for something that won't last as long as you do." She reached over and squeezed Calliope's hand before she opened the door and got out. But before she walked away, she leaned down once more. "But I'm certain there's something between us. Something totally different. Maybe it's just because you're one of them. But what if it's not? What if there's something more going on? It would suck to lose out on seeing what it might be, wouldn't it?" She closed the door softly and loped up the stairs to the hotel, turning to give a quick wave before she headed inside.

Calliope drove back to her place, contemplating Jordan's questions. But she'd already been down this road. She'd had magical times with mortal women, and every time they passed away, they took a little piece of her with them. Not to mention that as they aged and their bodies changed, they usually grew to resent her. She reflected on something they'd never have. A life unending, a face without wrinkles or age spots. A body without stretch marks. What they didn't realize was that sometimes she envied them.

Chapter Thirteen

Was it a good idea? Probably not. At least, not from a personal perspective. From a business perspective, it might be what she needed to do. But what if it backfired?

Jordan stood on the bridge looking down at the river, her hands shoved deep in her pockets. She'd come up with the idea in the middle of a sleepless night where all she could think about was the way Calliope's eyes lit up when she smiled and the delicate way she held her glass when she drank.

With a quick swear word under her breath, she turned and headed toward Calliope's house. She passed the temple and saw the girl she'd seen there before, who was lighting candles and straightening things shifted by the wind overnight. The girl glanced at her and then quickly away. Jordan wondered if she felt the way Calliope did about her business venture.

Calliope was sitting outside on her deck, a steaming cup of something in her hand, her eyes closed, and her head tilted toward the early morning sun. Her dark hair glistened and fell over her shoulders in soft waves. She looked every inch the immortal she was, and Jordan couldn't help but fall under her spell. A branch broke underfoot, and Calliope opened her eyes.

"You're out early," she said.

"I have a proposition for you," Jordan said, stopping to lean on the stone wall.

"I'll admit that sounds enticing, but I'm not sure I'm your type." Calliope took a sip from her mug, staring at Jordan over the rim with a playful challenge in her eyes.

God, how Jordan wanted to take up that challenge. But gods weren't something you trifled with. "You couldn't be more my type than if I'd created you in a computer program. But when I make *that* particular proposition, I promise it will be under circumstances where I don't have to state my intention to do so." She grinned as Calliope rolled her eyes. "I want you to take a road trip with me."

"Where are we going?"

That was a far more promising response than a flat-out no. "I'd like to surprise you. But it's a distance away, so we'll have to stay overnight. I promise we'll be back for the meeting at Tweed tomorrow night."

Calliope looked off into the distance without responding, and Jordan wondered what was going through her head, but she waited patiently. Mostly patiently.

"Okay." Calliope set her mug down and stood. "When do we leave?"

Jordan wanted to raise her arms in victory but that wouldn't look very cool at all. "As soon as possible."

"And I assume you want me to drive?"

Jordan shook her head, already backing away. "We're going with some friends of mine, and they're happy to drive."

Calliope frowned slightly. "You left that bit out."

"I know how to pitch things so I get a yes first." Jordan ducked the twig Calliope threw at her. "You'll like them, I promise. We'll pick you up in an hour. Okay?"

Calliope folded her arms, her head tilted thoughtfully.

"Wear comfortable clothes and shoes!" Jordan called over her shoulder as she headed back toward the bridge. She needed to pack herself, as well as call Leith to tell her that she and her girlfriend of the minute were about to take an overnight trip with her. She'd planned on it being just her and Calli, but when faced with that she'd chickened out. At least having someone else there would give them a buffer against whatever it was building between them.

❖

"This is one of the weirdest things you've talked me into. And you once convinced me to skinny-dip in a volcano." Leith looked in her rearview mirror at Jordan.

"That's a story I want to hear." Amber, Leith's latest girlfriend, fluttered her eyes, which, with the amount of mascara on them, looked like tired goth butterflies.

Leith grinned. "Some things stay on the mountains they happen on." She looked at Jordan in the mirror again. "Are you sure about this?"

"God no. But it may help, and if it doesn't and she calls in some god for backup, I'll need you beside me."

"What, so we can get fried or turned into beavers together?" Leith drummed on the steering wheel. "I guess it's just another Jordan James adventure, huh?"

"Exactly."

Amber looked over her shoulder at Jordan. "I think it's super cool that we're going to be traveling with a muse. Like, how many people get to hang out with the immortals?"

"More than there used to be, that's for sure." Jordan winced at the bit of iron in her tone, but she couldn't help it. Her issues with the gods needed to be set aside for this to work, that was certain. They pulled up in front of Calliope's house and Jordan jumped out. The door opened before she could knock, and Calliope's smile gave her that delicious weak-kneed feeling once again.

"I'm not usually one for surprises," she said, allowing Jordan to take her overnight bag from her. "But I'm making an exception because there's something about you that makes me want to."

Jordan's heart sped up at the simple admission. "That's awesome. I'm glad you feel that way, and hopefully you'll enjoy it." She walked behind Calliope to the car and opened her door for her, then popped her bag in the trunk before running around to her side. They were making their own introductions as she strapped in.

"You don't look like one of them," Amber said, looking distinctly unimpressed.

"No, I don't suppose I do." Calliope smiled gently. "No wings or fangs or snakes. Just me."

"Huh." Amber gave a polite, goth butterfly smile and turned back around, where she immediately started playing with her phone.

Leith looked at Amber like she might toss her from the car before she set off toward the motorway. Jordan had a feeling their relationship wasn't going to last much longer. But Calli's smile suggested she'd heard Amber's kind of admonition before and wasn't in the least fazed by it.

"Have you known one another long?" Calli asked.

"Long enough for Jordan to get me in all kinds of trouble in all kinds of places." Leith glanced in the mirror and then back to the road.

"It's not like I had to force her. Ever." Jordan lightly flicked the back of Leith's ear and got a swat to her leg in return.

"Jordan tells us you're a muse, Calliope? That must be interesting…work." Leith grimaced at her word choice.

"It is. I've met some incredibly creative people over the years. And being dedicated to justice, I've also stood at the side of various rulers."

Jordan turned so she could look at Calliope comfortably. "Like who?"

Calliope hesitated and then smiled. "King Arthur was probably my favorite."

The car swerved slightly, throwing them against the side until Leith righted it again. "King Arthur? Like, the guy in the fable?"

"The guy in the fable was actually very real. But there wasn't a lot of emphasis on written records in his kingdom, so what you have is handed down oral stories that have become fable. But he was an exceptional king, and I was able to enhance his sense of justice so he could rule well."

She said it as simply as though she was talking about what she'd made for dinner the night before. There was no pride or ego, just genuine admiration. Jordan was reminded once again of the differences between them. "Did you wear those long dresses? Was it as beautiful as they portray it?" She wiggled her eyebrows. "Did you get it on with Maid Marion? Where was his kingdom actually located?"

Leith and Calliope laughed. Amber was engrossed in her phone but glanced up at the laughter.

"Yes, I wore the fashion of the times, which was less restrictive in a lot of ways than it is today. No, it wasn't nearly as beautiful as they portray it now. It was smelly and dirty. People bathed maybe once a year and toilets, when there were any, emptied into shallow holes or ditches. Granted, people in the court were cleaner, but even they just used perfume to cover up the smell of bodily odors." She shook her head, clearly disgusted at the memory. "I could tell you where the kingdom was located, but that would ruin the mystery. And as for Maid Marion…" She gave Jordan a wicked grin. "Well, let's say she wasn't really a maid."

Leith and Jordan burst out laughing again. It had been a good idea after all, to invite Leith and Amber to go with on this spontaneous and possibly ill-fated adventure. It provided the buffer she'd hoped for, it was true, but it also allowed her even more time to spend with Calli, who was open and kind and seemed to have no problem answering any of Leith's and Jordan's questions. Eventually, as they went farther north, Amber lost phone reception and threw it on the dashboard petulantly. She shifted in the passenger seat so she could look at them in the back.

"What do you *do*?" she asked. "Like, I know you're a muse and all, but what does that mean? Like, do you cast spells or something?"

Although she'd been curious about how Calli's power worked herself, Jordan winced at the tone of Amber's question. Calli, however, didn't seem to mind.

"Give me your hand, Amber," Calli said, holding out her own.

Amber narrowed her eyes a little but put her hand out. Calli held it between both of hers and looked into Amber's eyes for a moment. "I thought so. You like to sing, don't you?"

Amber slid her hand away. "Yeah."

Calli motioned for Amber's hand back. "Sing for us."

"I can't just sing. Like, with no music or whatever."

Leith turned on the radio and switched it to her iPhone connection. A country song began playing. "She likes this one."

"Country music is good for telling stories. Sing along." Calli continued to hold Amber's gaze as well as her hand.

Amber swallowed and then began to sing, and it was only a line or two in before she began to sing beautifully, her eyes closed as she fell into the lyrics. Emotion poured from her as she sang about heartbreak, about going home, and about missed chances. Jordan's breath hitched as tears welled in her eyes at the despair and longing in Amber's voice, and she barely noticed when Leith pulled into a turnout and turned the car off.

The song ended, and after a moment Amber opened her eyes. Tears streamed down her cheeks and the silence was heavy before she broke it. "I've always loved that song, but I've never felt it like that. Deep down."

Calliope released her hand and sat back. She was glowing faintly, as though lit by some inner light. "In answer to your question, that's what I *do*. I touch the gift you already have, the desire to use it, and I amplify it. I make it so you truly connect with it. And if I'm by your side long enough, I can help you grow and learn how to bring it to life."

"And all your sisters do that too?" Leith asked.

"We do. But we all have specialties, things we're most passionate about, and those are the people we reach out to. We all love song, to some degree, but we often have a second passion too. Like mine is justice."

Amber sat back in her seat, quiet and thoughtful. Leith started the car and they got underway again. Jordan couldn't help but reach out to take Calli's hand.

"That was incredible. Why don't you have pop stars lining up at your door?" It brought to mind the young singer who'd been at Calli's house the other day. "Or do you?"

"There are lots of reasons, and there are plenty of pop stars who write to ask us to be part of their crew." She smiled at Leith's huff of indignation. "But it takes something special, something deeper than a desire for fame and a basic enjoyment of singing. It takes emotion and passion on a level deeper than many people feel. When I got in the car, I could feel Amber's passion and I sensed the song in her soul. She has something rare, and with training and ambition, she could touch the world with her voice."

Amber stared at her, wide-eyed. "Do you mean that?"

"You'll find I never prevaricate. That's the justice side." Calli smiled kindly.

"And what about world leaders? Wouldn't they want you at their sides too? Like King Arthur?"

At this, Calli's light faded a little and Jordan wished she could take the question back.

"Sadly, not anymore. Through the centuries there have been a wonderful number of leaders who genuinely wanted to be the best rulers they could for their people. But in the last hundred years, those leaders have become far fewer. Most are only interested in numbers and a title, not real justice."

"But what about the movements? Like the BLM movement? Do you get involved in those?" Amber asked, eliciting a surprised look from Leith.

"I'm the only one in my family who gets involved in politics, but it can get extremely messy. But sometimes I do, if someone asks and I can see how they're genuinely working to make the world better. But after JFK and Martin Luther King were shot, I guess I became a little…" She drifted off for a moment as she stared out the window. "Jaded, I suppose. They were men who wanted real change, real justice, and I walked beside them both on many occasions."

"But then the people who work against real justice stepped in." Jordan squeezed Calli's hand, which she still hadn't let go of.

"Right. And from then on, the groups who want, and need, real justice have become smaller and more spread out."

"But couldn't you help them? Like, make their voices louder?" Amber asked, once again eliciting a look from Leith like she'd just found an alien in her car.

Calli looked at Jordan, who could practically see the thoughts whirling in her mind.

"Yes, I suppose I could. I've been so busy I've left the world behind. Maybe it's time to look at that."

Conversation became lighter and laughter more prevalent as they seemed to silently agree to leave the heavier subjects behind. Amber sang along softly to the music, and the trip went swiftly. Too quickly for Jordan, who was so immersed in Calli's beauty and stories she didn't want it to end.

But then Leith turned into the parking lot and the road trip part had come to an end. Now was the bigger test.

Calliope read the sign at the entrance and turned to Jordan with her eyebrow raised impossibly high. "An adventure park?"

Jordan threw open her door. "What better way to show you what you've been missing?" She watched as Calli slowly got out of the car and looked at the people milling around. Happy people, children laughing and darting around, people excited about what they were about to encounter. Jordan was familiar with the customer reactions. The question was, would Calli see the good parts? Or would it just reaffirm what she already feared would happen to her little piece of paradise?

CHAPTER FOURTEEN

There had been rare times in history when Calliope had envied the gods their powers. The ability to turn people into creatures or plants, for instance. Zeus and his lightning bolt. The fury sisters and their snakes. It usually only happened when something truly egregious had occurred.

If she'd had any of those powers, she would have used them now, just as she was about to go flying through the air held up by nothing but thick, uncomfortable straps, and a cable meant to inspire confidence in the idea that you wouldn't go tumbling through the air to end up impaled on a tree or broken by the rocks. Jordan and Leith would have made cute sloths, she thought as she listened to the instructor tell her how to slow down and how to land once she came to a stop.

Jordan, on a line parallel to hers, was looking at her expectantly and with no small amount of concern. "On a scale of one to ten, how magically pissed are you right now?"

"You're lucky I can't turn you into an anteater."

Jordan winced and she heard Amber giggle behind them.

"You're about justice and things being fair, right? Well, once you've experienced the type of thing I'll be building, you'll have a better idea of what we're in discussion about. Only fair, right?"

The nervousness in Jordan's voice would have been funny had Calliope not been about to step off a platform a hundred feet up. "I can't die, but I can feel pain. And my sisters will be terribly upset with you if I feel pain. As will my father." She looked down at the ground far below.

"Who's her father?" Leith asked.

"Zeus," Jordan said, a little breathlessly. "Maybe this wasn't a good idea."

Calliope took a deep breath. "You're buying dinner." The attendant called out that it was time to go, and adrenaline like she hadn't felt for centuries rushed through her as she stepped off the platform. In a sitting position, she began her descent past the trees, and once she'd settled, she began to look around. Sunlight glinted off lochs in the distance and an eagle soared in lazy circles over the pine trees. The wind was chill and invigorating, and she looked at Jordan, flying along almost beside her and gave her a wide smile.

Jordan raised her arms. "You're flying! Who needs wings!"

Calliope laughed, a free, open laugh as she tilted her face to the sun. She wished she could slow down a little so she could take it in a little more fully, but she wasn't going too fast. A large river flowed in puzzle piece pattern, and she could swear she'd seen fish in it before the river was quickly left behind. When they got to the platform her heart was racing.

"On to the next," Jordan said.

"Next? That wasn't it?"

Jordan hooked onto the next line. "There are fourteen lines. It will take us about two hours, give or take."

She wouldn't say outright that she was glad. She'd save the admission for when Jordan could really savor it at the end of the day. Line after line, she flew through the air, past towering pines and ash, past startled birds, and sunbeams that she careened through. The final line was the longest, according to the sign that said it was five hundred and fifty meters long, which was nearly two thousand feet. It was also the fastest, which meant she wouldn't be able to talk to Jordan at all this time, as she had on a few of the other lines as they'd pointed things out to one another.

The final line flashed by and she understood, if only for a moment, what the fury sisters must feel as they launched into the air and flew through the sky. It was a magnificent experience and one she'd treasure forever. She landed and the vibrations continued in her arms even as she took off her rigging. Impulsively, she threw her arms around Jordan. "Thank you. I might have wanted to turn you into some kind of fauna when we got here, but that was absolutely wonderful."

Jordan held her tightly. "I'm so glad you enjoyed it. And that you couldn't turn me into anything else."

They parted, keeping eye contact, and Calliope saw Jordan's gaze linger on her lips before they were interrupted by Amber and Leith arriving on the platform as well. Both seemed as exhilarated as Calliope felt, and the enjoyment of being a part of a group adventure made her tingle. That, too, hadn't happened in a very long time.

They made their way down the platform stairs to the café below, where they got drinks and shortbread and dissected the trip, sharing things they'd seen. Jordan checked her watch and stood. "Ready for the next one?"

"There's more?" Calliope didn't want the day to end.

"That was one zip section. The second one is a little more intense, but it goes over waterfalls and a beautiful gorge." Jordan held out her hand. "If you want to, of course."

Calliope took her hand and her breath caught at the surge of electricity between them. Jordan's eyes widened, and with a slow smile, she held a little tighter.

The four of them walked to the next launch point, and although she knew it was a bad idea, she allowed Jordan to continue holding her hand as they made their way over. It felt so good to be touched in such a simple and sweetly intimate way. She was almost sorry to let go once they reached their destination.

This experience was different from the last one, steeper and with even more incredible views. Calliope's heart sang as she moved through the trees and over stunning, crashing waterfalls. She also took note of something she bet the others hadn't seen. By the last platform she was pleasantly exhausted, and once again, she hugged Jordan tightly. This time, Jordan only let go enough to lean back so she could look Calliope in the eye.

"You're amazing," she said softly.

How desperately Calliope wanted to be kissed. For Jordan to lean in and bring them together. Her eyes were just starting to close when laughter inserted itself into their moment, pulling it apart. She smiled slightly and moved back, noting the disappointment in Jordan's expression.

Leith and Amber came in fast, and Jordan caught Amber as she tripped slightly. This time, they skipped the café and went straight to a pub serving dinner, where they chatted and ate and drank for quite a while. Jordan was humble when Leith told them about the charities Jordan's parks helped keep going, including programs for homeless LGBTQ youth.

The pub was empty by the time they got up to leave, and fortunately, the hotel was only across the road. The night sky was a blanket of blinking stars, and Calliope took a deep breath of cold, clean air. An owl hooted and Jordan jumped and looked around.

"Afraid of owls?" Calliope asked with a knowing smirk.

"I knew you had something to do with it!" Jordan said, pulling Calliope to her.

"I have no idea what you're talking about."

Leith had her arm around Amber as they headed up the stairs to the hotel. "See you bright and early."

And then they were alone on the sidewalk, with Jordan's arms wrapped around her. "I'm so glad you enjoyed today. I had a feeling you would."

An idea began to form around the thing she'd seen earlier. "You know that final waterfall? The one that fell over three levels?"

Jordan nodded. "It has some really long Scottish name."

"Do you think you could find your way back? On foot?"

Jordan looked confused. "I think so. We could probably go early tomorrow, before we head back."

Calliope shook her head, paying attention to her instincts. "Tonight. You've shown me some of your world. Now I want to show you some of mine."

Jordan stared at her for a moment, then let her go. "Let me go get the keys from Leith."

Calliope took out her phone, found the waterfall on the map, and set the directions going. Fortunately, it was a well-known place with a trail leading to it.

Jordan came loping out. "After you."

She drove while Calliope gave directions. There was no light at all, and the turns were well hidden. When they got to the trailhead, Jordan parked and turned to Calliope. "If you wanted to go somewhere to make out, you could have just said."

Calliope got out of the car. "As you once said, if that's my intention, I won't have to say it out loud." She took Jordan's hand, and they made their way down the trail. "I saw something today. Something really special, and I wanted to share it with you."

The roar of the waterfall could be heard easily, and she followed the sound to the end of the trail, where the bottom third of the waterfall was clear. But she needed to get higher and, using her phone flashlight, she searched for a trail. She found one, a narrow gap between bushes and nothing more. "This way."

"The muse of justice can't kill someone and leave their body in the forest, right?" Jordan whispered. "It must be against some rule or something."

Calliope smiled but didn't respond, aware of the sensitive nature of what they were doing.

They made their way along slowly and she closed her eyes periodically, feeling the way by instinct. When she heard the tinkle of a bell, she stopped and looked around. "Listen," she whispered, once again taking Jordan's hand.

Jordan jerked a little when the singing began. Soft, beautiful sounds that barely rose over the sound of the waterfall. "It's like the trees themselves are singing," she leaned over and whispered.

"Dryads. Water nymphs who live among the trees." Slowly, she led Jordan forward toward the singing. They stopped at the edge of a small clearing, and what she saw made her heart leap.

A group of five dryads played by the river's edge, picking flowers, singing, and splashing one another. They were naked, their pale green bark-like skin and flowing green hair allowing them to blend into the forest that was their home. Calliope had caught a glimpse of one at the edge of the waterfall, so quickly she would have thought she'd imagined it if she hadn't known better.

She held her hand up to tell Jordan to stay put and then slowly made her way into the clearing. The dryads startled and backed toward the river until Calliope began to sing. She sang an old Celtic lullaby, letting the feeling of the wind in her hair and the feeling of belonging to infuse the melody. It also marked her as other, as one of the immortals rather than as a human. The dryads drifted closer, one even sitting on the ground to listen. When she finished, she too sat down as a way to be less threatening. She wasn't surprised when the tallest of the dryads, nearly seven feet tall and as slim as a seedling tree, spoke to her in Gaelic.

"Before I answer, I have a friend with me. I'd like to bring her out, if I may? I swear to you by the gods she means no harm and will tell no one of your existence here."

The leader looked past Calliope into the shadows and gave a curt nod.

Calliope waved Jordan out and heard her careful footsteps as she moved to Calliope's side and sat down beside her. Calliope glanced at her and saw the wonder in her eyes. "She's asked me why I'm here."

She replied in Gaelic, a little rusty but clear, hopefully. She explained that her friend wanted to build something like they had here, with people flying overhead. She wanted to know how they felt about it. She relayed the question to Jordan, who looked like she now understood why Calliope had brought her here.

Another of the dryads moved closer before the leader could respond. She touched Jordan's shoulder, then her face, her hair, and her biceps. She said something that made her sisters titter, and then slid her hand up Jordan's leg toward her crotch.

Jordan jerked slightly and the dryads tittered again.

She said something and Calliope dipped her head and smiled. "She said you'd be welcome not to build anything, but to stay here and let them see how strong you are." She glanced at Jordan. "She doesn't mean for manual labor."

The sound that came out of Jordan was something between a laugh and an embarrassed cough. "Tell them I'm honored, but—"

"But you're spoken for." Calliope relayed the message, and the dryad retreated a few steps, but the look in her eyes said she didn't care who Jordan was with.

The leader spoke sharply, and the dryad closest moved back, hardly looking sorry. She smiled, and her sharp, pointed teeth glinted in the moonlight. Once again, Jordan jerked slightly, but this time Calliope put her hand on Jordan's leg. Dryads were easily insulted and rather unpleasant when irritated.

The leader sat cross-legged in front of them and repeated her answer. Calliope translated. "She says they can't be free like they were. They have to be careful that no human sees them, as they were once hunted nearly to extinction. Before, it was easy to live unnoticed in the mountains, but now humans are all over those, too. They still play in the rivers and falls, but now they do it mostly at night. There's more noise and the sound from the wires hurts their ears."

Jordan leaned forward, listening intently. Calliope's instinct to bring her here had been correct. But then the dryad continued, and Calliope continued to translate.

"But the forest is also healthier. The dead trees are taken away, the underbrush is cleared, and if there's sickness in the water, the people help make it right. The laughter and joy that ring through the forest makes the trees happy."

The dryad leaned toward them, directing what she was saying at Jordan.

"If you're going to make something like this, then you must be sensitive to those who are part of the forest. If it dies, then they do too. If it hurts, they do. If it cries or becomes ill, so do they."

She looked at her sisters and turned back to them, her expression sad.

Calliope translated as she spoke. "They're like the animals who lose their homes because humans want their land. They cut down trees to make buildings from those trees, and then the animals have no home. Like that, the dryads may have to leave this forest and find another so that they can roam freely once again."

The dryad looked at Jordan, her oblong pupils black as the night around them, and said something else.

"She's afraid at some point there will be nowhere left to go."

The dryad stood and her sisters did too. They moved to the edge of the river where the second tier of the waterfall dropped into the third. She began to sing, and the sisters joined, as did Calliope. The forest entered her, rooted her, let her feel what it was to be earth bound and reaching for the sky, to flow like water around any obstacle.

And then the song stopped, and the dryads walked into the water and were gone.

Chapter Fifteen

Jordan leaned back on her elbows, the look of awe still on her face.

"You didn't look that stunned when you found out I was a muse," Calli said.

"You don't have strange eyes, green skin, and pointed teeth. That I know of, anyway." Jordan ran her hand over her face. "That was something else."

Calli scooted back to lean against a boulder. "I couldn't believe it when I saw them as I was flying past. They're incredibly rare. You've been able to see what many gods haven't even seen."

"Really? I thought the gods saw everything?"

"Some things are outside their realm. Dryads are older than the gods. They're an aspect of human evolution, I guess you could say."

Jordan sat up. "You're telling me those things are related to people?"

Calli winced. "*Things* is a bit harsh, don't you think?"

Jordan tilted her head in apology. "Sorry. You're right. Bad word choice. But can you explain?"

"You know the Darwinian idea of evolution? Humans crawled out of the primordial ooze and such? Eventually you went from primate to neanderthal. Well, one group didn't. They climbed from the ooze, but they became dryads, shy creatures tied to the land and water. Human-like, but not human. They're extremely rare and well hidden, and they live long lives, and rarely procreate." She took a deep breath and closed her eyes for a moment. "As much as humans think they know about their planet, there will always be more they don't know. They're still finding new species of fish, after all this time."

It was hard information to take in. There was another evolutionary strand of humanesque being and hardly anyone knew about them except through fairy tales. "Thank you, Calli. It was an astounding surprise."

Calli stood and brushed the dirt from her butt. "And has it given you something to think about?"

It had given her reams of things to think about, beyond what Calli was probably referring to. "It has, and I promise to give what they've said serious thought."

Seemingly satisfied with that answer, Calli led the way back down to the car. Once there, she guided them back to the hotel. Jordan couldn't think of any conversation starters that didn't include questions about other primordial beings walking around on the planet. Sure, she needed to apply what she'd heard tonight to her venture, but until she could fully come to terms with what she'd experienced, that could wait.

She walked Calli to her room and took her hand. "Thank you for being such a good sport, and for being so much fun." She lifted Calli's hand, she then kissed it lightly, not dropping eye contact, which meant she saw the way Calli's pupils dilated as her breathing sped up.

Jordan leaned forward, brushing her lips to Calli's, and then pressed closer when Calli's hands held onto her hips. She deepened the kiss, growing dizzy at the softness of Calli's lips, at the way she kissed her back like there wasn't anything in the universe she wanted more. When Jordan broke the kiss, her body on fire, Calli's hands slid from her hips.

She backed against her door, groping with her free hand for the door handle. "I had an amazing time. Thank you." Calli got the door open and gently pulled away. With a quick smile, she went in and closed the door behind her.

Jordan sighed right down to her toes and rested her head on Calli's door. She'd hoped that whatever had transpired between them might lead to more. There was no question something *had* transpired. Fucking hell, that had been a hell of a kiss. She'd felt it in her soul, a warm wind coursing through her. But Calli shut it down. Why? Okay, so she said she didn't date humans. And Jordan didn't do the relationship thing. But had Calli had a connection like this with one before?

The thought that maybe she had and that's why she was so reticent left a bitter taste in her mouth. Maybe it wasn't as special as she thought. In fact, it was absurd to think she could be special or unique to someone who'd lived as long as Calli had. What did she have to offer someone who'd inspired Plato? And if a human woman could make demands on her time, then how much more intense would an immortal's demands be? She pushed away from the door, one hand still touching her warm, tingling lips, and went across the hall to her own room. She got ready for bed and crawled under the cold comforter, alone.

She woke drenched in sweat, early morning light peeking through the thin curtains. She ran her hands through her damp hair and counted to slow her pounding pulse. The dream had been so real. Beings she didn't know existed ran from her bulldozers but didn't make it and were crushed beneath the huge tires. Women and children cried out as their trees were ripped from the ground, and as it happened, their bodies turned to charred wood and then to ash. And all the while, Jordan ignored the carnage and gave directions on where to build next.

Horrified and sick to her stomach, she got up and took a hot shower to wash away the despair that lingered in the shadows of her mind. She thought about the other places she'd built. Had she done irreparable harm to creatures she didn't even know were there? Calli had said the dryads were rare, so it was unlikely she'd encroached on their territory. But were there other creatures? It didn't seem impossible.

Her dream venture was turning into a nightmare. Last night she'd been so overwhelmed by what she'd seen she hadn't taken time to consider the ramifications. But clearly her subconscious was ready to delve into the darker places.

She dressed and left her room, fortified in a thick sweatshirt, jeans, and ski socks. It was extra cold this much farther north. In the restaurant, she made herself a cup of tea from the ever-present kettle and carried it outside to a wooden table. Early morning birds sang as they darted to the bird feeder and away again. An impossibly fluffy black and white cat sat watching the birds from a fence, looking only vaguely interested in their comings and goings. In the morning light, with such normal things as birds and cats, she began to feel better, and the dream began to fade.

Leith came out, looking well rested and content. She sat opposite Jordan and sipped her own tea. They sat in silence for a while, which Jordan appreciated.

"I may need to rethink the park," she said eventually.

Leith raised her eyebrows. "The muse of justice touch on your sense of right and wrong?"

Jordan hadn't even considered that aspect, but she didn't think Calli had done anything like that. "Maybe, but I don't think so. She showed me something last night. Something amazing, and it has me thinking about my impact."

Leith sipped her tea and tracked the fluffy cat as it made its way toward them. "I don't know what you saw, and I'm guessing you probably shouldn't tell me since we weren't invited. But I can tell you this. I've never met a more considerate, conscientious builder than you. You're environmentally aware, you use sustainable materials, and you minimize impact any way you can." She shrugged noncommittally. "Maybe that helps, maybe it doesn't. But don't give up on your dream. Maybe you just need a different perspective on it."

The thing was, Calli had provided her with a different perspective last night. But Leith was right. Jordan did everything she could to make it fun but green. And even the dryad had said the forest was better off in some ways. The whole extinction thing, though, made the healthy forest less of a bright side.

"Thanks, buddy. I think yours was the voice of reason I needed. But I may have to make some adjustments. Maybe." It was entirely possible no immortal or almost human or creatures older than God lived in the area she wanted to transform. But how would she know? Even Calli had been surprised at finding the dryads by the waterfall.

The fluffy cat leapt onto the table and stuck its nose in Jordan's tea. "Help yourself, why don't you? And what kind of cat likes cold tea?"

Leith held hers out of reach. "A Scottish cat, obviously."

It finished lapping at her tea and lay down in front of her, purring loudly. She stroked it, her thoughts drifting in currents this way and that. There were more questions than answers, and tonight she had the meeting at the Tweed center. How could she say that her place was truly safe, truly environmentally friendly?

Unbidden irritation began to rise. The gods and their ilk always seemed to mess things up. A world of humans had been fine. Messy, yeah, but they'd managed on their own for several thousand years. And now the gods were out and about, and it was all about…well, she wasn't sure what it was all about, but it rubbed her the wrong way. It was an illogical thought process, but she needed a place to lay her frustration, and the gods were an easy target.

And so, when Calli came out looking serenely beautiful in all her immortal gorgeousness, Jordan wasn't nearly as happy to see her as she should have been. Maybe Leith was right and Calli had used that special muse thing she did to enhance Jordan's sense of justice. But if that sense of justice went against Jordan's business, her plans, her future, then wasn't it an unfair way to play the game?

Calli seemed to sense Jordan's reserve, and she just gave them a brief smile before going back into the restaurant.

"Cold, mate." Leith looked unimpressed.

"What do you mean?"

"Come on. You've got your panties in a twist because you're having doubts. And if it were some god with their own agenda, I'd back you up. But to take it out on a muse, who is all about beauty and peace and being fair? That's harsh."

Irritation was quickly replaced with guilt. "I'm being an ass."

"Not the first time, won't be the last." Leith ducked as Jordan flicked a bit of cold tea at her. "But we have a long car ride back. Don't make it weird."

"It might already be a little weird. We kissed last night, too."

Leith whistled softly. "And I bet it shook you to your old hiking boots."

"Yeah." Jordan stood and the cat did that weird juddery cat jaw thing where it didn't make any noise but looked utterly pissed off. "Sorry, buddy. I have to go apologize."

Leith took over talking to the cat about whether it preferred tuna or salmon. Jordan headed in and found Calli sitting by the window, a far-off look in her eyes. When Jordan sat, she blinked as though coming back to herself and gave Jordan a wary smile. "Everything okay?"

Jordan took her hand. "I'm sorry. Last night has thrown me into a tizzy, and I'm all over the place. And it isn't fair to take it out on you."

Calliope squeezed her hand in return. "I forget sometimes that not everyone has adjusted to the new way of life. Not everyone wants to know there are beings among them they've never conceived of. Or at least, never taken as real. It might have been unfair of me to take you to them."

"No, not at all. No matter what the end result, I never want to live in ignorance just because it's easier." Jordan let go of Calli's hand, needing the separation in order to think clearly. "I'm insanely glad you took me to them, and I'm really glad to know their perspective on it." She hesitated, trying to find the right words. "But I won't say it hasn't thrown a wrench in the works. I'm just trying to wrap my head around things."

Calli's smile made Jordan's heart thump painfully in her chest.

"I understand completely. These things challenge us, but challenge can mean change." She winced. "I sound like a fortune cookie."

Jordan was going to respond in kind, glad they were back to bantering and hoping they might be able to talk about the kiss, when a young woman came over to the table. Jordan glanced at her, surprised when she sat down. She looked more closely. "Wow. Amber?"

She blushed and looked down. Her brown eyes were clearly visible without the heavy makeup, and her hair was pulled back in a simple braid. She was pretty in a natural way that suited her perfectly.

"Calli and I had a little talk yesterday, and she told me I don't have to hide. That people will see my real talent even more when they can see my real face." She gave Calli a shy smile.

Jordan winked at her, making her blush. "I agree, and Leith is lucky to have found you."

Leith joined them at the table. "I am. But let's not forget how lucky she is too, eh?"

"Like you'd allow that." Jordan was glad the car ride back wouldn't be weird, but it was going to be a long day. There was time yet for things to go off track. "We should get on the road. Big meeting tonight." She didn't miss the quick flicker in Calli's eyes before they all stood.

"I have a strange request." She handed her phone to Leith, showing her a location on a map. "Can we stop there on our way? It's not too far off the road we'll be on, but I think it might be important."

Leith shrugged and tapped the address into her own phone's GPS. "I bet you don't have a lot of people who say no to you."

"They rarely have need to," Calli said with a mischievous grin.

Laughing, they went to their rooms to gather their things and were soon back on the road. Early morning light filtered through the trees, throwing thin shadows across the road. Highland cows stood near the fences, their boy-band bangs covering their eyes as they languidly surveyed the world beyond their field. It was idyllic, and an aspect of traveling that Jordan loved. But her thoughts kept going back to the night before and what she needed to do next. And how would her actions affect whatever might be happening between her and Calli? As was often the case, Calli seemed to be lost in thought as she stared out the window, and as much as Jordan wanted to take her hand, just to touch her, she couldn't bring herself to invade Calli's thoughts. Not to mention the feeling of inadequacy that still hung like a dark cloud in the back of her mind.

They pulled off the motorway and followed the GPS to a driveway almost hidden by trees. The drive wound for a long while through dense forest before it gave way to a clearing with an enormous house in the middle of it.

"Is that an actual thatched roof?"

Calli smiled. "The largest thatched roof home in all of the UK." She looked at her phone and tapped something in, and as they parked, the front door opened.

"Is that Nova Stokes?" Amber leaned forward, her eyes wide as the singer came out barefoot and gave them a small wave.

"It is." Without further explanation, Calli got out of the car and went to Nova, giving her a big hug.

Jordan, Leith, and Amber followed and stayed a respectful distance away until Calli turned to them and waved them forward.

They all shook Nova's hand. Amber held on a little longer than the others. "I've always loved your work."

The fleeting sadness in Nova's eyes was clear, and Calli wrapped her arm around her and squeezed her shoulders. It seemed to give her the grounding she needed, and Amber immediately looked chagrined at the faux pas.

"Thank you. It's always been a part of me. Come on in."

The inside of the house was stunning. Broad, dark wood beams stretched across the house, but the white walls and light furniture kept it from feeling too closed in. The ceilings were low, and Leith had to duck in the doorways. They went to a living room with several large sofas, where a tray of drinks was already laid out.

After they sat, Nova turned to Amber. "Calli tells me you have a gift."

Amber glanced at Calli, clearly surprised that she'd been a topic of conversation between a muse and an internationally known singer. "I don't know about a gift, but I love to sing. It's all I want to do from the time I wake up till I go to sleep."

Nova shared a brief smile with Calli. "If Calli says you have a gift, then you do."

"Nova has offered to mentor you, Amber. I believe the two of you working together will create wonderful things."

Amber gasped and moved to the edge of her seat. "Seriously? I can't pay…I mean, I don't have a lot of money, you know?"

Nova shook her head. "Calli has shown me how to redirect my gift, and by mentoring you, it will give me the chance to do that. We'll both win."

"You'll start today." Calli stood, apparently not expecting any argument. "We'll get your overnight bag out of the car, and Nova can help you if you need anything else."

There was a moment of silence. Leith stood with her head tilted, a small frown in place. "How will she get home?"

"I'll bring her home after we've got some training basics done and when we've figured out a schedule." Nova, too, stood.

A little perplexed, Jordan headed out to the car. "I'll get her bag."

Leith followed her out. "Do you get the feeling no one else has a say in this plan?" she asked as Jordan pulled the bag from the trunk.

"Amber doesn't seem to mind, and it's a hell of an opportunity." She squeezed her eyes closed and rolled her neck. "I think there are two women in there who are used to telling people what to do. But when you can see that they're right, it's hard to argue, isn't it?" The thought was like a hot needle under her skin as she considered applying that to Calli's argument against her adventure park.

"I guess. I just wish—"

"That someone had asked you if the girl you've been dating for a few weeks could go and stay with a Grammy winning singer instead of coming home with you?" Jordan grinned, hoping to ease the tension. She punched her in the arm and then hefted Amber's bag over her shoulder. "You're just pissed because she didn't put up a fight to stay with you. Don't make the ride home weird."

Leith harumphed and they went back in. Jordan handed Amber her bag, Calli hugged both Nova and Amber, and then went outside. Leith pulled Amber aside and had a quick, quiet conversation with her before she gave her a deep kiss and joined Calli outside. Jordan had no idea why she was the last one there, but she awkwardly held out her hand. "Good luck with everything. If you need whatever, Amber can get in touch with me."

Nova didn't let go of her hand. "Can I say something?"

Jordan wasn't about to tell her she couldn't.

"I think one of the things I've figured out is that you don't come across a muse by chance. They show up when you need them most. If you're on Calliope's path, then she's got something to teach you. You should listen."

Jordan gently extricated her hand from Nova's. "Thanks. I'll give that some thought."

Nova's enigmatic smile matched the look she gave her. "No, you probably won't. Until you have to." She walked Jordan to the door.

What could she say to that? There wasn't anything that wouldn't sound like a platitude, so she just smiled and headed for the car. Calli sat in the back so Jordan took the passenger seat, even though she wanted to sit beside her. Both of them in the back with Leith driving would make it weird.

They pulled out and headed back to the motorway.

"She'll be fine," Calli said, meeting Leith's gaze in the mirror. "Right now, they need one another more than you can know."

Leith sighed and looked back at the road. "What about what I need?"

Jordan was about to make some quip, but Calli said, "Your needs lie elsewhere."

Leith pulled into a lay-by and turned to face Calli. Jordan had never seen her look so serious. Or angry. "What can you know about my needs?"

Calli didn't flinch at the intensity of Leith's question. She simply held out her hand, and after looking at it like it might bite for a second, Leith took it in her own. Calli's eyes didn't leave Leith's, but Leith began to tremble, and tears slid down her cheeks. Jordan desperately wanted to ask what the hell was happening but didn't want to interrupt something that looked important.

Calli let go and sat back, giving Leith a small smile before she turned to stare out the window. Once again, she was surrounded in a kind of hazy halo, like she was lit from inside.

Leith wiped at her eyes with the back of her hands and took some deep breaths before she pulled back onto the road.

After a few minutes of silence, Jordan couldn't stand it anymore. "So…that was weird. Anyone want to clue me in?"

Calli didn't say anything, just glanced at Leith and then back out the window.

Leith began to laugh. "You have no idea what you're up against, Jordan."

She didn't say anything else, and when Jordan looked over her shoulder at Calli, she just gave her that same small smile that didn't give anything away.

"Not an answer to my question, and not an answer that makes me feel better about my life choices."

At that, both Calli and Leith began to laugh, and Jordan couldn't help but chime in. Okay, so whatever had happened was between them. So be it. But watching Calli's simple power, or whatever it was, change the people around her was daunting. What did it mean for Jordan's plans? What did it mean for her heart, if she let it get involved? If Calli affected everyone that way, then Jordan's planning permissions wouldn't get off the ground, and she could be in over her head when it came to how damn badly she wanted Calliope in her arms again. It didn't seem like a muse would be up for a quick fling, but Jordan wasn't interested in anything more permanent. She slumped in her seat. This venture was turning into something she'd never anticipated.

CHAPTER SIXTEEN

They dropped Calliope off first, and she was glad to be home. It had been an incredible trip and one she wouldn't regret. Even if it did mean she was far more attracted to Jordan than she'd been before, and she was also aware that the attraction meant something. What that something was, she had no idea. In all likelihood, Jordan had no idea they were already attached to one another in a mystical kind of way. And if Calliope told her so, she'd likely scoff and laugh it off.

But her instincts were never wrong. Jordan was special in many ways, and Calliope's heart was going to be involved. When Jordan had kissed her in the hallway, she'd very nearly opened the door and pulled her into her room for a night of passion that would have changed them both. And that would have been a bad idea. There were issues between them, ones Jordan hadn't even spoken about yet and things she'd be bothered that Calliope already knew without her saying them out loud. Such was the power of a muse to see into a person's soul.

She quickly unpacked and got everything tidied away before she made herself a cup of tea and relaxed in the sunshine on her porch. It wasn't surprising when Duncan ambled her way, and she went into the house to make him a cup of tea as well, which she handed him when she came out. He was already seated in the chair beside hers, his ever-present cap resting on his knee. The sun created diamonds on the river and children played on the hill below the temple as dog walkers crossed the green suspension bridge. How she loved her little corner of this big world.

"Was worried you'd gone back to the land of sunshine and left us to figure this out on our own." He closed his eyes and tilted his face to the sun.

"Did you stop by yesterday?"

He sipped his tea as he watched the river. "Aye. Brought my great-niece to meet you."

Calli smiled. "Is she still here?"

"Aye. Sleeps like a heifer after giving birth, she does. She's coming with me to the meeting tonight."

It wasn't the most flattering description of a person she'd ever heard, and she pictured Duncan's relation as half-woman, half-cow. Not exactly dating material, at least, not in her world. Several of the gods would find the combination enticing. "It will be good to meet her."

"The thing with a muse of justice is that you don't always call a spade a spade, eh? You go all around the houses so you don't offend anyone or commit to a position." He finally glanced at her and grinned. "But you can't fool an old Scotsman." He tilted his head toward the sun again. "You'll like her. You'll see."

They sat in silence for a bit, smiling at the occasional person who walked past. Calli was lost in thoughts of the last twenty-four hours and thinking about what she wanted to say tonight. What would Jordan say?

"Duncan, how do you feel about all this? After hearing the arguments on both sides."

He shifted to look at her, his expression serious. "Spade a spade, Calli?"

She nodded. Just because she didn't do it didn't mean she didn't appreciate the ability of others to do so.

"I think it should go ahead. Better that it goes to someone who knows what she's about than to someone who puts up one of those huge ugly eyesores. You know, those box businesses who sell every scrap of nonsense someone can think to waste money on. Or, not as bad but still bad, that the land goes to waste. Goes fallow and overrun and becomes an eyesore of its own."

"I wonder if those are the only options." She couldn't fault his logic, but there simply had to be another way.

"Course not. There are always options. Get the gods to build some outpost or some such. Have them invest in the land."

Calli winced. "Then I'd never get away from work. I bought this place to escape."

"See? There are always options, and always reasons that do away with those options."

She sighed and slid deeper into her chair.

"And the jobs will be good, Calli. You know that little villages like this die out eventually if nothing new comes in. The young people are moving closer to the city and they're not coming back. This place will be empty houses and irritable ghosts after all us old folks die off."

That, too, was true. The houses in the village were beautiful, but she'd noticed more than one with boards over the windows as she'd driven in. Was she being selfish by wanting this to stay the way it was? "Thank you, Duncan. I needed to hear the side of things from someone not invested in the long-term outcome."

"Well now, there was no need to play dirty and remind me I'll soon be dead." He stood and popped his cap on. "I'm going to go wake the niece and then we're having tea with Jacob. See you tonight?"

She smiled as he headed back to his place. Why couldn't she let go of the notion that Jordan's park would upset the balance of everything here? Was it instinct, or was it her need for solace and quiet? There were plenty of other places on the planet where she could find solitude. And with better climates, too. But this was hers, and it was special. The temple made it clear that this place mattered to other people too. What it meant was that she had to find some balance. A way to allow for Jordan's park that would benefit the people of the village, but also a way to keep the area around the temple a sacred space.

She checked the time and went inside to shower and change, all the while her thoughts pursuing different avenues of options that led mostly to dead ends.

By the time she was walking toward the Tweed center, she wasn't any closer to a solution. She still didn't like the idea of Jordan's park anywhere near here, but she couldn't deny that there were important sides to consider, and Duncan's views were logical. But then, it wasn't just her concerns. The townspeople had their own concerns, too, that didn't align with Duncan's.

The Tweed center was full to bursting when she arrived. Every seat was taken, and people stood against the walls. Tension was heavy in the air, and more than one conversation sounded heated. It didn't bode well for the night.

Jordan was sitting on the edge of the stage, swinging her legs, watching the crowd. Calli knew her well enough now to know she didn't feel as calm as she looked, and she'd be taking in every conversation she heard in preparation for the evening to come. When Calli joined her on stage, Jordan stood to face her. Awkwardly, she stuck her hands in her pockets, clearly unsure what protocol was in this situation with regard to hug or not to hug. Calli chose not to hug. She didn't want any semblance of being on one side or another, although she couldn't deny the desire to pull Jordan in and quell her concerns, preferably with a kiss like the one they'd shared yesterday.

Stephen from the council hurried onto the stage and gave Calli a quick kiss on the cheek and then nodded at Jordan. "Calli, will you run this?" He bobbed his little bald head apologetically. "I can't think of anyone better to hear all sides and keep control of the situation."

"And you don't want your house egged." Calli smiled gently, hoping to put him at ease.

"Right. That too." His relief was almost palpable.

"Of course. You know I have my own feelings about this, but I'll do my best to be impartial."

Jordan frowned slightly and shrugged. "Okay by me, as long as we get to hear all sides."

The insinuation that Calli might not be able to be impartial irritated her instantly. "I've been doing this job for a while. I think I can handle it." It came out sharper than she meant it to, and Jordan took a step back, her shoulders hunched.

Calli turned to the crowd and stepped up to the mic, putting aside her emotions so she could focus on the issue at hand. "Everyone, please quiet down so we can get this meeting started."

The room settled, but the emotion was running high enough to send pulses along her skin. This kind of intensity had led to cities burning in millenniums past. "We're here to discuss the planning permissions applied for by Jordan James, who runs Alpine Entertainment. Her intention is to build an adventure park that will include a number of activities, which I'll let Jordan tell you about when she comes to speak. This adventure park would be built on the Bemersyde property, which extends for twelve hundred acres and incorporates the edges of several of our villages."

The word "our" slipped out. As a mediator, she shouldn't have any skin in the game, so to speak, but she couldn't help it.

"You may not have noticed, but the issue has become a little fraught." She was glad when there was a titter of laughter. "And rightfully so. It's a big decision for a location like this one, and hearing everyone's thoughts and opinions is a good way to make certain whatever happens is for the best." She glanced at Jordan, who looked at ease, but the little lines around her eyes were tight. "I'm not here to argue my case. Jordan knows my feelings on the issue." She turned back to the crowd. "I'm here to help get your voices and concerns heard. Jordan is here to hear them and to respond as best she can. Please direct your comments to us on the stage, and not to one another." She looked around the room and then pointed at a man who looked like the love child of a brick wall and a bulldozer. "Little Tim, I'm placing you in charge of gently refocusing people if things get out of hand."

Little Tim gave the crowd a big grin and flexed his biceps, earning a laugh. For all that he'd often been written off as a big, dumb oaf, he was an exceptional violinist. Something few residents here knew, as he preferred to keep it to himself although he'd taken lessons with Calli when he was young. She noticed the gray in his hair and was reminded that time had passed.

"Okay, that's settled. I'm going to ask Jordan to come to the mic. Please raise your hand, and she'll call on you to ask your question. This isn't parliament. No booing or catcalling if you don't like what she's saying. Listen closely to what she's saying all the way to the end." She motioned to Jordan, who looked a little less concerned as she stepped forward.

And so the night went on. For three hours, people stood and called out their questions. Most were directed to Jordan, but some were directed toward members of the council, and a few were even directed toward Calli, although those were of a more spiritual nature, and therefore were harder to apply to the situation. They went over everything from environmental impact to the restoration of old buildings and the design of new ones, as well as how the narrow roads would handle the kind of traffic she'd be bringing in. A shouting match began when the owner of a horse ranch began to argue with a woman whose four sons were looking forward to having work so nearby. And then their husbands joined in, and soon they were belittling one another's villages and ancestors. Little Tim stepped between the shouting people and spread his arms, effectively keeping them from seeing one another, until they stopped their shouting. He looked at Calli and then lowered his arms and moved back to his position at the wall.

Toward the end of the evening, Iona stood. Pale and trembling, she raised her chin when Jordan called on her. "The Temple of the Muses is sacred space. How can you encroach on sacred space? Don't you have any regard for the prayers of creative people? How can you expect people to come to pray and leave offerings among people having a picnic and talking about climbing ladders in the trees?"

Calli gave Iona a small smile. She'd been surprised to see Iona show up at all, and more so when she raised her hand. But she shouldn't have been, really. It was clear she felt strongly about the temple, more so than many people in the area.

Jordan turned to look at Calli. "I have the utmost respect for Calli and the temple. And you're right, Iona, this is a serious issue we need to give some more thought. I admit that I don't have an answer to your question at the moment, but I promise I'll do my best to make sure your temple gets the respect and consideration it deserves."

Iona gave a curt little nod, her shoulders tight and her jaw working. It was a good answer, politically speaking. It didn't promise anything, but it also allowed Jordan to do what she needed to do. As Duncan had said, it wasn't calling a spade a spade. It was prevarication that allowed for interpretation when it came down to action.

Calli looked toward the council members, and Stephen took Jordan's place at the mic.

"Thank you, Jordan and Calliope, for being willing to come here tonight. I think we've all heard many, many things we need to give considerable thought. I think I can speak for all the council members when I say we've heard your concerns and your hopes, and we'll take them into account when determining planning permission. We're on break for a fortnight, and then we'll reconvene the council and decide, which we'll post online and also let local businesses know so they can spread the news of our decision. Good night."

The crowd began to disperse, and conversation was muted. Opinions aired, the people were content they'd been heard. It was down to the lawmakers now.

There were dark smudges under Jordan's eyes when she moved to Calliope's side. "That went well, I think. Exhausting, but well."

"Better than I expected. I was sure we'd have more than a few fistfights." Calliope took Jordan's hand in hers, that same feeling of electricity making her smile. "You did well."

Jordan's gaze searched Calliope's. "And have I changed your mind?"

Calliope let Jordan's hand slip from her own. "A little, maybe? But many of those concerns tonight were ones I have too. Noise, trash, traffic, pollution...you have some good ideas about them, but it won't change the fact that they'll be a part of this place no matter how good your policies are." She lowered her head slightly. "And there's the element we discussed yesterday with regard to the creatures of the forest."

Jordan sighed and tilted her head back to stare at the ceiling. "I've never faced so much opposition on one of my projects. It's exhausting, and the possibility that I've bought the land and won't be able to build on it makes me a little sick."

"I can imagine," Calliope said. Duncan's logic aside, it was still impossible to conceive of this little haven as anything other than that. And knowing Jordan, it wasn't surprising she'd gone full steam ahead without considering anyone being entrenched against her.

A throat clearing behind them made them turn. Duncan stood there with his cap in hand, a young woman beside him. "Calli, this here's my great-niece. Emma."

Emma did not, in fact, look like a heifer. She had thick, long dark hair, full breasts that pushed at the low V-neck T-shirt, and eyes the color of milk chocolate. Her full smile was genuine. "Ms. James, I thought you did an excellent job fielding those questions. I would have been cacking myself."

Jordan held out her hand and shook Emma's. "Thanks. I won't say it wasn't grueling."

"Maybe I could buy you a drink and you could tell me more about your park? I'd love to hear your plans." This time, the smile wasn't just genuine, but genuinely flirtatious.

Duncan gave her a slight bump with his shoulder, his frown lines deep.

"Oh, and, Calliope, of course, you could join us. A muse is always good for conversation, right?" This time, Emma's smile was a little less genuine.

Calliope hooked her arm through Duncan's, not just to make clear her intention to leave with him, but so she didn't drag Emma out back and drown her in a mud puddle. "No, you go ahead. I'm tired, and I can walk back with Duncan."

"Great!" She slid her hand around Jordan's bicep. "Off we go, then."

Jordan looked baffled at what had just occurred. She and Calliope had been in the midst of an important conversation, and now she was taking out some woman for a drink.

Calliope practically dragged Duncan along with her out of the center. The last thing she wanted to see was Jordan going out with a gorgeous woman. In her three thousand years she'd rarely felt jealousy. Life and love were, after all, fleeting, even when you loved another immortal. But right now, she'd gladly have turned Emma into a toad and whisked Jordan away into a tower where she could be all hers.

Distance was good. It would help remind her that it wasn't just that she and Jordan were on different sides when it came to the business at hand. Jordan had made it clear where she stood when it came to relationships, and while Calliope respected that, she already knew she wouldn't be able to handle something brief, because it wouldn't be meaningless. Getting your heart broken for something deep and true was one thing; getting it broken over something you knew was doomed from the start was another. Pragmatism in emotion helped stave off heartbreak. Usually.

But Calliope didn't miss the look of longing in Jordan's eyes as she looked over her shoulder before she too was pulled away.

Chapter Seventeen

I f ever a person had been born to be an octopus, it was Emma. Duncan's niece was handsy, and it seemed like every time Jordan moved, Emma was ready with her arm around her or her hand on her thigh or on her bicep. How she'd gotten herself into this situation she wasn't quite sure.

She'd been talking to Calli, and it had been reassuring to speak to her after the event. With everything that had been said she could see how the opposing sides both had valid arguments, but given how much she wanted her park, it had been hard to really open up and listen to the people who were against the idea. She'd done her best to allay concerns and promise to look into the things she hadn't considered, and she'd hoped to be able to deconstruct it after with Calli and a stiff drink.

Instead, she was fending off Emmapus, who seemed to grow more hands with every beer she slugged down. And she wasn't unaware of the stares of the other patrons, either, who probably thought she was celebrating in her own particularly lesbian way with the hot young woman from the nearby village. It couldn't be further from the truth. She wanted quiet, time to think, and someone to talk to. It was only two in the afternoon in California, and if she could get rid of Emmapus without causing offense, she could maybe give her sister or Austin a call.

When Emma began to get slur-sloppy, Jordan went to the bar with the excuse of getting another drink. When the bartender came over looking less than friendly, Jordan tried a smile. "I don't mean to be a hassle, but I don't suppose you know where Emma lives? You don't have Lyft or Uber here, do you? I don't want to take her back myself and give her the wrong idea."

He looked suitably mollified. "We've a small taxi service. I'll call and let them know they're taking her. No worries."

"Thanks. I don't mind paying for it, just let me know how much."

"She's staying with Duncan. He'll pay for it, and you can pay him back when you see him." He was already on the phone.

She went back to her table. Duncan was Calli's friend. He'd said he wanted to introduce her to Calli. The thought nearly made her spit out her water. Was he trying to hook Calli up with his niece? Maybe she hadn't had a big conversation about what type of woman Calli liked, but she was fairly sure Emma wasn't it.

The bartender came over and tilted his head toward the door as he picked up their glasses. Jordan stood and helped Emma with her coat while trying to fend off the ever-present groping hands, and then led her out to the waiting taxi. When she closed the car door behind Emma, she heard her complaining and said she'd meet Emma at her place, which calmed her down. It was clearly illogical, but that didn't matter. She'd be passed out by the time the taxi was at the end of the street and wouldn't be waiting up for Jordan to arrive.

Relieved, she walked to her hotel. Normally, an Emma-like distraction would have been just the thing to take the edge off. They'd never have stayed in the bar that long. Clothes would have been off, and a night of surface, fun passion would have ensued. But this place, this project, this moment in her life…it was all different. She could still feel Calli's lips on hers, she could still see her sitting in the forest in the moonlight, she could still smell that particular sweet apple scent she seemed to exude. She'd never felt a connection like theirs. It was beyond shitty that they were on opposite sides of this issue. Although, what the hell she'd do if there wasn't the issue between them, she wasn't sure. She wasn't relationship material, but damn if she didn't want to see what spending every minute with Calli would feel like.

She pulled out her phone and headed toward the river, where she found a bench not far from the suspension bridge. Across the river, on the hill, she could see the flicker of candlelight from the temple and an occasional whiff of incense was carried on the breeze. No lights were on at Calli's place, at least not that she could see from the front. The thought of her in bed made her shiver. She called her sister, the one person who would totally understand the mechanics of what she was up against legally, as well as the emotional roller coaster she was on.

"Hey, Mona."

"Jesus, I thought the Loch Ness monster had eaten you." There was the clatter of restaurant noise in the background. "But I know you get busy, so I was going to wait to call the Mounties."

"Pretty sure they don't have Mounties in Scotland. It's good to hear your voice."

"Hold on." She excused herself to whoever she was with, and then the restaurant noise faded. "Okay, now I can hear you. What's wrong?"

Where to start? Jordan kicked at the pile of leaves at her feet. "Things are messy."

"Things are often messy. What makes this different?"

Once Jordan started talking, she couldn't stop. She filled her in on the opposition to the project, on Calli's involvement as a muse, and on the issue of the temple. She even mentioned the possibility of building on a place where creatures they didn't know existed might be living. "And to top it all off, I have feelings for her."

"For a muse? Sis, you know better." Ramona actually sounded disappointed.

"I know. I do. But I can't seem to help it. She's beautiful and talented and smart—"

"You mean she's a muse?"

Jordan sighed. "Yeah. I guess."

"I'm flying out. I'll email you as soon as I have my flight info. Have a driver pick me up, though, okay? I saw the pics of those things they call roads. No way I'm driving."

When Jordan began to argue, she was cut off.

"I'm coming. I'm in this business with you, remember? If you don't hire me to design any more of your parks, I'll end up living under a bridge. I love you, and I'll see you soon."

Jordan tucked her phone back in her pocket and relaxed against the bench. It was silly to have her sister fly all the way over here to rescue her, but in truth, she did feel like she needed to be rescued. There was still time to pull out of the sale. This country allowed a thirty-day cooling off period, and she still had time to reconsider. She could pull out, buy land somewhere else and start again. It would be an expensive decision, given that she had her crew and a lot of the building materials already in place, but if she had to do it, then it had to be done.

But the thing was, she didn't *have* to do it. There was no guarantee that there were mystical creatures living in the area she wanted to build. There was no law she was aware of that said she couldn't build near the temple. If she moved her park, she was doing it solely because Calli felt strongly about it not being there. Because it really was the perfect place for it. Every option she wanted to put in fit perfectly. She could work around the villagers' concerns.

If her planning permission wasn't granted, then she'd have to make a decision about what to do next. But making one based on the needs of an immortal was stupid. They had the world at their feet. Hell, right across the bridge there was proof of that. People flocked to them, asking favors, stroking their egos. And what did they get in return? The promise of an afterlife. Rules, regulations, books that told people what to do and not do, even though those things often contradicted themselves and so the books were constantly being revised.

She only had a certain amount of time on this big blue rock. She didn't give a toss about what came after. This life had to be all she could make it, which meant doing what she loved, where she wanted to do it. Allowing an immortal, who could just as soon do away with Jordan's park after she was dead and gone, to mess things up went against everything Jordan believed in. And Mona was right. Falling for a muse was the dumbest thing of all.

But…Calli was special. There was something special between them. She *knew* it. She felt it every time they touched. And damn, did she want to touch her. Constantly and everywhere.

She pulled out her phone. "Hey. Sorry, I know it's late. What do you say we check out that cave tonight?"

Leith agreed readily. "Need to work off some steam?"

"You know me well." Jordan began the walk back to her hotel, ready for action instead of relentless thinking. An owl called in the distance, and she walked faster.

"Well enough to know you're twisted up like that knot the guy in mythology had to cut through. I'll get the gear and a guy ready and pick you up in twenty."

Jordan headed to her hotel room and changed. Whenever things got too intense, she turned to physical activity. It focused her and drove away all the stuff she couldn't deal with. It often created mental space, too, that allowed for answers she couldn't dredge up consciously.

She was outside on the sidewalk waiting when Leith pulled up. She jumped in and they drove to the site in silence. The guy who would handle the ropes at the top gave a tired grunt and then closed his eyes.

"Are you sad about Amber?" Jordan asked, her thoughts once again turning to Calli.

"Nah. I thanked her for spending time with me and wished her good luck. We both knew it wasn't going to go anywhere." Leith glanced at her and then back at the road. "You know how I feel about love. A lot like you do. Why settle for drinking only one type of beer all your life when there are so many to try?"

Jordan tried to smile, but she had a feeling there was more to Leith than she let on, if the scene with Calli had was anything to go by.

"Calli's nice, though," Leith said.

"Nice lead in. Subtle." Jordan wasn't sure if she was ready to talk about this stuff yet. "Yeah, she's really something."

"If you take away the immortal thing, what would you see in her?"

"You can't take that out of the equation. It's a pretty big part of her." Jordan rested her head against the cold glass. "But in theory, it's that she's kind. She's a good listener, she has a great sense of humor, she's crazy smart, and she's dedicated. And she's wicked sexy."

"Nice. Now, what about the negatives?"

"She's pretty rigid about stuff. I get the sense she's one for routine and spreadsheets. She's three thousand years old and has forgotten more than I'll ever know."

"Sounds like one outweighs the other." Leith threw the truck in park.

"Yeah. She also doesn't date humans, and I swore off the gods a long time ago." Jordan got out and started hefting gear out of the truck. The full moon meant she didn't need a flashlight right away, which was a bonus. The waterfall echoed quietly off the hills around them, sounding like wind if you didn't know what it was.

"Well, that creates a right conundrum, doesn't it?" Leith took a duffel bag. "Let's go work shit out of our systems. Maybe we'll have answers when we come back above ground."

So, Leith was looking for some answers too. Jordan allowed the meditative process of gearing up to settle and focus her. Pulling all the straps on the harness into place, hooking carabiners into the right slots, tightening her helmet, and turning on her headlamp. By the time they descended into the third cave system at the waterfall, her pulse was steady, and she was ready to immerse herself in nature. It was her cure-all.

They made their way along the wall, crab-climbing sideways after they rappelled down to the bottom. Spray made the stones slippery, and she made sure her grip and feet were secure with every move she made. The waterfall, illuminated by their headlamps, looked like something out of a fairy tale. Even more so when they made their way behind it to find that the pool split. Part of it went on to the river system they'd already been along. But the pool created another waterfall that dropped down the other side, too, creating a massive pool larger than two swimming pools put together. The cave walls sparkled like they had diamonds embedded in them, and Jordan pictured the way she could do the lighting to bring it to life.

"Where do you think that empties?" Jordan asked as she landed on a huge granite boulder beside the lower pool.

Leith took out a flashlight and searched the area. "I can't tell. There's no whirlpool suggesting a massive drain, but it must let out somewhere." They walked the edges of the pool, but there was no indication of anything.

"We could get a diver in to check it out. It would be an amazing end to the ride. Or maybe even an extra."

Jordan knelt to feel the water. "It's damn cold. I'll have to give it some thought. I can't heat it without changing the geophysics of the place."

Leith lifted her flashlight. "The rock looks solid enough to hold an entry staircase. We could build it in pretty easily and that would create an outlet for steam."

Throughout their exploration Jordan watched carefully for anything unusual. Were dryads who lived in caves possible? What else lived in caves? Dragons seemed unlikely. But there could be other things. After exploring some more and not seeing anything out of the ordinary, they made their way back to the original opening and climbed back out, helped by the guy on the surface keeping their ropes taut.

Puffing, they lay side by side under the blanket of stars.

"Do the trick?" Leith finally asked.

"Yeah. I still don't have any answers but at least I don't want to pull my skull open and dig around for them anymore."

"Disgusting visual. Thanks for that." Leith stood and pulled Jordan to her feet. "If the new world has taught me anything, mate, it's that things have a way of working out. Sit back and watch it happen. Strain too much and you'll give yourself a mental hemorrhoid. And things will still turn out the way they would have anyway, you just have a hemorrhoid to deal with now too."

"Is that the answer you found down there? Nice." Laughing and lighter, Jordan helped store the gear and they headed back to the village along the pitch-black narrow roads. Leith was right, but sitting back and waiting for things to happen wasn't in her DNA. Yet, maybe, that's all she could do. For the moment, anyway.

Chapter Eighteen

"Mickey Mouse could set up a kiosk at the bottom of your hill and you couldn't do a thing about it."

Calliope watched the cows grazing outside her kitchen window. It wasn't the news she'd been hoping Themis would come back with. "I was really hoping I'd have the law to fall back on."

Papers shuffled in the background. "I've searched all the current laws and plenty of old ones. There's nothing saying something can't be built near a sacred site. Just the regular laws about property ownership. Who owns the land the temple is on?"

"The council, I think. The old earl had it built, and his estate has passed on to other owners, except for my house. But I think the temple was gifted to Scotland."

"And it's the local council deciding whether or not to grant permission. Do you have Scotland on your side?"

She considered the expressions of the council members from the meeting the night before. "I don't know. Honestly, both sides have valid points."

"Don't they always?" There were raised voices in the background. "I don't know how you deal with the gods and their egos all day long. I'm ready to drag at least three of them to the fates and let them be thrown into the void."

Calliope winced, the guilt of not being at her post rising quickly. "I'm sorry. Do you need me to come back?"

Themis scoffed. "If a goddess can't handle a bit of godly ego, she isn't much of a goddess, is she? No, enjoy your time, do what you need to do. I'll hold the fort until you get back. And if there are a few less gods for you to deal with, then it's a win-win, isn't it?" The voices in the background were louder this time. "Okay, gotta run before Hades tries to set fire to Poseidon again."

Calliope set her phone on the windowsill and smiled as a little cow ran after its parent. If only her days were so simple. Inspired by Themis's information, she began drafting a document to put laws in place around sacred sites, detailing distance from the site as well as the possible parameters that should be considered. It felt good to put things in place. It might not help her with the Jordan situation, but it could certainly help with other sites that might face similar issues in the future.

It was early evening by the time she had a suitable draft that she could put into motion when she returned to the office. Unlike the old days, she couldn't just hand it to Zeus and make it happen. Now there were other offices to go through. Ultimately, the fury Tisera would be in charge of passing it by the other religions and making it official. Then Selene, who was the primary conduit between gods and humans, and Kera, who was in charge of business expansion and marketing, would be in charge of spreading the word among the humans. It would take time to come into effect, but it was more than they had now.

She sighed and set her pencil down. Whether or not her beautiful spot would be irrevocably changed was in the hands of the council. Jordan wasn't going to back down, and Calli couldn't bring herself to either. Thinking of Jordan made her wonder about her impromptu date with the voluptuous Emma. Calliope knew her type well. Jordan was successful, sexy, and smart. Anyone with a pulse was attracted to those qualities, and women who wanted an easy ride were especially drawn to them.

And although Jordan had looked bewildered, she hadn't put up a fight when she'd been tossed to that particular wolf. There was little question as to whether Jordan would find Emma attractive. The bigger question was whether or not she'd taken the opportunity to enjoy her company for the night.

The thought made her itch, and she touched her lips. Their kiss had been electric, like their touches, like their conversations, and the idea of Jordan kissing Emma that way made her want to burn things down, as out of character as that was. She checked the time and decided to get out of the house and out of her head. Grabbing her rain jacket and slipping on her rain boots, she knew she needed to talk to someone. Maybe she'd call her sister Thalia. Later, once she could use words that were less sweary and would make more sense.

She made her way through the drizzle at dusk to Bemersyde House. The lights were on in every window, lighting her way from a distance. Once there, she didn't have to knock but rather had to swiftly move around people who were roaming the house, official looking clipboards in hand. They'd called to say they'd begin the process, and she'd been a little put off at how abrupt they'd been. There'd been a time when customer service meant being polite and establishing a connection. Now it seemed that time was money and even extra words were considered superfluous.

She found Jacob in the kitchen, a towel twisted in his hands, a cold cup of tea in front of him. When she touched his shoulder, he startled and looked up at her with tears in his eyes.

"Ah, lass. Good of you to come." He stood slowly and moved to the kettle. "It's good to see a friendly face."

She hung her rain jacket on the hook by the back door. "Has something gone amiss?"

He was quiet as he made their drinks and shuffled back to the table. "Nay. Not amiss. Just…" His old shoulders were hunched more than usual. "None of these things are mine. But I've cared for them for much of my life. And now outsiders are here, talking about how much things are worth, saying some things are and some things aren't."

"But they're all worth something to you." She took his leathery hand in hers. She was growing far more accustomed to physical touch again, and it was easier to comfort someone when she could touch them. She'd forgotten that somewhere along the way.

"Silly, isn't it? To be attached to someone else's things."

"Of course not." She let go of his hand to stir her tea, the feeling of his sadness making her eyes water. "You're not just letting go of material things. It's a life change and that's never easy."

He appeared grateful for the understanding. "I'm happy to be able to live out my days here. Just sad to see the vultures circle this way."

At that moment, an officious looking woman in a tailored navy skirt suit came in. "I assume you're Ms. Ardalides?" She butchered the pronunciation but didn't look flustered.

Calliope stood and held out her hand. "I am."

The woman gave her a limp fish handshake, barely touching her. "We'll be wrapped up with our valuation in the next hour or so. You've got some truly exceptional pieces here that will sell well. Others you may as well send to a charity shop. You'll see both in my report."

Pragmatic and direct were qualities Calliope understood. They were also qualities best tempered with compassion and empathy. Jacob sighed quietly and sipped his tea, looking like he was miles away. "Thank you. I trust you've taken into account the history of the items you deem unworthy?"

The woman frowned. "Personal history is only important to the people who lived it. It's rarely important at auction."

"If that were the case, no one would care about Charles Dickens's original manuscripts or Anne Lister's private letters." The woman wasn't just pragmatic, she was callous.

"But they were important people. Most of us aren't." She gave a tight-lipped smile. "Not that you would understand that, I imagine."

Irritated, Calliope reached out and grabbed the woman's hand. "Let me show you something." She allowed the feeling of creativity to run through her. For the beauty of music to swell through the woman, for the sense of right and wrong to infuse her soul, though that took a little pushing on Calliope's part since the woman's armor against that was thick. She showed her the emotion put into a painting deemed unworthy, the history and desire in the photographs, the deep appreciation that flowed into the pieces collected throughout the years for various reasons. And then she did something she rarely did. She allowed a glimpse of the world without the arts, without beauty and creativity. She showed her what a lack of empathy and true justice were. In essence, she showed her aspects of World War II, which were death and destruction and loneliness.

Mascara tears ran down the woman's face, erasing the cold facade and leaving in place someone who had plenty of thinking to do about the way she worked with people. Hopefully, it would make her better at her job. "I understand," she whispered, disengaging her hand from Calliope's and stumbling backward.

"Good. Perhaps you could take these things into consideration before you send me your final report."

The woman backed out of the room, her eyes still wide. Jacob stood and gave Calliope a fierce hug. "I don't ever want you to do that to me, whatever it was you did, but I'm damn glad you did it."

She hugged him back, feeling the frailty in his frame. "Sometimes you just have to be reminded about the beauty of the world."

They sat and talked for a while about what he wanted to do when the house was sold and when she might be going back to LA, which was a question she couldn't answer.

She felt marginally better by the time she left Bemersyde. Jacob promised to come to her cottage for afternoon tea one day the following week and she made her way back. The night had dropped cold, and she pulled her jacket tight around her. Heavy clouds threatened a late spring snow, and the air was icy on her face as she moved along the path beneath the tall pines and along the plowed fields. When she got to the bridge she stopped. Jordan stood with her elbows on the bridge railing, her chin in her hands as she stared out at the water.

Calliope's heart leapt. The possibility that Jordan had come to see her, even after a night with Emma, made her giddy. She stepped onto the bridge, her footsteps on the wood planks echoing in the still night. The bridge bounced slightly as she walked, and Jordan looked away from her thoughts toward Calliope. She straightened and stretched her back.

"Hey."

"Hey yourself." Calliope stopped beside her, waiting.

"I don't know why I'm here."

Calliope felt it. The understanding, the need, the desire. The destiny. She took Jordan's hand. "I do."

Silently, she led the way off the bridge, past the temple, to her cottage. She let go of Jordan's hand only when she went to take off her jacket and turn on a dim light before she lit the fire in the fireplace. Her pulse raced but she knew it was right. She quickly pulled off her boots and ran her fingers through her hair before turning to face Jordan.

Before she could say a word, Jordan swept her into an embrace. She kissed her, long and hard, pressing her against the counter. Calliope returned the kiss with everything she had, every sinew of her body reaching for what Jordan had to offer. Jordan's hot lips slid over Calliope's neck, her teeth nipping lightly as she made her way over Calliope's collarbone. Her hands were firm as they slid beneath her shirt, skimming her back and stomach.

Calliope shoved away from the bar, pushing Jordan back, and then took her hand and pulled her into the bedroom. As hot as sex anywhere else in the house would be, she wanted their first time to be in her bed, where they could take their time and not worry about their legs shaking with exertion or slipping on the tile floor.

Jordan wasted no time in pulling Calliope's shirt over her head and throwing it on the floor, quickly following it with the rest of her clothes. She stopped for a minute and stared at her, her gaze leaving a trail of fire as she took her in.

"Fucking hell." She pressed herself to Calliope once again, kissing her hard, her tongue demanding access.

Calliope lifted her shirt and traced her fingertips along the clenched and trembling muscles of Jordan's abdomen. "Are you sure—"

"No." Jordan tore off her sports bra and kicked off her boots.

Calliope wasn't either, but it didn't matter. She took one of Jordan's nipples in her mouth and sucked hard, biting the tip. Jordan's hand tangled in her hair as she groaned and pushed into her, need evident in the flush of her skin and strength of her hand. She let go of Jordan's nipple and gasped softly when Jordan pushed her back on the bed, following quickly, covering Calliope's body with her own. Her jeans pressed against Calliope's hot, sensitive clit and she pushed against Jordan's leg, her back arcing in pleasure.

Jordan clasped one of Calliope's breasts in her hand, squeezing it, pinching the nipple, as she sucked and bit at the other nipple. Her body was on fire and the feel of Jordan's hard, heavy body on top of her was a kind of bliss usually reserved for the gods. Jordan jerked her knee against Calliope's clit, and she moaned and bucked as Jordan paid attention to every sensitive spot at once.

"Please," Calliope whispered.

"Please what," Jordan asked, her eyes wild and hard. "Tell me."

"Please fuck me." She didn't need to ask again. Jordan slipped her fingers inside her, two at once, and Calliope cried out in pleasure, pushing down on Jordan's fingers as she pushed in hard and fast, fucking her deep.

"Look at me." Jordan's words were barely a growl.

Calliope stared at Jordan through the haze of lust enveloping her. She gripped the sheets as her body responded to Jordan's thrusts and never lost eye contact. Until she came, slamming herself onto Jordan's fingers as Jordan kissed her deeply, not stopping until Calliope's body began to settle. She slid her fingers out and lay back, and Calliope automatically turned toward her, resting her head on Jordan's shoulder.

The tears were surprising, but she let them come. Not sobs, just slow tears of release.

"You okay?" Jordan asked softly, smoothing the hair from Calliope's face.

"Overwhelmed, I think. That was...I can't find the right word."

"You'd think a muse would always have the right words." Jordan's tone was teasing as she continued to caress Calliope's hair. "But yeah. It was that, whatever that was."

Calliope took another moment to compose herself before she pushed up on her elbow and sucked Jordan's nipple into her mouth.

"Fuck," Jordan whispered.

"Can I touch you?" Calliope asked as she moved to the edge of the bed and unbuckled Jordan's jeans.

"I'm more of a giver than receiver generally, but I might explode into stardust if you don't touch me." Jordan grinned that sexy lazy grin that Calliope loved.

She tugged her jeans off, quickly followed by her boxer briefs and socks. In the dim light she could see the hollows and surges of Jordan's muscles. The tremble in her stomach muscles, the tension in her thighs. The damp curls waiting to be parted. Calliope knelt at the edge of the bed and pulled Jordan to her, letting her be in the perfect position. She parted her and licked her in a firm swipe, making Jordan's hips buck.

"God damn fuck trolls." Jordan gritted her teeth and raised her hips.

Calliope managed not to laugh at Jordan's creative swearing and began a slow, firm rhythm against her clit, her hands on Jordan's thighs. Jordan's swearing and breathing grew more rapid and finally her hand was firm on the back of Calliope's head as she cried out and came hard, her pussy pressed to Calliope's mouth.

She fell back on the bed, still softly swearing, and Calliope rose to lie next to her. Jordan held her close and pulled the comforter over them. Jordan's heartbeat soothed her to sleep, and the feeling of being wrapped in her arms made her wonder if Jordan was the person she'd been waiting for throughout her existence.

CHAPTER NINETEEN

The morning call of blackbirds and the bickering of magpies woke Jordan slowly. The patter of heavy rain against the windows explained the lack of morning light. She looked down to see Calliope still asleep on her shoulder. No wonder she couldn't feel her arm.

What had they done? Aside from have sex twice more, that is. She knew full well that Calliope had reservations about having a relationship with a human, and she most assuredly had her own issue with Calliope's kind, not to mention relationships in general. And then there was the wrangling they were doing when it came to the business.

But damn if that hadn't mattered one iota last night. When she'd seen that look in Calli's eyes on the bridge, there'd been no question where they were headed and why. And she wasn't about to put a stop to it. Naked desire had shown in her eyes, and for some reason, she knew it was for her and her alone. The feeling of Calliope's body on hers, under her, writhing as she pushed into her and took her like it might be the only time...she shuddered, her heart simultaneously soaring and petrified. She rarely let a woman touch her the way she'd allowed Calli to. It made her too vulnerable, and she couldn't always let go, which could lead to frustration. She got her pleasure from making the other woman beg for more, from the flush of her breasts, and the way her body screamed to be touched. But Calli had torn that wall down, and she'd have begged if Calli hadn't asked to do it. She was glad Calli had fallen asleep before she'd seen the tears in Jordan's eyes.

"Good morning." Calli stirred, her ethereal sleepy eyes looking up at her.

"Morning, beautiful." Jordan wanted to pull Calli back down when she sat up, not ready to give up this truce, this moment of bliss.

"Coffee?" Calli stood, fully naked, next to the bed.

"Can I drink it off your body?" Jordan leaned across the bed, reaching, but Calli danced away, laughing.

"That would be messy, and I still wouldn't have my coffee." She smiled at Jordan over her shoulder. "Be right back."

Jordan flopped back on the pillow, her arm over her eyes. She almost never spent the night with a woman. The next morning was always way too awkward. Even if they were both on the same page, that the night had been nothing more than a bit of fun and tumble, there still seemed little to say in the exposing light of day.

But she couldn't fathom *not* waking up to Calli. Her beauty rivaled any sunrise she'd seen on the top of a mountain. She wanted to see that smile again, tomorrow morning, and the morning after that. Could feelings this intense happen this quickly? Maybe it was a lesbian cliché, falling for someone you'd known for such a short time. But there was no question in her mind that her heart was involved. And that was beyond terrifying.

She shifted when she heard Calli come back into the room and sat up to take the cup of coffee on offer.

"Those look like heavy thoughts on a stormy morning." Calli scooted into bed beside her and pulled the comforter up over them.

"I was thinking about how beautiful you are. And how much I enjoyed last night." It wasn't a lie. Those thoughts had been part of the larger picture.

"And yet there was a frown line on your forehead." Calli sipped her coffee, looking at Jordan over the top of the mug. "Duncan says I'm too political, that I don't call a spade a spade. So that's what I'll do." She took Jordan's hand and lightly bit and kissed her knuckles. "Last night was special. Delicate and sweet and hard and hot. It was transcendent. For me, anyway. And I haven't felt that way in an exceptionally long time."

Jordan could breathe again for a moment. "I like the sound of that."

Calli's smile slipped slightly. "Me too."

Thunder rattled the window, seeming to underline the feeling of hesitation in her tone.

"There's always a but, isn't there?" She tried to keep her tone light, not wanting to ruin the afterglow that was already fading under the weight of reality between them.

"But…let's not talk about the real world." Calli's gaze searched Jordan's. "Let's pretend, just for now, that we're a normal couple who have woken up together after a stupendous night of sex."

Jordan grinned and set her mug down. "Do you cook?"

"I do. Is that your way of asking if I'll make you breakfast?"

"It's my way of knowing that I'll get fed after I've enjoyed you again." She took Calli's mug from her hand and set it aside before turning back to her and flipping her over so that Jordan was pressed against her back. "I want you. I love the way you sound when you come." She slipped her hand between Calli's thighs and nipped at her shoulders as she pushed into her, moaning when Calli gasped and begged for more. She would take as much of this fantasy as she could before it drifted away like a dream at dawn.

It was lunchtime before they rose again, the sheets a tangled mess on the floor, the storm outside having abated and allowed through a watery glow of hazy sunshine.

"Okay, now I need food." Jordan let her head fall to the side so she could look at Calli from where she rested on her stomach.

"Agreed." Calli pushed up from the bed, forcing Jordan to roll off awkwardly. "If we have food in bed, we'll get distracted and it will go cold and we'll both pass out from dehydration. Come into the kitchen." She wrapped herself in a silky black robe and left the room.

Jordan sighed and stretched sore muscles. Thanks to her being physically fit, it took a lot to make her muscles ache, but last night with Calli had done the job. She dug around until she found her boxers and sports bra, then headed into the kitchen. "My hotel room is never this warm."

"A holdover from LA. I dislike being cold and keep the house at a constant seventy degrees. Duncan thinks I'm crazy."

"I like it." Jordan watched as Calli pulled eggs and veggies from the fridge before pouring her another cup of coffee. "Can I ask you something personal?"

Calli glanced up and then continued to focus on her cooking. "By all means."

"Have you felt like this before?" Jordan quickly clarified. "I mean, this electricity that keeps making me feel like I've stuck my finger in a really good socket. This feeling that I'm being pulled toward you…" She drifted off, realizing she might sound needy.

Calli chopped a red pepper thoughtfully before she answered. "No. I haven't felt that connection you're talking about before. I've been in relationships that were wonderful and intense, but this feeling with you is different. And no, I don't know why."

She didn't sound exactly thrilled by it, either. "And are you okay with it?"

Calli took a deep breath. "The bigger question is, are you? You made it clear you're not a relationship person, Jordan. Last night was incredible, and I wouldn't change it for anything. But the fact remains that I am what I am, and I get the feeling you have a problem with that which we've not discussed as yet."

There was no judgment in Calli's tone. And yet, it felt like a minor accusation. Perhaps it was time to lay her cards on the table. She wrapped her hands around the mug and took a deep breath. "I was twelve when my mom died. She was deeply religious, and of course this was before the gods came strutting down off their mountain. So, she had faith, the real kind, that everything was going to happen the way it should. But her faith, the rules she chose to live by, kept her from getting medical help. That damn book they referred to told her that she just had to pray and be a good person, and God would listen." The coffee tasted bitter, and she pushed it away. "But he didn't listen. She died of a treatable cancer because of the rules of her religion. I had to grow up without her because of ignorance and faith."

"I'm so sorry, Jordan. That's awful." Calli continued to cook, but there was no question she was listening intently.

"After my mom died, I was lost. My dad did everything he could, but losing a parent is hard. I took it hardest, I think, because I understood that it was preventable. My brother and sister hurt too, but they seemed to heal. My world just got darker. I got in more trouble, lost interest in everything, and basically just gave up. My aunt, my mother's sister, stepped in when I was at my lowest and my dad felt like he couldn't reach me. She lived here in St. Boswells. I only spent one summer with her, but she saved my life and helped me move forward again. Any time I saw her after that she came to the States. She loved adventure and encouraged me to travel and experience all life had to offer."

Calli set beautifully cooked omelets on the counter and sat beside her.

She picked up her fork and began to eat. "Putting the park here is my way of thanking her, of telling her I'm okay and giving people the sense of excitement and adventure she instilled in me." She glanced at Calli, then back at her food, the feeling of vulnerability making her shake inside. "You see, it's a place of inspiration for me, too. It inspired me to live again."

Calli's eyes were wide. "I had no idea you had an actual connection to the village. I assume your aunt isn't still in the area?"

"No, she passed away a few years ago, when I was scuba diving off the Italian coast. I had no idea until I got back. I didn't tell you because I'm not one to talk a lot about myself." Jordan gave her that adorable little smirk. "I'd rather show people what I am."

Calli ate quietly. "I wonder if I knew her?" she finally said.

"She never mentioned knowing a muse, but maybe she didn't know you were one. I think, though, if she'd have known you, she would have told me about the beautiful woman in the little cottage. When I came here as a kid, we never crossed the bridge, so I didn't know about the temple. I wish she'd shown me that back then. Although I probably would have drawn rude pictures on it and left dog poo on the altar, given how I felt about the gods."

Calli gave her a quick, understanding smile. "I can imagine a young Jordan doing just that."

They finished their breakfast and Jordan helped Calli clean up. It felt so sweet, so domestic, to have shared something so personal and then to be clearing up dishes together. The thought that she could get used to it was worrying.

"I can't imagine, Jordan, what you went through. I've seen people grieve for their loved ones. I've felt grief myself when a human lover of mine moved on to the afterlife. But to lose a parent one loves is truly crushing. I'm so glad you found peace here." She held Jordan's hand in her own. "Would you still have found that peace if you'd been surrounded by climbing rigs and zip lines?"

Once again, it was a question without rancor, and one Jordan couldn't answer honestly. "I can't know what might have been. But I do know that this place is special, and it gave me what I needed." She paused to allow the thoughts time to breathe. "In fact, what if that peace I found here is part of the temple?"

Calli tilted her head as she considered Jordan's question. "I'm not sure I follow."

"You said music is part of your gift, but not always. That sometimes you help people find peace in other ways. What if the peace I found here was part of that? And by bringing other people here I'm helping spread that feeling? I'm just using the land as a way to bring people to it."

Calli leaned against the counter, her arms crossed, her brow furrowed in thought. "I'll need to give that some consideration. You'd have made an excellent lawyer."

Jordan laughed, feeling lighter after sharing her reasoning and the wounds of her past. "That's harsh. There's no need for insults."

Calli's brow quirked. "And sending an insult right back."

Jordan's phone rang from the other room, and she ran in to get it. "I'm expecting a call from my sister," she called over her shoulder. She looked at the screen before she answered, not wanting to interrupt her time with Calli for anything less than family. "Hey, Mona, you made it okay?"

"I've left three messages. Whoever is in your bed better be worth it. I'm only about half an hour away, I think, if no more sheep wander in front of the car."

Jordan had been so caught up in Calli she hadn't given any thought to when Mona would be landing. "Sorry. I'll be ready and waiting for you." She hung up and returned to the kitchen, where the sight of Calli in that silky robe made her want to head straight back to the bedroom.

"Everything okay?"

Jordan held up her phone like it was an explanation. "My sister has flown in, and she'll be at my hotel in about half an hour. I'm sorry to cut our morning short."

"Family comes first. You know I understand the call of a sister." She smiled, but there was a flicker of something in her eyes. "I hope it won't be our last morning together."

Jordan came around the breakfast bar and pulled Calli close. "We have some things to work out, and I don't know what this is between us. But I know I've never felt this way before." She kissed her gently. "So yeah, more mornings like this definitely have to happen."

Calli seemed to relax. "In that case, you should shower before you go. You reek of sex." She nipped her earlobe and then led her to the shower.

Chapter Twenty

It had been an exceedingly long time since Calliope's stomach had twisted at the thought of a woman she wanted being with someone else. If nothing else, she was pragmatic. It was impossible to be everything someone needed, and trying, or wanting someone to fill that role, was what often caused heartbreak. In most all of her relationships over the years, she'd understood that and allowed her lovers the freedom to see and enjoy whomever they chose, as long as they remained respectful and courteous to her.

That wasn't going to be the case with Jordan. After Jordan left, Calli enjoyed the physical aches and afterglow as she cleaned up the house. The night had been arguably one of the best she could remember having. Jordan's hard body, soft lips, and stamina had proved to be the perfect way to break her long run of unintended celibacy. And now she fully understood why Jordan had some issues with the immortals, which made sense. Hopefully, having sex with one would begin to diminish that anger she'd held on to for so long, anger Callie had sensed from the first time she'd touched her.

She hadn't asked about Emma and whether or not Jordan had enjoyed that pursuit with her, but she couldn't help but hope that Jordan meant what she said about feeling like they had something special. One night of sex didn't equate to an exclusive relationship. She'd never been one to think so, anyway. So why did it feel so different now?

The day ahead was hers. She hadn't asked when she'd see Jordan again since she didn't want to intrude on the time she'd spend with her sister, but it would have been nice to have lunch, curl up in front of the fire, and talk about whatever came to them.

She shook the thoughts from her head. Expectation often led to disappointment. She needed to let whatever was happening between them do so as it would.

She dressed and headed out into the bright spring sunshine as she made her way to the temple. Predictably, Iona was there, lighting more incense and looking like she was where she belonged.

"Good morning," Calli said as she climbed the steps, not wanting to startle her.

Still startled, Iona turned, her hand on her heart. "Oh, morning."

"I thought I'd see if there was anything you thought I should attend to." She surveyed the fresh flowers, the freshly swept ground, and the small stack of letters ready to be taken out.

"Me? I mean, no. The usual, I guess. Not like Nova's." Iona stared at her intently.

"Iona, can I take your hand?" It felt like the right time. No one was around and only the birds kept them company.

Iona swallowed hard, her eyes wide. "Why?"

"So I can understand better how to help you. So I can get to know you on a deeper level."

"Most people just ask."

Calli hadn't considered doing it the human way. It was a good reminder. "Yes, I suppose that's how it usually works, isn't it? And we can do that if you want to." She motioned to the bench overlooking the river valley. "Why don't we sit and talk? You can tell me more about yourself."

She led the way, hoping Iona would follow. That strange shadow on her left side remained, and this close to her and the temple, Calli could clearly feel that there were damaged parts in need of care.

Iona sat on the very edge of the bench, her hands pressed between her knees, her mouth pressed into a firm line.

"Do you live nearby?" Calli asked. This would be easier if she could simply touch her, but Iona clearly wasn't ready for that. And she was right, normal people had to do it this way.

"At the top, in Bemersyde village."

That was nearly two miles away. Not far when you'd grown up walking in Scotland, perhaps, but it was a steep walk, too. And as far as Calli could tell, she did it at least once a day.

"But I'm not from there. Not really." She glanced back at Calli, who gave her an encouraging smile. "My mum is from Iona, the little island in the Hebrides. That's why she named me that. She missed it. She married my da when he was there with a few friends on a stag do. He was from Jedburgh, but his mum, my gran, lived in Bemersyde." She was silent for a moment. "I'd like to go there, to Iona. Do you know, only a hundred and twenty people live there? The island is three miles long and a mile wide."

"That sounds idyllic." Calli didn't mention that she'd been there to oversee the interment of a Celtic king well before the Christians had claimed the island as their own.

"I'd like it, I think." She eased back slightly on the bench. "Mum and Da loved the arts. He painted and she sang. They said between them they could put color to all the emotions in the world."

The fact that she was speaking in past tense didn't bode well. "What happened?"

"I was nine. We were on our way to the theater in Edinburgh. It would have been my first musical. But coming off the hills, we got caught in a flash flood that swept the car into a ravine. The car got wedged and water flooded in so fast. Da was unconscious but Mum wasn't. Her seat belt was jammed, and her leg was stuck. I was able to get loose and I climbed out of the car and onto the roof. I held Mum's hand through the crack in her window so I didn't get swept away by the water."

Tears ran down her face and her shoulders were hunched in to protect herself. Her left hand clasped her knee so tight her knuckles were white. Calli gently draped her arm over Iona's shoulders and was relieved when she leaned into her.

"She let go. The water had filled the car. They both drowned that night. The storm passed and a passing car caught sight of me on top of the car, otherwise they would have gone right by." She took a shuddery breath and scrubbed at the tears on her cheeks. "I was sent here to live with my gran. But she and my da weren't close. She's angry and bitter. Hates…well, she hates everything, I think. And if it had only happened once my parents had died, I'd understand, but she's always been that way."

Tragedy was something the gods didn't have to deal with. It was also something they had no control over, though humans rarely believed that was true. Maybe now that they were among humans they'd begin to understand the depth of despair and grief that came with being human. It might not change anything, but a little more empathy and help in processing that grief wouldn't go amiss. The shadow attached to Iona's left side was the memory of holding her mother's hand as she drowned that night.

"How old are you?" she asked.

"Seventeen." She looked small, like letting out her history had wrung her out like an unwanted rag.

"If you could do anything in the world, what would it be?" She already had a sense of it from having her arm around her.

"Paint, like my da. I still have some of his paintings hidden in a trunk in my room. Gran tried to get rid of everything to do with them when I moved in. Said it was best to forget and move on. But I still have some things of theirs. And I want to do what my da did. The way he captured a place, made it come alive so you could almost step into the world on the canvas…" She shrugged and gave a deep sigh. "But I've not the money for supplies, and I can't afford to go to college or uni. I'll be stuck here and become the same angry granite as my gran."

It was an apt description for someone who denied the beauty of life, and with Iona pressed to her, she could feel the girl's talent waiting to emerge like a bird ready to fly the nest.

"You know what one of the benefits of having a muse on your side is?"

Iona turned to her, looking warily hopeful. "What's that?"

"Not only can I help with the actual emotion of your painting, but I can help you find a way to help you follow your dream." She hugged her close and then let her go. "Why didn't you ever write a letter like the others?" Calli motioned toward the temple behind them.

"I didn't want to be a bother, I guess. And I don't even know if I'm any good. What if I waste your time?"

"The arts aren't meant just for people who excel at them. They're an expression of the soul, a way to tell the world how you feel. Even if you sound like nails on a chalkboard or you can only draw stick figures, you should still do it if it feels good in your heart."

Iona nodded like she understood, but that kind of self-doubt would take a long time to undo, if it could be done. In the meantime, though, Calli would find a way to help.

"You can move out of your house at sixteen, right?"

She looked puzzled at the question. "Aye. But the part-time job I have at the bakery doesn't pay enough for me to go out on my own."

"Let me worry about the specifics." She stood and looked down at Iona. "Why do you take care of the temple the way you do?"

Iona pulled her feet onto the bench, her knees to her chest. "At first it was just a place where I could be by myself. Calm, and quiet. Then I started to think that maybe if I saw someone's prayers being answered, I might get the courage to ask for help too. The longer I stuck around, the more it gave me... I don't know, purpose, I guess. And I like the way the creative people feel." She looked up at Calli, her heart in her eyes. "Is that stupid?"

"Definitely not. I like the way creative people feel too. And the fact that you can feel them that way means your creative soul is begging to be let out. You're in touch with people and the world around you, and that's something special. I promise we're going to work out the next step for you, okay?"

Iona unfolded herself and stood, her lanky frame looking a little less fragile. "You mean it?"

"I don't break promises. And I'm promising you, we'll get a paintbrush in your hand."

Unexpectedly, Iona threw her arms around Calli in a crushing hug. In the moment of touch, Calli got a glimpse of Iona's life. It was shadows and anger, hiding from a hand quick to strike, hugging walls and walking as silently as possible to stay unnoticed. It was fresh air, incense, and calm when she was at the temple. It was the first hug she'd had in years as they stood there overlooking the river.

"You won't let them take the temple away, will you?" Iona asked, her voice muffled against Calli's shoulder.

"Never." She held Iona at arm's length. "I will do everything in my power to make sure it stays a sanctuary."

"But that woman. She wants to make it something stupid. Something to make money."

Calli pictured Jordan sitting at her breakfast bar in just her underwear, her short hair tousled from the long night of lovemaking. She could still see the pain in Jordan's eyes when she talked about the loss of her mother. "You might have more in common with her than you think." She brushed away the last of Iona's tears. "Remember that everyone has their reasons. Even your gran has become the way she has for a reason. It doesn't make her behavior acceptable, but sometimes understanding people's reasons can change your mind about how you feel about them."

Iona searched Calli's face. "You like her."

It wasn't the time to hide behind uncertainty. Iona deserved the truth. "I do, very much. I don't like her plans, but as a person, I like her a lot. I think you would too."

Iona stepped back, putting some distance between them. "Maybe. But I think I'll keep my distance anyway."

"Fair enough." Calli's phone buzzed with a text, and she checked it. "I have to head home. Stay strong, and I'll let you know when I come up with a plan, okay?"

"Thank you." Iona shoved her hands in her pockets. "I haven't had anyone to talk to in a long time. There's hardly anyone left my age around here."

Duncan's assertion that the village would become a ghost town didn't seem as far off as it might have before this conversation. "Any time you want to talk, come by the cottage. Or track me down in the village." She smiled, liking the part of village life that meant you were so accessible.

"I will." Iona checked her watch. "Better run. My shift starts at the bakery soon."

Calli watched as Iona ran down the path away from the temple that would lead across the field and then up through the forest at the base of the village. That land was part of the Bemersyde estate that Jordan had purchased. It was only about fifteen houses, if that, which had once belonged to the people who worked the estate. Now they were private homes. What was Jordan planning on doing with those houses? Would she evict people? It seemed unlikely, given the way she'd allowed Jacob to keep his home beside Bemersyde House. For Iona's sake, she'd find out.

She headed home after picking up the neatly stacked letters in the temple. She'd taken to reading them often and loved the sense of people reaching out to her and her sisters in such a tangible way.

Once she was home, she opened the email Themis had sent her. Included was a licensing renewal form that included protests against the renewal based on issues the locals had with the company. The company was an adventure park, complete with roller coasters and zip lines, just like the one Jordan wanted to build. It cited problems with noise, traffic, and pollution, just as the locals here had been worried about.

She sat back after reading the document in full. While that renewal had gone ahead after much discussion, there hadn't been much choice in the matter since the park was already up and running and making use of the land. But if she handed this document over to the council here, the likelihood was that they'd deny Jordan's planning permission. It would put a stop to her plans. To her dream of the legacy she wanted to leave in memory of her aunt.

She sent Themis a thank you and then shut the computer. In her bedroom, she looked at the rumpled bed she'd been in so recently, her body on fire, her emotions raging. Justice, in her case, wasn't blind. There were always at least two sides to every argument and both sides felt theirs was the more valid. Arbitrating meant finding the overlap, where the sides had common ground they could work with. There'd never been a time when she couldn't find that overlap.

Which meant that it was extremely irksome that she couldn't find it now, when she was one of the sides involved. The issue with middle ground was that there didn't seem to be one. Jordan wanted to build something huge, something that would bring people to the area. That, in itself, wasn't a bad thing. It was the destruction and difficulty brought about. The road construction, the noise, the people who didn't care about history or temples. Bringing any of that into the area would increase the chaos, thereby decreasing the serenity people found here. The serenity Jordan herself had found here. The peace and refuge that people like Iona needed.

Frustrated, she changed her bedding. Jordan's musky cologne lingered, making it hard to think clearly as her body replayed their night together.

CHAPTER TWENTY-ONE

Jordan couldn't stop grinning, and it was making her face ache in the best way. She pushed the thorny issues aside and thought about nothing except the way Calli's body felt against hers. The way her breasts felt in her hands, the way her whispers of ecstasy sounded in her ear as she pushed into her, over and over again.

There was a knock at her door, and she opened it quickly, smiling when she saw her rather bedraggled looking sister leaning against the doorjamb like she might fall over if she didn't. She pulled her into a strong hug. "You look like hell."

"You would think that now that the world has gone all mystical and shit, we could move around the fucking globe easier." Ramona dragged her suitcase into the room and then fell face down on the bed. "And why does this place smell like grandma's attic?"

"Grandma's attic smelled better."

Ramona slowly flopped onto her back. "I'm the weirdest combination of famished and stupefyingly exhausted."

Jordan bounced onto the bed next to her. "Jet lag is a nightmare. Let's get you some food, then you can sleep for a little while. But it's best to get into this time zone as quickly as you can, so I'll wake you up and then take you to the building site."

They made their way to the bookstore coffee shop, where Ramona got a slightly more friendly welcome than Jordan usually did. As he was making their breakfast, he looked over his shoulder at Jordan. "Will you make use of the businesses already here? Or will you focus on your own?"

She played with a sugar packet, flipping it between her fingers. "What would you prefer?"

He looked surprised. "I want to die in this place, under a pile of books that haven't been read in fifty years. I don't want to have an empty shop because everyone is bypassing it to get to your place."

At least that was a concern she'd dealt with before, and one she knew how to alleviate. "Makes sense. As I see it, main streets like this one are imperative for a place like mine. Variety and the essence of village life are what make my places unique. No big chain stores or conglomerates. When we're at the marketing stage, we'll make sure to include shops like yours in our location section on the website and in the brochures."

He grunted and gave a quick nod. "Right, then. Good enough."

Ramona looked at her coffee and the plate of wet scrambled eggs on top of a crumpet, which was essentially a rubbery English muffin. "I said I was hungry, not desperate."

"You'll get used to it."

"Yeah? Why aren't you eating it too?"

Jordan grinned. "I had a homemade breakfast. Way better than this."

Mona squinted at her over her forkful of eggs. "Sounds like there have been developments." She ate quickly, like she was trying not to taste it as she shoveled it in.

"There have. But it can wait until you're rested and even grumpier from jet lag." In truth, she wasn't ready to break it down yet. She wanted to keep the flutter of hope a little while longer.

Mona finished and they got back to the hotel. She curled up and was asleep in seconds. In the meantime, Jordan called Leith and asked her to assemble her crew so they could meet Ramona. As the architect, they could ask her more detailed questions now that they'd had the time to walk the different sites, giving them time to think about the project ahead. She also emailed Austin to check in and see how things were going back home and caught up on work things she'd ignored since she'd been in Scotland. When she woke Mona after a two-hour nap, she received the expected grumbling.

"Come on. After we go to the site we'll drive into the bigger city for a late lunch."

Mona got in the car and held tightly to the door handle as they made their way down the narrow roads. "I had to close my eyes most of the way here. The guy driving thought nothing of the other vehicles that looked like they'd shove us off the road."

"I'm still getting used to it too. I try to find enough room to pull over instead of trying to figure out how the hell we'll both stay on the asphalt." As if to emphasize her point, an SUV passed them going the other way and Jordan pulled as close to the side as she could, branches scraping along the window. The other driver gave a smile and half wave from the steering wheel and Jordan did so in return.

"People are really friendly. Everyone wanted to talk to me, and I couldn't understand half of what they were saying. How we're speaking the same language I don't know." Mona shivered and turned up the heat. "And it's so cold."

"They consider this a nice spring day. Not raining, sun is out. Perfect."

"Perfect for an Eskimo."

Jordan pulled over at a good viewpoint and pointed. "So, we bought the land basically from this road to that hill in the distance, just above that black and white house."

Mona scanned the area critically. "You know, it's weird how I can draw up plans on paper based on maps and surveys, but seeing it is something else, isn't it?"

"You should do it with me more often." Jordan put the car in gear and headed to the area where the crew would be waiting. "So, one of the issues brought up throughout the debates has been about the roads. Now that you've seen them, you know what people are worried about."

Mona leaned closer to the window to look at the side of the road. "Widening these is imperative with the traffic you'll be bringing in. But it's not going to be easy. Is there any other way in that wouldn't require the changes?"

"Nope. Every road in this area is just like this one." It was so good to have her sister there to bounce ideas around with. Mona was the best at what she did.

"When we talked about extending the roads, I didn't realize how overgrown they were, or how there are so many ditches. Looks like a fair amount of water, too. We may need to do some revising."

The relief that ran through Jordan wasn't minor. Knowing she didn't have to figure this out on her own made things so much easier. They pulled up at the site where a chunk of her crew were standing around chatting. Leith turned and waved as they pulled up.

"Who is that?" Mona asked, gripping Jordan's arm harder than was necessary.

"Leith. She's the one you've been emailing with about the plans." Jordan tugged her arm away. "And ow, by the way."

"I didn't know she was so…" She swallowed and bit her lip.

"*So* not someone you're going to date in this lifetime or any other." She pinched Mona's leg to get her attention. "She's not one for anything serious, little sister. She's awesome in a lot of ways, but she's not interested in settling down."

"Neither are you, but it sounds like you're already planning baby muses with your new flame."

She got out of the car before Jordan could retort and was already halfway to the group by the time Jordan was out and following. When she caught up, Leith was shaking Mona's hand and holding it for far too long, as far as Jordan was concerned. She punched her in the arm, making her drop Mona's hand.

"Thanks for gathering everyone," she said, sending Leith a warning glance and getting only a sly grin in return.

"It's so great to meet Ramona after all this time. I had no idea there was someone so good-looking in your family. I figured they all looked like you."

The crew threw in their own tidbit insults until Ramona finally held her hand up for order. "Okay, teenagers, let's get to work. Show me things."

Jordan shoved Leith forward before she could respond to that particular nugget, and they began to walk the property, discussing what would be where. It was a long afternoon as they traversed the forest where the coaster would be, the sections where there would be zip lines, and the area for the treetop adventure. Then they drove to the cliff walls where the rock-climbing area would be, and then even farther off to the cave system. Mona refused to do more than look through the hole, though, as she hated enclosed spaces.

While Mona spoke with some of the crew at the cave site, detailing what they'd be looking for and asking questions about the landscape, Jordan and Leith hung back a little.

"You never told me your sister was gay." Leith was watching Mona like she'd never look anywhere else again.

"You've never said you don't look good in yellow. So what? My brother is gay too, incidentally. My parents hit the trifecta."

"I look fabulous in yellow." Leith finally looked away from Mona. "Would you really have a problem with me asking her out?"

There was no joking in her tone, and Jordan flinched a little. How did you tell someone they were good enough to be your friend, but not good enough to date your sister? "Tell me something. That day with Calli. What happened?"

Leith rubbed at her eyes and then leaned against the car. "You and I are a lot alike when it comes to women. We don't settle down, we don't let anyone else call the shots." She paused and waited for Jordan to agree. "But that isn't what I want. Not what I need, as Calli said. I want someone to come home to. I want someone to wonder where I am and what I'm doing and if I'm okay. I don't want to be *alone* on this planet full of people. The no-strings thing is fun, but I need more. I want that cheesy kind of love you see in romantic movies, where they say the stupidest shit and it makes you all gooey inside." She laughed when Jordan made a gagging sound. "I know. But it's true. I'm not getting any younger, and I want someone to experience this life with me."

"I experience a lot of this life with you. Since when am I not enough?"

"Since we don't have sex at all hours, and you don't give a rat's ass what I want for breakfast." Leith rolled her eyes at Jordan's fake pout. "So, can I ask your sister out or not?"

Jordan watched Mona laugh with the crew. Her sister had been alone too long too, and Leith really was a good person. Knowing the truth of what Leith wanted made it easier to answer. "You can ask her out if you're looking for something real. But make sure that's what you want, okay? Break her heart, and I'll drop you in that cave and leave you there."

"Fair enough, mate."

They made their way to the group, and Jordan listened to what they had to say. Mona's input was already invaluable and allowed Jordan to look at the area differently, and the crew, having been hanging out with the locals while waiting for the go-ahead, had some thoughts about ways they could help with the environmental aspects. They left the area and headed back to the village for dinner at the pub. It was loud and raucous, and she didn't miss the looks and tentative flirtation between her sister and Leith, and although she couldn't help but worry at least a little, they did look good together.

Throughout, Calli had never left her thoughts. She'd considered calling her and inviting her to have dinner with them, but given that it was the crew about to begin work on the project Calli was opposed to, that didn't seem like a good idea. Still, she wished she were there, which made her think of what Leith had said.

She and Mona went back to the hotel after she'd made plans to see Leith for breakfast. As they were getting ready for bed, Mona looked at her in the mirror.

"You okay with it?"

She didn't need to ask what it was. "Yeah. We had a little talk, and she knows that if she hurts you, no one will ever find her body."

"And what if I hurt her?" Mona stopped wiping off her makeup.

"If you do, it will because it's not working out, not because you're a callous player who bed-hops. Big difference."

Mona started her facial routine again. "You don't have to protect me. I'm a big girl."

"And I'm your big sister. Deal with it." She kissed the top of Mona's head before she got into bed. It protested as it always did, and Mona winced.

"I'm finding us another place to stay tomorrow. I can't deal with this whole Victorian crypt vibe." Mona got into the other bed and switched off her bedside light. "And tomorrow you can tell me all about the woman that Leith says has you twisting in the wind."

"Sleep well." Jordan turned out the light and stared at the ceiling. Should she have sent Calli a text, just to say hi? Was that too juvenile? Calli had seemed worried that Jordan might not be serious about what had happened between them, and then Jordan had spent the day with her sister and working. She should have sent a text, if only to allay any worries that she was already flaking out.

She grabbed her phone and sent a quick message. *Missed you today. If you're free tomorrow, want to meet my sister and have lunch? Xx*

She wasn't one to put x's and o's in texts and had no idea what had possessed her to do it now. She was about to set the phone down when it buzzed.

Would love to. Will be home, just let me know what time.

No x's. Did that mean anything? Probably that Calli was a grown-up.

Perfect. See you then.

She wanted to say more. She wanted to tell Calli she had crazy feelings that she didn't know what to do with. She wanted to tell her she was falling for her and that she didn't care about her being immortal. She wanted to say she'd move her park anywhere Calli wanted her to, if only she'd give them a chance.

But all of that was emotion driven, and none of it was strictly true. She did have crazy feelings and she was definitely falling for her. That part was undeniable. But the other things… She punched her pillow and flipped over.

"The thing is, how do I know? Can you help me?" Jordan continued to dig into her pie, which wasn't a pie in the California sense at all. It was some kind of meat and potato thing in a heavy crust, covered in brown gravy. It was dense and aromatic, and she loved it.

Mona, on the other hand, was far from impressed by her chicken salad, which was barely a side salad and had very little lettuce or chicken in it.

Calli smiled sympathetically. "I should have warned you. The UK hasn't quite caught on to the idea of salads as a main meal yet. I have to ask for extra lettuce even when I get a salad at Subway." She looked at Jordan and laughed when she took an exaggerated bite. "As for your question, I'll have to ask around, but I'm sure we can find a way to make sure you're not infringing on anyone's territory."

Mona pushed her non-salad away and scooped up a handful of Jordan's fries. "You really mean there could be creatures no one knows about out there?"

"You should have seen them, Mona. They were incredible." Jordan had described the dryads and their translated message, agreeing wholeheartedly when Mona said it was like finding out Bigfoot was real. They'd discussed the ramifications of that kind of thing with regard to the park, and Mona had suggested they simply ask Calli for help when Jordan had said she had serious concerns now.

"It's possible, and it wouldn't hurt to check." Calli pulled out her phone. "Bear with me."

Jordan listened to the one-sided conversation as Calli asked someone on the other end for a contact in this area.

Mona leaned forward. "How weird is it to be sitting with a god who is asking for another godly contact?" she whispered.

"As weird as you think it is," Jordan said, spearing a fry.

"Okay, there's a pixie not far from here. Epona is going to try to get hold of him and see if he'll help."

Mona raised her hand like she was in school. "What's a pixie? And who is Epona?"

Calli took one of Jordan's fries, receiving a swat, and then Jordan pulled her plate out of their reach. "Epona is the goddess of horses. She's ancient and well known in this country, hence the revival of people dedicated to her. But in her downtime, she did a lot to take care of the mythical creatures who needed help as the humans continued to spread over the planet. A pixie is a little harder to explain."

Jordan finally had to put her plate on her lap so they'd stop stealing her fries. "Order your own, you gannets."

Mona stuck her tongue out and went to order fries for her and Calli to share. While she was gone, Jordan took Calli's hand in hers. "Thanks for agreeing to this. My sister means the world to me. I'm really glad you got to meet her."

Calli squeezed her hand. "It makes me feel good that I'm important enough to be introduced to your family."

"Can I come over tonight?" Jordan asked.

"What about your sister?"

"She's going to dinner with Leith." She grinned at Calli's look of surprise. "I know. But they seem to have a connection already. Like, one of those attraction at first sight things."

"I believe the phrase is love at first sight," Calli said, running her thumb over Jordan's knuckles.

"I think the L word gets thrown around too easily. Do you believe in love at first sight?" Jordan shivered at the way Calli's touch made her weak.

"I do. But you're right, I think it's far rarer than we believe. I think it takes a truly special connection at just the right time in the universe."

The possibility that theirs was one of those connections was thrilling. Had she fallen in love with Calli that first time she'd seen her? Mona returned to the table with more drinks, cutting off that train of thought.

Calli's phone buzzed, and she read the text. "Excellent. The pixie is willing to help. How about we start with your cave system?"

Jordan gave Calli directions, which Calli then sent on.

"So, a pixie?" She hadn't let go of Calli's hand and saw the quick glance Mona gave the interaction, but she simply couldn't release her.

"Pixies have been in Britain for eons. Like dryads, they were a type of human. But they were small and got smaller, until they could hide easily almost anywhere in nature. They're shy and kind, although they can be mischievous. You'll want to put your car keys deep in your pocket, or he may hide them in a flower somewhere."

"Pixies are like fairies, right? Why are they considered fairy tale creatures?" Mona asked.

"Humans have a funny relationship with time. They forget things or pass them on with just enough errors that the stories morph into other stories. There was a time when humans knew full well that pixies existed and were simply a different race. But when pixies began to hide away, and stayed only on this little island, never spreading out, humans forgot their true existence and they faded into fairy tale. Like many creatures have."

Jordan slipped her hand from Calli's with the excuse of taking a drink. The reminder of being human and flawed was also a reminder of their differences.

"Were unicorns real?" Mona asked, again glancing at Jordan with that sisterly look of understanding.

"They were. They weren't magical, mind you. They were simply a breed of horses that had a single horn, not unlike the narwhal. But they were terrible at breeding, being too lazy and obstinate, and they died out of their accord."

They ate and chatted a while longer, with Mona telling Calli a few silly stories of their youth and Jordan's penchant for causing trouble, before Calli looked at her watch. "I'm sorry, I promised Duncan and Emma I'd have tea with them this afternoon."

Jordan shivered dramatically. "Be careful. She's got more hands than you'll know what to do with. It took every ounce of my considerable charm and flexibility to get her into a taxi without losing articles of clothing along the way."

Calli's eyebrow quirked.

"A taxi to take her home. Alone. Not with me," she clarified quickly, earning her a smile.

"Good to know I won't have to call in a favor to turn her into a tree." Calli stood, and then leaned down and kissed Jordan's cheek. "The pixie can meet us at midnight at the caves. Why don't you come to my place for dinner?" She looked at Mona. "You and Leith are welcome too, or she can drop you at my place after you're done. If, of course, you want to come. Jordan and I can do it on our own if you're otherwise occupied."

"Gross," Jordan mumbled.

"I'm not missing a chance to meet a fairy tale creature, no matter how hot the woman is." Mona threw a cold fry at Jordan. "I'll be there before midnight."

Calli seemed to hesitate for a moment and then gave them a quick wave and left the pub. Jordan sat back, already missing Calli's company.

"I can see what you meant about her being beautiful and smart and sexy," Mona said. "And she's wonderful. But it doesn't make her one of us, J. She calls up goddesses and asks for favors. She's in charge of the complaints humans make against the gods. Are you sure you're doing the right thing?"

The light feeling she'd been enjoying immediately sank like a stone with depression. "I don't know, Mona. In my head there are all these reasons to stay away from her. Like, I'm going to die, and she isn't. She's part of that whole religious system that pisses me off. She's trying to put an end to my park here. Those aren't small things." She picked at a fleck of paint on the table. "But then I look at her and none of that shit matters. My heart feels like it's going to explode, and I want to hold her to me and never let go."

Mona looked at her for a long moment. "Wow. That's intense."

"Yeah." Jordan looked at her watch. "Let's go check into that hotel I said I'd never go to."

They made their way to the Dryburgh Hotel, which sat right behind the old abbey. It was closer to Calli's place, which would have felt a bit over-the-top if it weren't also the nicest hotel in the area. The parking lot was still empty and the guy who checked them in did so with the enthusiasm of dead grass. But the room was far nicer and didn't smell of mothballs, so that was a plus. This time, Mona got her own room and Jordan didn't need to ask why.

Mona, still tired from her trip and her morning breakfast with Leith, lay down for a while. Jordan took a notebook and headed to the abbey to write out the thoughts thrashing around in her head. Maybe putting them on paper would help her find a way through the maze her life had become.

Chapter Twenty-two

Emotions and justice were an intricate balance. Calli had found that justice without emotion lacked empathy, and that ended up being false justice. Too much emotion, though, and there could be a lack of practicality and pragmatism that clouded the outcome that should have been the right one. Calli, born to be what she was, had never had a problem walking that line and helping others to do so as well.

But as she served tea and fresh scones with cream to Duncan and Emma, she couldn't help but wonder if the more ambiguous sides of justice would allow her to poison Emma's food. If she went on and on about how wonderful Jordan was any longer, Calli would have no choice but to kill her off.

Jealousy was an emotion, apparently, that didn't work well with actual justice. Still, she'd feel justified in turning Emma's hands to stone if she mentioned how muscular Jordan's arms were again. No matter that she didn't have that power—she'd find someone to do it for her.

"And she was so right, you know, not to come back with me the other night. I mean, I had way too much to drink, and you want to remember your first time with a woman like that, right?" She took a too large bite of scone, smearing cream around her mouth.

Duncan had been staring at her silently for some time, but as he handed her a napkin, he said, "I think I was remembering the child you were, instead of the woman you are." He looked at Calli, his expression contrite. "I'm sorry, lass. If I'd known…"

Emma looked baffled as she munched her scone, looking between them as if for clues.

"No matter, Duncan, really." She squeezed his hand and then looked at Emma. "You're right about Jordan. She is all that and so much more. But before you go further, I should let you know that we've become intimate, and I don't think she'll be seeing anyone else, at least for the time being."

Emma choked on her scone, flinging chunks of bread and jam across the table. Duncan pounded her on the back, none too gently, and she finally wiped the tears from her eyes and food from her mouth. "You can't be serious?"

When Calli simply looked back at her implacably, she pushed back from the table.

"But you're one of them. I read in that article how she feels about you people, or whatever you are. And you're *old*. I mean, yeah, you don't look it, you're all right looking, but still."

"Emma!" Duncan cuffed her upside the head, earning him a glare. "I'm quite sure your mum would be mortified if she knew you were behaving this way. How dare you speak to Calli that way?"

"What, because she *inspires* people? She's not a god, Uncle Duncan. And she's not supporting Jordan the way I would."

He stood, dragging her up with him. "Calli, forgive me, but I think we'll go."

Calli simply nodded, hoping it didn't show that Emma's barbs had struck home. "Before you do. Emma, what article, please?"

Emma's expression changed to one of vindictive delight. "Your phone?"

Calli handed it to her, and Emma tapped hard on it before handing it back. "There you go. Now you'll know you're not right for her."

She turned and flounced out the door. Duncan looked over his shoulder at Calli and glanced at her phone. "People say things, lass. What was said then may not be what's felt now. Remember that."

"Duncan, before you go. Do you remember a woman named Sue Abernathy from St. Boswells? She was Jordan's aunt."

He tilted his head, thinking. "Aye. Died some years ago. Friendly enough, but away on her travels a fair amount and I don't think she was well known. Jordan would have had an easier time of it if she'd have let people know she was tied to this place." He looked out to where Emma was waiting on the road, her arms crossed, her foot tapping. "I'm sorry again, lass."

She gave him a quick smile, and when the door was closed behind them, she set the phone down like it might burn her. Then she cleaned up the remnants of tea and scones, debating on whether or not she should read the article. Jordan had already told her how she felt about the gods because of the death of her mother, but she'd set some of that anger aside as they'd come to know one another. Shouldn't that be enough?

Once the kitchen was spotless, she leaned against the counter and stared at her phone on the other countertop. Ignorance wasn't acceptable. Choosing to look away from something just because it might say things she didn't want to hear was choosing to stick her head in the sand, and that wasn't who she was.

She made herself a cup of tea and took her phone to the deck to read.

By the time she finished the article, the tea was cold and bitter and wouldn't wash away the taste left by the printed word. The article was an interview done by a business magazine focusing on young entrepreneurs, and Jordan's sexy, smiling face was the first page of the article. The questions had focused on a wide variety of topics as a way to get to know Jordan as more than just a businesswoman, and when the interviewer asked Jordan how she felt about the Merge and if she'd chosen an afterlife, the article had exploded.

Jordan was almost vitriolic in her anger against everyone associated with the religious world. She made it clear that the world would have been better off if the gods had not only stayed away but had ceased to exist completely. She blamed religion for everything wrong with the world and said that if people wanted to be truly successful and truly free, then they had to release themselves from the shackles of the immortal beings.

Trembling, Calli set her phone down before she dropped it. She'd known that Jordan had issues, but she'd hoped they only went as far as the old hurt from her mother's death. But what she'd said in the article went far deeper than that. If even a portion of it was still at play, then how could they be together when Calli worked in a world Jordan so despised?

She curled into herself, hugging her knees. The first woman in years to make her heart hammer in her chest was one who couldn't possibly accept it in full. She sent Jordan a text message. *Can we take a rain check on dinner? Something has come up. See you at midnight.*

Jordan texted back almost right away. *Bummer. Was looking forward to it. See you soon. Hope everything is okay.*

Calli's fingers hovered over the phone, but she couldn't find anything to say. Things weren't okay and she'd been looking forward to it as well. But she couldn't sit with Jordan over dinner and not discuss the article. Discussing said article, though, would most certainly drive a wedge between them, one that would splinter and cause pain. At some point she'd have to discuss it with her, but for now, she wanted to sit with her pain and let it flow through her, allowing her to feel again. She put on a jacket and went to the temple, where she sat on the cold concrete floor and leaned against one of the pillars.

She started to sing, letting the words fill her heart as the tears slipped down her cheeks. With her eyes closed, she pictured Jordan in bed, in the forest, over lunch. She felt the happiness that came over her when Jordan smiled like Calli was the most interesting woman in the world, the passion that flooded her when Jordan touched her, and the crushing fear that Jordan's feelings about the gods would end whatever they might have had. The song ended and she opened her eyes and wiped her cheeks.

There were several people seated in the temple around her, staring wide-eyed, tears running down their cheeks too. Iona was one of them, and she moved across to Calli and sat down beside her before taking her in a strong hug.

The others who'd been listening drifted away respectfully, leaving her and Iona there in peace.

"People never think about the immortals having feelings." Iona finally let go of Calli and sat with her knees up, her chin resting on them.

"No, I don't imagine they do. At least, not deep ones." Calli smiled and stood, brushing off her jeans. "Thank you for listening." She left Iona sitting in the temple and headed back to her place to get ready for their trip out to see the pixie.

When Jordan knocked, Calli had to take a deep, settling breath before she opened the door. With her mask fully in place, she hoped Jordan wouldn't have any idea how she was crumbling inside. She opened the door and her stomach turned. Jordan looked so sexy in her dark jeans, thick wool jacket, and leather gloves.

Fortunately, she could concentrate on Ramona instead.

"That's your temple, right?" Ramona asked, pointing toward the flickering candles on the hill.

"It is." Calli motioned them toward the car and didn't miss the confusion in Jordan's expression when she gave her only a light kiss on the cheek. "We need to get moving. Pixies are patient, but they get bored easily."

They got in the car and Calli didn't acknowledge Jordan's hand on her leg, which meant that she slowly pulled it away. She avoided looking at her so she didn't see the hurt in her eyes.

"Everything okay?" Jordan asked.

Calli took a chance and glanced at her, and immediately wished she hadn't. She looked worried, and more than that, she looked hurt. But she'd never been able to lie. "Not really, but I'm processing. Maybe we can talk about it later?"

Jordan's frown made Calli ache to hold her and tell her everything would be okay. But it was a promise she couldn't make. The tension for the rest of the drive was heavy and silent except for Jordan giving directions. When they arrived at the dead-end road in the hills around the cave system, Ramona jumped from the car and shook her arms.

"Whatever you two need to deal with, you should do it sooner rather than later. That kind of tension causes avalanches."

Calli wasn't about to argue geology with her; she'd made her point. She moved ahead of Jordan toward a large boulder shaped like a spearhead. Once there, she sang a few notes and waited, and then smiled when the notes were returned. She heard the muffled surprise behind her when the little person, about a foot tall with yellow eyes, jumped onto the boulder beside her.

"Hello, Puck," Calli said, holding out her hand palm up. The pixie stepped onto her palm and held her thumb as she raised her hand so she could look him in the eye.

"Muse. I understand you need my help?"

She held up the bag in her other hand. "We do, and I've brought you a little gift as a thank you."

The pixie continued to hold onto Calli's thumb, while he peeked into the bag. His face lit up. "It's good when you remember the old ways." He let go of Calli's thumb and climbed into the bag.

She held it at a distance to give him privacy and then reopened it when he tugged on the bag. She put her hand in and lifted him out, and he preened in his new clothes, the rags he'd been wearing left behind in the bag. It was an old custom. Pixies loved new clothes but never had any to wear. If you wanted to make them happy, you brought them new clothes. Finding adult clothing for a one-foot-tall person wasn't always easy.

"What is it you need, Daughter of Zeus?"

She winced at the title, knowing it would reinforce Jordan's idea of who and what she was. "My friend here is going to be building on much of the land. She wants to make sure that none of your kind, or mine, are going to be made homeless."

He peered around Calli at Jordan, who gave him an awkward wave. "Unusual for a human to be so aware."

"She's rather different, I'd say."

He tugged on her thumb like a joystick and Calli brought him closer to Jordan. "Show me where you're building, and I'll scan the area to make sure it's clear." He stepped from Calli's palm and onto Jordan's. "What are you going to do if I tell you there are creatures here?"

Jordan looked from the little man to Calli. "Honestly, I have no idea. But I refuse to hurt anyone."

He tugged on her thumb. "C'mon then."

Jordan looked at Ramona and Calli and then shrugged slightly and set off, Puck holding her hand and looking around them. He stood on her shoulder as she descended the stairs into the primary cave, but Calli and Ramona stayed above ground, allowing Puck room to work.

"My sister was lit up like a glow stick when she was talking about you earlier." Ramona looked at the ground and scuffed at a pile of rocks. "But I don't see that now."

It seemed inappropriate to talk to Jordan's sister about what she was feeling before she'd spoken to Jordan, but she didn't want to be rude. "Things are complicated. They always are when it comes to relationships between immortals and humans."

Ramona snorted. "You say that like it's been happening forever."

"It has." Calli smiled at her. "At least, for me and my sisters it has, since we've been among the humans for so long. The gods were often among people thousands of years ago, and then they stayed out of sight when the world began to change, but we didn't."

"So you know what you're talking about."

Calli inclined her head, stopping when Puck and Jordan emerged from the cave and moved farther away. He turned her by her thumb, moving her in a circle, as he made the clicking noises that sounded like a strange bird. When nothing responded, they continued on.

"How do you feel about the Merge?" Calli asked, wondering if Jordan's sister felt the way she did.

It took a while for her to answer. "You know those movies where robots live among humans? Like, they're two separate races existing in the same place, and then the robots go insane and try to take over?"

Calli's eyebrows rose. "You're comparing the gods to killer robots?"

"Not exactly. It's just, there's us and there's you guys. Like, two separate races living next to one another. And who knows what you'll all do one day, right? Like that war where gods were fighting other gods at the time of the Merge, when they brought down the Vatican. What if that happens again? What if you all go crazy and turn on us?"

"Not exactly benevolent, then." The comparison seemed silly on the surface, but she understood what Ramona was saying. The war between the gods had been a terrible wake-up call, both for gods and humans. Their sci-fi and fantasy films had become reality, and many wished it had stayed in the realm of fiction and faith. "The gods who fought, though, fought for the humans. To keep them safe."

"Sure, and that's awesome. But what if they change their minds down the road?" Ramona reached out and took Calli's hand. "That's how I feel overall. But now?" She looked at Jordan and Puck. "You're showing us new things, the magic of things all around us. And that's really cool, and it makes me feel like maybe you're not all that different from us." She sighed quietly. "But then, you show us things like this, and it shows us that you're totally different, too."

"So there's no real answer, is there?" Calli didn't expect an answer and didn't receive one. Jordan and Puck turned back to them.

"Puck says there's nothing living here, but the cave system once belonged to a tribe of boggarts, whatever those are."

"You wouldn't want to come across one, I can tell you that." It was good news, in a way, that there was nothing to disturb up here. But there was plenty of land to cover. "We should move on. Pixies don't like to be out in the daytime, so we need to hit all your sites before sunrise." She looked at Puck. "Are you okay to ride in the car with us?"

He looked up at Jordan and then around at the car in the distance. "Trust."

They made their way back to the car, and Puck climbed off Jordan's hand and onto the dashboard, where he tucked himself in and held onto the windshield, making lovely little noises of excitement as they drove to the next spot, which was the rock face she'd be using for the climbing area. That area wasn't as spread out, and it took only a few minutes for Puck to decide that the area was clear. Their final destination was the largest, as it included the area for the zip lines, coaster, and sky trails.

On the drive there, Jordan said, "I don't mean to cause any offense, but I did think pixies and dryads and such were part of fairy tales. I know you've explained the biology, but surely there are other creatures who don't fit into that example?"

Calli took the turn a little too sharply and received a little hiss from Puck. "Sorry." He settled himself again. "Yes, but I'm afraid I have little to do with the actual fairy tale things. My understanding is that a young woman named Maggie is dealing with those, out of a portal in New York."

There was a moment of silence before Ramona began laughing in a way that didn't sound entirely tethered. "You're telling us fairy tales are real?"

Calli glanced in the rearview mirror. "This world is so, so much better than most humans give it credit for. Time and space expand to allow for so much creation, but most humans only ever know a tiny fraction of what's out there."

"Like us, and not like us," Ramona said, sitting back and meeting Calli's gaze in the mirror.

Jordan frowned but didn't say anything, for which Calli was glad. It was exhausting, trying *not* to touch Jordan, not to reach out and take her hand and reassure her. And, honestly, to reassure herself. But reassurance wasn't what they needed. They needed to know where they stood, and right now, it seemed like they stood in radically different places.

She pulled up at Bemersyde House, and Puck uncurled from the dashboard but turned away from Jordan's hand, holding his arms out for Calli. She let him climb on, and tears welled in her eyes when he hugged her thumb tightly, his yellow eyes glowing up at her. Pixies were incredibly sensitive creatures, and he must have picked up on her emotional distress.

"Thank you," she whispered.

He began to hum and she joined in, and he led her by pulling on her thumb as they walked through the forest, and soon she was singing softly to accompany the tune he hummed in the background. He led her this way and that, and she lost track of Jordan and Ramona and allowed herself to get lost in the melody and the grounding energy of the forest around her. Time moved past unnoticed until they ended up back at the house. Puck hadn't stopped her throughout their walk, and he confirmed that there'd been no creatures of their kind in the forest. There had been, once, but there were enough humans in the area to make them uncomfortable, and they'd headed north, farther into the Highlands.

She thanked him and asked if they could return him to where they'd picked him up, but he leapt from her hand to the ground as easily as a bird.

"I'll find my way. I haven't been here since my grandmother's time, and I want to remember." He bowed his head. "Be well, Daughter of Zeus. Remember who you are." With that, he ran off toward an oak tree and was gone.

"I think it's safe to say this will be a night I'll never forget." Ramona linked arms with Jordan and looked up at the night sky. "You remember just how small we are when you're out here."

Jordan didn't respond. She was looking at Calli, her eyes full of questions.

"If nothing else, at least you know your area is safe for creatures you might not have known were there. It was good of you to check." The words were insufficient when it came to any kind of emotion, but it was all she had right now.

They drove back to Calli's place in silence, and though she ached to reach out to Jordan, she couldn't bring herself to do it.

When they arrived, Ramona said, "Can I use your bathroom before we walk back?"

Calli groaned. "I'm so sorry. I automatically drove back here instead of taking you to your hotel." Impulsively and knowing it was a bad idea, she said, "Why don't you just stay here? I have plenty of room, and I'll take you home in the morning."

Ramona jumped in before Jordan could respond. "Perfect. Can I borrow pj's?"

Calli unlocked the door and ushered them inside. "Of course." She showed Ramona the bathroom and then found a set of pj's that would work for her and left them in the guest room. Back in the living room, Jordan stood with her hands in her pockets, looking like she carried the world on her shoulders.

Calli closed her eyes and held out her hand, and when Jordan's warm, solid hand gripped hers, the world righted itself again, if only for now. She led her to the bedroom, and they undressed quickly and got into bed. They lay facing one another.

"Can you tell me what's going on?" Jordan asked, lightly caressing Calli's arm.

"I read an article. An interview you did for a business magazine."

Jordan looked confused for a moment before she flinched. "Ah. Now I understand."

"Is it true? Do you think we're all parasites who feed off humans without giving anything in return?"

"You have to understand. It was the anniversary of my mother's death, and I was angry. Worse than that, I was pissed off. There I was, being interviewed for my success, and she'd been taken from me."

"I understand that. But do you still think that, Jordan?"

Jordan stopped caressing her but didn't look away. "I think there are real problems with the system. All of it. Books that detail rules that contradict themselves. Leaders who tell people what to think, what to do, and how to do it. A system that allows people to do terrible things and then confess and poof! It's all okay again. I know a lot of things have gotten better in the last five years. Wars, poverty, hunger…they're all massively reduced, and that's great. But if the gods left us again, where would that leave us? People lost their minds during the Merge. What would happen if they were suddenly abandoned? And what kind of deity requires sacrifice?"

She reached up to wipe away Calli's tears.

"I'm sorry you feel that way."

"But you're not like that, Calli. You've shown me the woman you are. How beautiful you are, and how you make the world beautiful too. That singing you were doing with Puck…I couldn't breathe, it was so beautiful." She held Calli's hand and kissed it. "You're not like them."

"Can't you see, Jordan? I *am* them. I work at Afterlife. I have dinner with the gods. Zeus is my *father*. If I worked as an accountant and had nothing to do with them, then maybe I could see your point. But I don't. I'm firmly attached to the world I come from, and I do believe in the good they're doing." She allowed the sob to escape. "You can't love me but not what I am or where I come from. I'll represent everything you distrust so deeply. How could you be part of my world without hating every moment?"

Jordan searched her eyes but didn't seem to know what to say, though she looked grief stricken. "Turn around."

Calli flipped over and allowed Jordan to pull her close, wrapping her arms around her tightly. Tears fell on the back of Calli's neck, adding to her own.

"I'm sorry," Jordan whispered into Calli's hair.

"Me too." Calli pulled Jordan's arms tighter around her. Eventually, she cried herself to sleep.

Chapter Twenty-three

When Jordan woke, Calli was still asleep. She looked beautiful as always, but her eyes were puffy, and even in sleep she was frowning slightly. Careful not to wake her, she got out of bed and gathered her clothes, then slipped out to the living room. It was too early to be up, but the desperation and despair in Calli's voice last night was still dragging at Jordan's heart and she couldn't sleep any longer. She went to Mona's room and gently shook her awake, then nodded toward the door, not wanting to wake Calli. Mona threw off the covers and yawned.

Jordan went to the living room to wait and sat on the couch with her head in her hands. A piece of paper on the table caught her eye, the words "adventure park" in bold at the top. She picked it up and began to read through it, and the more she read the angrier she became.

Mona came out, and Jordan jumped up and stalked to the door, and this time, she slammed it behind her.

"Whoa, what's going on?" Mona jerked at Jordan's arm when they were halfway up the hill toward their hotel.

Jordan held up the paper. "This. She lay in my arms last night crying about how it can't work between us because I've got such a dim view of her world. And what do I find this morning?" She rattled the paper. "This. She's found a damning report from another park similar to mine in this country that details all the complaints from villagers. She's going to tank my project, and she didn't have the guts to show it to me first." She stomped off up the hill.

"Give me that," Mona said, grabbing the paper from Jordan's hand. "And slow down. You're going to give me a heart attack." She read as they walked at a slower pace, and by the time they reached the hotel, she'd finished scanning it.

"The nerve. This is exactly why you can't trust them."

"I love you, but you're being an ass."

Jordan spun around. "What the hell? One night with a pixie in the forest and you're on their side?"

Mona turned red and put her hands on her hips. "I'm on your side. I always have been, and I always will be. But being on your side doesn't mean I don't get to tell you when you're being an ass."

Jordan crossed her arms. "Fine. Tell me."

"I need coffee first." Mona went inside and headed to the always empty restaurant, where there was a kettle and tea and instant coffee always available. "Why on God's green earth do they still drink instant here?"

Jordan didn't respond. She didn't care about coffee. She didn't care about anything except the feeling of betrayal raging through her.

They sat at a table by the window looking out at the abbey. A ruin, just like her time here.

"Have your permits been denied?"

"You know I haven't heard back yet." Jordan stirred her coffee angrily.

"But if she'd given them this, then they would have been, right? I mean, there's clearly a precedent for all the things the villagers here are worried about."

Jordan slammed her spoon down. "Right. What's your point?"

"My point, irritating sister of mine, is that she doesn't seem to have provided this information to them yet. Why not?"

"We don't know that she hasn't. They aren't due to give me an answer for another week or so. They may be sitting with it in their pretty little hands, waiting for the day they hand over the verdict that I can't build anything on twelve hundred acres of land."

"Find out." Mona stopped Jordan from tapping on the table by covering her hand with hers. "Call and ask if any further documentation has been provided. Hell, I'll do it as someone involved in the business. Then you'll know."

"And if they have it?"

"Then you'll know she did this behind your back. But if she didn't give it to them…"

Jordan waited, but nothing else was forthcoming. "Then what? She still dug it up. She still had it sitting on the table like she was debating what to do with it. It wasn't in the trash, was it?"

"You're on different sides of this issue, Jordan. Of course she found something to support her cause. And this is what you were worried about, right? Both of you, I think. That your attraction to one another is complicated by this very thing." She tapped on the paper.

The anger slid from her body, replaced with disappointment. "You're right. But damn it to fucking hell. I want her so bad."

"One of you may have to give up on what you want, if you want the other bad enough." Mona held Jordan's hand. "I can't imagine how hard this is. I'm sorry."

Jordan let her sister come around the table and hold her as she started to cry. She'd cried more in the weeks she'd been here than she had in years. What did that mean? The pain in Calli's eyes when Jordan had told her the truth about how she felt about the gods had been devastating, but she deserved the truth and nothing less. And Calli's response, in turn, had been as honest, and as painful.

"I want more sleep. Maybe I'll go into one of those fairy tale sleeps and wake up in a hundred years." Jordan's feet felt heavy as they made their way to their rooms.

"Okay. I'm going to make plans with Leith this afternoon. I'll text you and let you know where I'm at." She hugged Jordan tightly. "I love you, big sister."

Jordan held tightly. "I love you too. I'm so glad you're here."

"Always." She kissed her cheek and then went into her room.

Jordan went into hers and curled into a ball on the bed. Why did it have to hurt so much?

Jordan was woken by a constant knocking on the door. When she opened it, she was surprised to see old Duncan, Calli's friend, standing there with his cap in his hands.

"Now, I don't know what you did or didn't do," he said, launching straight in. "But Calli is my friend. She's a good woman, no matter where she comes from. She's one of the best. You need to make this right."

Groggy, Jordan tried to make out what he was saying. "Duncan, what are you talking about? I only left her place this morning."

"Aye. And then she up and left, didn't she? Barely a good-bye."

"Wait, what? What do you mean she left?"

He banged his cane on the floor, making it echo. "Are ye listening, ya buffoon? She left. Packed her things and went back to La-La Land and took that temple girl with her. Said the issue is in the hands of the lawmakers now and she'll abide by whatever they decide. That she has to get back to work, back to her world." He shook his cap at her. "Fix it!" When she went to ask another question, he raised his cane. "Fix it!" He stomped back down the hallway, muttering to himself about foreigners and their stupidity.

She closed the door and leaned against it. Calli had left? Just like that, she'd left without even saying good-bye. She checked the time to find it was already late afternoon. She'd slept far longer than she'd meant to, notwithstanding the hundred years sleep comment she'd made to her sister. She picked up her phone, but there were no texts or missed calls. And then she saw the email.

Dear Jordan,

You have no idea how lonely I've been, and I didn't even know it until you walked into the bookshop the first time I saw you. I realized in that moment that I needed to start living again, and every moment with you has been one I'll remember forever. You have stolen my heart, and I don't know what I'll do without it, but I do know it's yours. Whatever happens with your project, I'll always be glad we had this time together. Our worlds may be too far apart to overlap, but I hope you know that I'll be with you, always. Thank you for giving me my song back.

Love, always,
Calli

Jordan couldn't breathe. She sat on the bed, her hands shaking. She'd potentially just lost the best thing to ever happen to her. How had things become so confusing and gone to hell so fast?

She showered, hoping the hot water would warm her chilled soul, but no such luck. It was like she was facing a stone wall and trying to figure out how to make it brick. There simply wasn't a way to change things. She slid to the shower floor and sat against the wall, letting the water sluice over her and hide her tears. The water started to turn cold, and she forced herself out.

On the bedside table lay the document that had propelled her out of Calli's place like she was on fire. Had Calli intended to use it? If she hadn't, why not, when it could mean she'd win? Her phone buzzed and she grabbed at it, hoping it was Calli, although she wasn't sure what else they had to say to one another. Cards had been put on the table last night, and a spade was a spade.

The text was from Mona. *Either you're moping or still sleeping. Either way, get your ass up and come meet us at the Gray Mare.*

She sent a thumbs up, not feeling like finding actual words, and slowly got dressed. She made her way through the empty halls and down to the foyer, where the only guy she'd ever seen in the place stood behind the counter. "Can I ask you something?"

"You're going to anyway, I imagine," he said.

"I am. Why is this place empty? It's stunning, and even if you act like it's the last place you want to be, most people would overlook your charm in order to stay in a place like this."

He stared at her for a moment and then gave a short bark of laughter. "Direct is good." He came around the counter and stood beside her. "Truth is, the owners live somewhere in the Middle East. Bought this place as an investment but haven't ever been to see it. They don't do any marketing for it, and they don't provide any funding to do it right. I refuse to do it halfway, so I don't encourage people to book. We're not on any of those hotel sites. We don't even have a website." He shrugged. "I keep it as best I can."

"And if someone else bought it and invested in it properly? Would you still retain your charming, welcoming personality?" She grinned to take the sting from her words.

"You can't change a cat into a mouse." He grinned back, looking far nicer now. "But I'd give it a go."

"Good to know," she said, and patted his shoulder. "Let's see what we can do." She headed down the lane toward the bridge to cross the river. In truth, she wasn't sure she wanted to go ahead with her plans anymore. She could stop the sale, move the location, and start all over again. Calli's presence would be a reminder of this feeling that her heart had split in half. When she got to Calli's cottage, it was dark, all the blinds pulled closed. She wanted to go in and smell Calli's scent, run her fingers over the bed they'd only just slept in, and feel Calli close to her. Her knees went weak, and she leaned against the tree, her heart racing and tears welling up once again.

She looked up when she heard a door open down the way. Duncan poked his head out and pointed at her.

"Fix it!" he yelled, then slammed his door shut again.

She couldn't help but smile a little at his simple vehemence. She pushed off the tree and looked up at the temple. It, too, was dark. No flickering candles bounced light off the inside the dome and there was no incense on the breeze. Duncan said Calli had taken Iona with her. Why would she do that? It was strange to think there were things about Calli she didn't know when she felt like she'd known her all her life.

When she got to the Gray Mare pub, she was glad to see Leith and Mona sitting on the same side of a booth, their heads together like lovers sharing secrets. At least her sister had found something she could hang on to. She ordered a drink and went to their table.

Mona studied her for a moment. "Something happen?"

"Calli is gone. She went back to LA."

Mona left Leith's side of the booth and moved to Jordan's. She put her arm around her and pulled her close. "I'm so sorry."

"Did something else happen? Mona told me about the document you found." Leith slid a menu toward her, but Jordan pushed it away.

"We had a serious talk when we went to sleep. She read some interview I did a long time ago, where I went off about how the gods and that whole system are shitty. When she asked if I still felt that way, I couldn't deny it."

Leith whistled. "Can't imagine that felt good to hear."

"No. Didn't feel good to say it, either." Jordan gently moved out of her sister's embrace, needing a bit of space.

Mona returned to her place beside Leith. "Are you sure you still mean it?"

Jordan let out an exasperated sigh. "I think so. I mean, don't you?"

Leith got up from the booth. "I'm ordering food. Since you didn't look at the menu, I'll order something for you."

"I'm not hungry."

"Tough shit. You need to eat." Leith walked away still looking at the menu.

"She's so damn sexy." Mona kept watching her, looking like a lovestruck teen.

"Gross. Don't tell me anything else." Jordan sipped her water. "So, don't you still feel that way?"

Mona looked away from Leith. "Honestly? I don't know. After meeting Calli and spending time with her, and that pixie thing last night... Maybe we've been too black-and-white, you know? Like, we've been so caught up in Mama's death that we haven't allowed for other options."

Jordan tipped her glass toward Mona. "Those, dear sister, sound like Leith's words."

Mona actually blushed. "We've been talking a lot, and she's smart. When you only talk to people who agree with you, it's not good. And you and I have only really talked to each other about this. Leith has made me think."

"I don't know if I can change my mind that easily." She hesitated, but she'd always been honest with her sister. "I'm thinking about pulling the park altogether."

Mona reached out to hold her hand. "I didn't know Aunt Sue the way you did, but I know she was special to you, and she loved you like Mama did. Your thing with Calli shouldn't take away what you've wanted to do here for so long."

Leith returned with fresh drinks and heard what Mona was saying. "She's right, J. You've put a damn lot of work into this, and you've got a lot of people counting on you for work. If it falls through because of the council, then that's one thing. But to pull it because your heart isn't in it right now is another."

Their logic was sound, and if Jordan didn't feel like she was sinking into an emotional pit she might have been able to hear them more clearly and even agree. The food came and she picked at it, listening to Mona and Leith chat and laugh. Eventually, she pushed away her plate and looked up. "I'm going home."

They stopped talking and looked at her. "You mean the hotel?" Mona asked.

"No, home to California. I've walked the sites. I've talked to the crews. I've signed documents and put my case forward to the council. There's no reason for me to hang around." They didn't seem to know what to say, since what she said was true.

"Will you oversee things here?" she asked Leith.

"Sure, of course I will." She looked at Mona. "Does this mean you'll be going back too?"

Mona looked torn. Stay with her new girlfriend, or go with her sister, who was heartbroken? Jordan helped her out. "Mona, you should stay. I'm going to want space and time. And if you're here when the council announces their decision, you can start whatever process needs to happen next."

Mona's relief was obvious. "Are you sure?"

Jordan stood and put some money on the table. "Yeah, I'm sure. I'm going to go find a flight. I'll let you know when I'm leaving." She leaned down to hug them both. "Thanks, you guys, for being here. You're the best." She left before they could say anything and set off the waterworks again.

It was time to get back to her everyday life. Why did that feel like such a bad thing?

Chapter Twenty-four

The flight back to LA was long and filled with heartache. When Calli had woken to find not only Jordan and Mona gone, but the document about the other park missing as well, she'd known things had ended. She'd written and rewritten the email to Jordan, only to find there weren't adequate words to express how she felt and how much it hurt to leave Jordan behind. She'd gone into practicality mode once the email was sent. She'd packed, closed up the house, and gone to the temple, somehow knowing that Iona would be there.

Iona had been surprised when Calli asked her if she had a passport. When she'd said yes, that she'd gotten one for the day she was able to escape, Calli had told her it was time. They'd gone to Iona's house, where her gran hadn't said anything at all as Iona had packed a bag. Calli had explained to Iona's gran that she was taking Iona to California to begin her training in painting, and she'd handed her the Afterlife business card so she could call and check on Iona at any time. Still, the gnarled old woman who exuded bitterness and anger had only pursed her lips even harder and said nothing.

It was only as they were walking toward Calli's car that she called out behind them, "She's not welcome back here, ya hear? You're taking her, you keep her." And the door had slammed.

Iona had stumbled and looked over her shoulder, but Calli had gripped her elbow and propelled her toward the car. "Look forward, not back."

It had been all the reassurance she'd needed, and she hadn't even asked where they were going for the first two hours of the drive. When Calli had told her they were going to Afterlife, in LA, Iona had stayed silent even longer. It had only been when they'd gotten to the airport that Iona had turned to her, tears in her eyes. "I don't have the money for this," she'd whispered.

Once Calli had reassured her that all she had to do was get on the plane, the spirit in her had seemed to rise. Now, on the plane, her hand moved almost nonstop as she stared out the window and drew what she saw, very nearly without looking. It was impressive and exactly what Calli had felt was possible.

As they drew closer to California, she felt Iona begin to tense. In an effort to drown out the doubts and despair in her own mind, she asked Iona what she was thinking about.

"I have so many questions. I can't believe this is happening." She played with a plastic fork on her dinner tray. "I guess my first question is why?"

Calli tilted her head. "Why?"

"Why bring me here? Why did we leave so fast? Was it because of Jordan?"

And there they were, circling back around to the reason she hurt down to her soul. "I'm bringing you because I made a promise, and I don't break my promises. And because I believe in you. I was going to do it a different way, but…" She sighed and closed her eyes, feeling Jordan's arms around her. "Yes, we left quickly because of Jordan. Not because of her, necessarily, that isn't fair. But because of my feelings for her."

"If you want to be together, then what else matters?"

It was the question of a teenager, someone who didn't yet fully understand the complexities of life. How Calli wished she could see things that way too. "It's complicated. We're from different worlds, and Jordan isn't a fan of mine."

Iona stared out the window for a while longer before she said, "Are you?"

"Sorry? Am I what?"

"Are you a fan of your world? Like, is it perfect?"

Taken aback, Calli wasn't sure how to answer at first. "It's far from perfect. There are a lot of issues."

Iona shook her head, looking puzzled. "I think adults sometimes create problems to make life more interesting."

The pilot announced that they were getting ready to land, and Iona quickly buckled her seat belt. "Will I be staying with you?"

Calli hadn't given it a lot of thought, but she'd now taken on a teenager. "Yes, for a while. Until we decide how to proceed with your training."

"Cool." Iona touched Calli's arm. "Thank you. For not leaving me behind."

In that single touch Calli felt the wealth of potential ready to explode from Iona's being and she smiled. At least she'd done something right. "It's my pleasure."

They landed and Calli tilted her head toward the California sunshine. Iona was looking around rapidly, trying to take it all in as they made their way through the airport. A van was waiting out front, the Afterlife logo of golden wings emblazoned on the side. As they headed toward the Afterlife campus, Calli pointed out various landmarks and areas Iona might be familiar with or want to check out. She looked overwhelmed at the amount of traffic and people everywhere.

"The campus is a little quieter." She considered what she was bringing Iona into and mentally chastised herself. The girl had never been out of her village and now she was taking her into the mouth of the gods. "But you're going to see a lot of odd things."

"I've watched the programs on TV about the gods. I know it's crazy."

At least there was that element. She wouldn't be walking in blind. The thick black metal gate swung open, and they drove onto the campus, past the main headquarters and smaller office buildings toward the housing section.

Hermes flew past, his garish gold sandals propelling him through the air. Shiva was gesticulating wildly with all four arms as she spoke to Athena, who wore her helmet and carried her spear.

Calli winced. Why was Athena in armor on campus? She was usually in ripped jeans and some old rock band T-shirt.

"This is wild," Iona whispered, her hands on the window as she took it all in.

They pulled up at Calli's house and the driver, a minion of Chammo Lan, the goddess of travel, helped unload their bags. He bowed low and left, silent as always.

Calli set her things down and looked around. It was good to be home, but it wasn't her quiet little cottage in Scotland. She closed her eyes and tried to understand what she was feeling. The house itself felt off, different somehow. She realized with a start that it was her energy she was feeling—the way she'd felt before she left for her vacation. Lonely, frustrated, sad, and even angry…all the things she'd felt before.

Now, she could add heartbroken and despondent. Perfect.

She led Iona to her room and showed her the bathroom that would be hers as well. "Tonight we'll go to the main hall, if you want to, and I'll introduce you to some people."

Iona gave a huge yawn, one that made her eyes water. "Can I sleep for a while?"

"Of course. I'll wake you later." Calli closed the guest room door and went back to her own room. She couldn't help but wonder what it would have been like to have Jordan here too, to share this part of her life with her. But that wasn't going to happen.

She busied herself sending texts to her sisters and to Themis to let them all know she'd returned, and then got laundry going. There was a kind of meditative aspect to setting things right, and when Themis knocked, she felt a little more grounded.

She surprised Themis by pulling her into a hug. "It's good to see you."

Themis backed away and looked at her suspiciously. "Have you snatched my friend's body? Who are you?"

Calli wiped away an unbidden tear. "It's been a good vacation, in a way. What's going on around here? Why is Athena in armor?"

Themis held up a bottle of wine. "First, this. Then the reason you look like one of Cupid's victims. Then work."

They did exactly as she said, and Calli gave her a rundown of what had happened in Scotland.

"I'm so sorry, Calli," Themis said, pouring out the last of the wine. "Love is difficult when it comes to mixing our groups."

There wasn't anything to say to that. She wasn't even about to deny the fact that she'd fallen in love. It just didn't matter.

"Now, about work?" she prompted her.

"Athena is acting as mediator between her father and his brothers. She feels like they take her more seriously when she's in uniform. But there's nothing serious to worry about."

"What are they arguing about now? Followers, again?"

"Nope. This time it's about food."

Calli tried to follow but couldn't. "Food?"

"Poseidon feels that serving fish in the canteen is an insult and is demanding that it be stopped. Zeus said he doesn't care because he doesn't like fish anyway, which Poseidon took as an insult. Hades said he thinks even more fish should be served and overcooked at that."

It was ludicrous, and exactly what she'd come to expect from them. "Why is Poseidon even here? Why isn't he in the seas?"

"I'll leave it to you to ask him. I'm off to Olympus where it's normal and quiet now that everyone is down here." She stood and kissed Calli's cheek. "If you need to talk, day or night, call me."

Calli hugged her tightly. "I may take you up on that."

Once Themis was gone, Calli sat on the couch with her feet up, pondering her next move. When in doubt, take it in smaller pieces. That's what she always told her students. She called Clio, who hadn't yet responded to her email.

"I didn't think you were talking to me," she said when she answered.

"I didn't say I wouldn't talk to you. I said I'd talk to you when you came to your senses about your benefit."

She huffed. "It would have been art, which is what we're all about, right? But fine, I've taken it off the table. I'll have musicians instead."

"Musicians from the school. Not some celebrity headliner."

Clio groaned. "You take all the fun out of everything. Compromise. One celebrity headliner to bring in the money, and then school musicians to showcase the talent from the school."

"Deal." The age-old contact with her sister made her feel a little lighter. "When does the summer program start?"

"There's an open house week after next. Why?"

"I have a young woman here with me—"

"Finally! You broke your spell!"

Calli grimaced. "Nothing like that. She's a teenager I met in Scotland. She's perfect for the program."

"Wow, that's fantastic. You've hardly paid any attention to the school."

"I pay attention to everything. You should know that by now." Calli's tone was sharper than she meant it to be.

"Yikes, someone needs a nap. Send me her details and we'll get her registered for the tour. And get me her flight details so I can pick her up. If she's special to you then she deserves special attention."

The thought of putting Iona on a plane and sending her off on her own when this was the first time she'd left her village made Calli uneasy. "Actually, I think I'll drive her up. Take Highway One and make a trip of it."

There was silence on the other end of the line. "What's wrong?" Clio asked.

"Nothing is wrong. I can take a road trip." Her sisters knew her far better than that.

"Okay, you can tell me when you get here. But are you okay? Tell me that."

She didn't feel okay. But she'd lived long enough to know that heartbreak didn't kill you, though sometimes it felt like it would. Like it did now. "I'm okay. Or, I will be, with time." She could practically feel Clio deciding whether or not to push.

"If you need me, or any of us, call. Remember that we're a team, okay?" Clio's tone had softened considerably.

"Thanks, Clio. I'll remember, and I'll see you at the school soon."

They hung up, and Calli heard Iona's door open. She shuffled into the room looking a strange combination of worn out and excited. "I thought I heard voices."

"My friend Themis just left. She was covering my position while I was gone. And I just got off the phone with my sister Clio." Calli got up and poured them both big glasses of iced tea. "You should get used to this, if you're going to live here."

Iona sniffed it and then took a sip and winced. "Who drinks cold tea?"

"Pretty much everyone in this country. A slice of lemon can help until you get used to it, as can some sugar if you prefer it sweet." She cut a slice and dropped it in Iona's drink, and she grimaced like it was only marginally better. "Have a seat."

Iona sat across from her, looking wary. "Are you sending me back?"

Calli's heart ached for her. How long would it take for her to trust that good things were possible? "Just the opposite, actually. Have you heard of the Ancient Center of the Arts in Big Sur?"

"Of course. The ACA is every artist's dream school." Iona held her glass tightly.

"Well, it was founded by me and my sisters. We decided it was necessary to have a school with all the arts involved, and we recruit tutors from all over the world." She paused to take a drink, enjoying the heightening of Iona's energy. "We offer scholarships to a number of students every year. The open house visit is the week after next. Would you like to go?"

Iona looked utterly speechless. "Do you mean it?"

"Of course." She was nearly knocked over when Iona flung herself into Calli's arms. "Your life is going to change, sweet child."

Iona pulled back. "What about the temple?"

Yes. What about the temple? She hadn't given it any thought as she'd practically fled from Scotland. "Well, now that you've shown us how important it is, we can make sure to get someone in place. In fact, maybe you could help me interview your replacement?"

In all her years on the planet, Calli had never seen such a remarkable change in someone so quickly.

Iona drew herself up proudly. "They have to be a very specific type of person, you know."

"I do. And you'll help me make certain they are."

That night they went to the canteen where the gods were gathering for dinner. There were plenty of welcomes, and Iona handled the situation well, though she stayed close to Calli's side.

"Will you go back?" Iona asked as she ate the Italian meal cooked by an Italian goddess who had branched out into restaurants.

"Back?"

"To Scotland." Iona looked around. "I can't imagine leaving all this, but you seem, like, I don't know, on the outside?"

Calli smiled at Iona's perceptiveness. "It can be hard being an arbitrator here. I can't be too friendly with any one person in case I have to handle a dispute that involves them."

"That sounds lonely."

"Yes, I think it is."

"Who is that?" Iona whispered, looking awestruck.

Calli followed the line of her gaze. "Ah, that's Dani. She must have just got in from work. Her official title used to be Death, but once people started worshipping her, she achieved goddess status. Now the cloak and scythe are mostly ceremonial, and she has someone else in her old position."

The tall figure in the midnight black cloak with the deep hood pulled over her head set down the silver bladed scythe she was carrying and pulled back her hood to reveal a strikingly handsome, short haired woman with a shy smile. Calli had always liked Dani, though her choice in the fury Megara had been surprising, given Meg's wild reputation and Dani's quiet ways. They'd managed to find a way to be together. Why was it so hard for her and Jordan?

"She's...wow." Iona hadn't taken her eyes off Dani.

"She's also happily partnered to a woman with snakes in her wings and a pair of very deadly fangs in her mouth." When Iona flushed at the warning, Calli smiled. The last thing she wanted was Iona invited to one of their rather sexual parties. She was still underage, after all.

They talked for a while about the college and what Iona could expect, and then they headed back to Calli's place, both of them tired from their journey. But sleep didn't come for Calli. She lay there wondering what Jordan was doing. There'd been no reply to her email, not that she'd expected one. She'd hoped, though. For what she wasn't sure. A plea to come back? She curled onto her side and let the thoughts run wherever they wanted. Feeling something again was a good thing. If only she'd been able to hold on to the magic of that delicious night spent in Jordan's arms.

CHAPTER TWENTY-FIVE

Jordan watched the fog roll in over the water from her hammock. The wraparound deck afforded her a view of the ocean in every direction, and she loved the peace and quiet it gave her. It felt out of the way, but the village of Big Sur had enough to keep her going, including the bakery she'd stopped at for fresh bread and carrot cake before she'd gone home.

The last week had been one of the most miserable of her life. She'd barely eaten, had been sleeping badly, and every thought revolved around Calli. She'd looked her up on the Afterlife website, read every article, every book, every poem that mentioned her. None of them came close to describing her beauty, her wit, or her singing voice. They had no idea how amazing she truly was.

Jordan desperately wanted to reach out but didn't know what to say if she did. Nothing had been resolved between them except that they wanted one another. Why couldn't that be enough?

Clumsily, she got out of the hammock and let the cool wood under her bare feet calm her thoughts. News from the council should be coming in any day now and she wasn't sure what she wanted the outcome to be. She'd talked to Leith and Mona, individually and together, and it sounded like they were having a great time. Mona had even jokingly asked if Jordan thought their dad would be upset if she stayed in Scotland.

She wanted her sister to be happy, but she'd be seriously bummed if she decided to stay there. She'd miss her, even though she traveled so much she didn't see her all that often. She needed to find a way to take her mind off Calli, but what with having to wait on the council's decision, it was all but impossible.

She hadn't allowed anyone to get close enough to give her a heartache, but when she'd even come close, she'd simply found another body to warm her bed and distract her until the feeling went away. With that in mind, she called Austin.

"I need to get out of my head. Go out with me."

"Day drinking on a Wednesday with my friend who is hardly ever around? I'm in. I'll pick you up in half an hour."

Not having to explain why you needed to go day drinking was one of the benefits of having a best friend. She needed someone, and Austin was always there. She got ready quickly, not really caring what she looked like. Anyone she picked up this time of day would be looking for exactly the same thing she was, and no pretense was needed.

Austin pulled up outside, the convertible top down and her long brown hair blowing in the wind. She honked, even though Jordan was already outside waiting. "C'mon, that tequila isn't going to drink itself!"

Jordan jumped in. "Let's do it."

The wind made it hard to talk, which was just fine with Jordan. The sea air and music were soothing, and her shoulders began to relax. By the time they made it to Easy Street she was in a slightly better frame of mind, and after the first two beers and games of pool, she could breathe again.

"So. What color are her eyes?" Austin shot at the two ball and missed.

"Pale blue. Like the sky in summer."

"Uh-huh. Go on."

Between shots and beers, Jordan spilled the whole story. "And now I'm back here, with you, playing pool. And you're great, but I really wish I was with her."

"I'll try not to be offended." She sank the eight ball. "Your round."

Jordan returned with the bottles and clinked hers to Austin's.

"Advice or sympathy?"

It was a question they always asked whenever the other had a problem. Sometimes people jumped in with advice when all you really wanted was a sympathetic ear. And sometimes they didn't offer anything up when you really needed help seeing a way forward. "Advice."

"You're being an asshole."

Jordan blinked and took a slug of beer. "That's not advice. That's just insulting."

"Nope. It's definitely advice." She racked the balls again. "I guess I could say stop being an asshole, and that would be more advice-like."

"How is this my fault?" Jordan took her shot and missed.

"You're letting old shit cloud your thinking. Your mom chose her path. Yeah, she followed rules and shit. But she *chose* to do that. You don't have to be religious to be with someone who is. You just have to respect their beliefs. And she's not religious, even if you do get on your knees for her." She gave Jordan a dirty grin, making her laugh.

"Isn't the ideological difference a big thing? Can you be with someone who works for a company you despise?"

"If you're not an asshole, you can." She sank the nine ball. "Hence, my advice."

"You're telling me that if someone worked for a company who, I don't know, felled whole forests just for fun, you'd still be with that person?" Jordan missed her shot again and drank a little deeper.

"If I loved them enough? Yeah. We might have to agree to disagree, but if they were my person, then we'd find a way to deal with it." She sank the six ball. "You're playing like shit."

"You're just full of compliments today." The more Austin talked, the worse Jordan felt, and the truer it began to feel.

"I'm your best friend. I'm full of a lot of things that allow me to deal with you." She pulled Jordan into a side hug. "Life can be shitty, but sometimes it gives you a chance to make it less shitty. This is your chance."

"You're terrible at pep talks."

"I'm awesome at everything." She sank the eight ball yet again, proving her point. She set her stick aside and crossed her arms as she leaned against the table. "Be brutally honest with yourself right now. Can you imagine never seeing her again? Not having her in your life?"

Jordan slumped onto a barstool. "It makes me sick to think about it. No, I can't imagine life without her."

"Then that's your answer, J. You need to fix it."

Jordan pictured Duncan shouting the same phrase at her. The world around her was a little blurry thanks to the amount of beer she'd enjoyed, but her original intention to pick up someone to take the edge off wasn't appealing in the least. Slowly, through the fog of beer and self-recrimination, an idea began to form, and she was reminded of Nova's cryptic remark, that she wouldn't listen to advice until the time came when she would. The time was now. She grabbed a handful of napkins and a pen off the bar and started sketching.

❖

"I love it. And you're doing the right thing," Leith said the next day via Skype, after looking over the plans Jordan had sent over. "We're taking them over to the council office right now. I'll let you know what happens."

"Mona, can you see how it all works? Do you see any problems with it?" Jordan looked at the architectural drawings on her screen, which she'd begun to create once the hangover had passed. It had taken a few days to work it out, and plenty of erasing and starting over, but once she had it, the feeling of rightness had filled her.

"I've made some tweaks. After we got your plans, we went to each site with the crew and rejigged things. I made changes based on landscape and a couple other factors, but for the most part, your ideas were solid. It's going to cost a lot to rework things. You sure about this?"

"A hundred percent. Thanks for taking care of it so fast. Let me know if you have any problems with the council." Jordan was satisfied with what she'd put in play. It might not bring her and Calli back together, but at least she'd know she'd done her best. And it was great for the park, too, which was a bonus. Sometimes setbacks allowed for a better product in the long run.

"Have you talked to Calli yet?" Mona asked.

"Not yet. I've been talking to Austin, though. She said I was being an asshole."

Leith laughed. "Good friends are worth their weight in gold, mate."

Jordan rolled her eyes, her soul a little lighter. "Yeah, they are. I mean, you're more in the silver range, but still up there."

"Call Calli. Stop being you." Mona giggled when Leith murmured something Jordan couldn't hear. "I love you, but we have to go. We'll call you tomorrow."

Jordan ended the call and then went to the Afterlife, Inc. page. She had Calli's email address, but she wanted to hear her voice, and the cell number she had for her said it was no longer in service. There was no direct number listed for Calliope's office, so she called the main one.

"I'm trying to reach Calliope Ardalides, please. She's the muse of justice."

"Yes, I know what her position is, thank you." The person on the phone clearly wasn't impressed. "Calliope is on vacation. She'll be back in a week."

"Oh. I thought she got back last week." Jordan had simply assumed that Calli had returned to California. If she hadn't, she had no idea where on earth she might be.

"She did, but she's away again. Did you want to leave a message?"

"Could you please tell her Jordan James called? Can I leave my number?"

The woman dutifully took down Jordan's number and promised to pass it on if Calli called in. Where was she, if she wasn't at Afterlife?

CHAPTER TWENTY-SIX

Calli loved the drive along Highway 1. The steep cliffs on one side, the high mountains and old trees on the other. The ocean far below, crashing against the rocks, the sea lions lounging on the beaches, their big gray bodies shining like wet boulders in the sunlight. In the convertible beside her, Iona tilted her face to the sun, her expression relaxed and smiling as it had never been in Scotland. In the week and a half they'd been at Afterlife, Iona had come bursting out of her shell. She'd carried a canvas around with her all the time and drew portraits of the gods that showed emotion and personality, and she was soon in demand. Calli had shooed several from the door so that Iona could get a decent night's sleep. It was good that she was off to the college, otherwise she'd get stuck at Afterlife pandering to the gods' egos.

The farther up the coast they went, the more she thought about Jordan. The verdict from the council should have been in by now, and she'd hoped, at least a little, that Jordan would tell her what they'd decided. She could call and ask herself, but for some reason, she couldn't bring herself to do it. If it went through, she'd be disappointed and upset about the temple. If it didn't go through, she'd be upset and disappointed on Jordan's behalf.

She and Iona had drafted a job description for the temple, and then Calli had posted it within the Afterlife organization. No one else in the area of the temple had seemed at all interested. At least if she got someone from Afterlife to do it, she would know it was being taken care of. They'd ended up choosing a woman from Death's domain, someone who had decided picking up dead souls wasn't for her, and who wanted to try something more contemplative and above ground. Iona had taken to her right away, and Calli had come to see that she had an extraordinary gift for reading people.

"What if I'm not good enough?" Iona asked as they sat at a small café overlooking the water for lunch.

"You've been told by a muse that you are. Do you think we're ever wrong?"

Iona gave her a wry smile. "I don't think anyone would ever tell you if you were."

"Come on, let's get going. We have a long way to go." Calli enjoyed Iona's company. She was kind and funny, and now that she'd stopped feeling like she might need to run every time someone came around, she was growing in confidence, too. She'd helped Calli sidestep her heartache so she wasn't sitting around wallowing. Once she was at the college, Calli wasn't sure how she was going to continue to avoid her emotions. She'd deal with that when the time came.

They stopped for photos occasionally, and Iona was growing more excited the closer they got. The ACA had been built into the cliffside above the ocean. It had extensive grounds and dramatic views, a meditative place as well as being a learning center. People with intensely creative minds could often be overwhelmed by the world around them and the difficulty in finding outlets for their gifts. The center made it possible not only to block out the world while they learned, but they also had programs in place to help them deal with the world once their training was over. The waiting list was long, and Calli's innate sense of justice was a little twisted around that she'd made it so that Iona jumped the line. But if nothing else, she was being reminded that flexibility was a necessary part of life.

They drove down the steep winding road to the center and were buzzed in at the gate. Clio came out, dressed in a flowing white suit that made her look like a fashionable nun of some kind. Calli turned to Iona. "Don't let her scare you."

Iona raised her eyebrows and got out of the car. She was then immediately swept up in the hurricane that was Clio.

"Aren't you adorable! I can see why Calli brought you here. Talent is just oozing out of you, isn't it? You'll be amazing, don't worry. And you can always call if you need anything. I don't live that far away, and I can be here in a jiff."

Iona looked over her shoulder, wide-eyed, and Calli gave her a shrug and smiled. This was what it was to be around Clio, and though her sister could be way over-the-top sometimes, and she didn't always agree with the way Clio did things, her heart was in the right place.

The tour lasted for over an hour, and Clio patiently explained the different areas and how classes worked. When she stopped at the art studio that overlooked the ocean, Iona sat on a bench, looking around in wonder.

"I think she's sold," Calli said, bumping her sister's shoulder.

"I should think so." Clio's stare was penetrating. "We'll get her settled in. She can start right away since our resident painter is already here. There's no reason for her to have to sit around the Afterlife campus waiting to start her life." She hooked her arm through Calli's. "And then we're going to have a chat about you."

If she were honest, she'd rather have talked to Thalia about what was going on, but Clio was here, and maybe her exuberance and spontaneity were what Calli needed, more than pragmatic advice.

They got Iona's things from the car and showed her to her dorm room, a private room with her own bathroom and a window that took in both the ocean and a bit of the rock face.

She hugged Calli tightly. "Promise you won't forget me?"

"How could I?" She held her at arm's length. "You'll be fine, and if you ever need me, or even if you just want to chat, call." She let her go and hoped the pride she felt in Iona showed. "Now, unpack and make this room yours."

Iona looked so happy it made Calli's heart burst in return, and she left before she started to cry. That wasn't very professional, and Iona had been subject to her unprofessional actions enough already.

She and Clio went to the staff quarters where Clio had her own office, complete with a deck overlooking the ocean. They sat outside with a glass of wine.

"Are you happy?" Clio asked, twirling her wine in her glass.

"I don't understand the question."

Clio gave her a look. "It's a simple question. Are you happy in the life you're living? Are you happy working at Afterlife as an arbitrator? Does it make you want to get up every day?"

Calli watched the waves roll in and crash, then roll out again. "No. I thought I was. I think at first, I liked the challenge of it all. But now?" She sipped at her wine, searching for the words to match the emotions. "No. After spending time away I realized that I want to get back to being what I was born to be. The position is too dry, too uncreative. It's turning me to stone inside, and every day it gets harder to take another step."

Clio had tears running down her face. "Can you see what a travesty that is? For a muse, inspiration of humans, creators of beautiful works of art in all forms, to have become something so grim?"

It turned out that Clio was exactly the right sister to talk to. "I know. I didn't see it, but I do now."

A delicious aroma filled the air. "Mm, it's time for dinner. I think you've had a big enough epiphany for the moment. Let's go eat so you can have more reluctant realizations later." Clio took her hand and pulled her up from her chair.

As they made their way to the dining area, Calli's phone buzzed. She checked the text and stopped walking, staring at the message from work that said someone named Jordan James was trying to get in touch with her. There was a phone number. She pushed her phone back into her pocket, her breathing shaky. She'd hoped for this, but now that it had happened, she wasn't sure where to go with it. All she knew was that she missed Jordan desperately, with the kind of soul ache sometimes only found once in a lifetime.

Calli thought about what she'd said to Clio as they filled their plates with beautiful food. It felt right, and she knew it was time for a change. But what would she do next? She'd always been a planner, and that part was definitely lacking right now. The one thing she knew was that the world was hers again, and it was time to take her place in it.

CHAPTER TWENTY-SEVEN

Jordan looked around her place for the tenth time, making sure it was spotless. When Calli had sent her a text, she'd nearly had a heart attack with relief. When she'd said she was already in Big Sur, she was baffled. What were the chances? Maybe they were better than average, since she was interested in an immortal. Maybe more cosmic things happened when you lived in their orbit. Whatever the reason, she wasn't about to blow the chance to love someone this much.

When the doorbell rang, she had to steady herself against the couch. This day would change the rest of her life. She opened the door and went weak kneed at the sight of Calli in a summer dress that went to her ankles, showing off her beautiful olive skin and gorgeous, trim figure.

"Although I appreciate the look on your face, could I come in?"

Jordan shook herself from her trance. "I'm sorry. You're just so beautiful."

"Thank you." Calli kissed Jordan's cheek, the subtle scent of apples floating around her. "I've missed you."

Jordan took her hand and led her into the kitchen. "I've missed you too. I hated that we left things the way we did." It was good that there was no small talk, no hesitant games or wishy-washy lead in.

"Me too." Call accepted the glass of iced tea and moved to look out the living room window. "Stunning."

"Indeed."

Calli looked over her shoulder at the timbre of Jordan's voice. She was far more interested in looking at Calli than the view outside. "Can I show you something?" She led the way into her office, which also looked out over the ocean, but had a beautiful view of the trees around them as well. The program was already set up to go. She motioned to the seat beside her. "You know planning permission should have come in last week. Or, the lack thereof, maybe." God, she hoped this was going to work. She pressed forward. "Well, before it did, I had an idea, and I called Mona and Leith and we redrafted our plans entirely. Totally revised the park." She pulled up the architectural drawings. "We've moved the locations of the coaster and the zip lines to over here so they're as far away as they can be from the village's houses, thereby decreasing the noise and the potential for disruption. And the handful of houses at the top of the village of Bemersyde won't be impacted hardly at all now. Here, we've put in a round restaurant that will allow for a quiet view of the scenery but also provide food and such. It will act like a boundary." She took a deep breath and studied Calli's expression. "And here, where the parking lot was going to be, we've put in the meditation and arts space. It extends from here, all the way to the base of the temple. The serenity garden will be landscaped with beautiful flowers and will also include sculptures throughout created by local artists. At the base of the hill will be a pond with benches around it for people to quietly enjoy the area."

Calli leaned forward, her gaze moving over the screen. "And this?" She pointed to a purple dot at the cave system.

"That one I'm going to need your help with." She took Calli's hand in hers and turned her to face Jordan. "Meeting you has turned my world upside down. Before you I was wandering the world, searching out adventures. I enjoyed beautiful women." She grinned and held on to Calli's hand a little tighter when her eyebrow quirked. "And I had no real ties to anyone, not even to family." It took all her courage to say the next part. "Nothing, not one adventure or any woman, has compared to what you've brought into my life. You're stunning, kind, intelligent, and in bed, you blow my mind." It made her heart sing when Calli smiled.

"Are you proposing to me, Jordan?" Calli asked teasingly.

"Not yet, and when I do, you won't have to ask if that's what I'm up to." Jordan motioned to the plans on the computer. "That blue dot is part of what you've brought to my life. That cave system has a waterfall. As I've planned it, we'll use it for private parties and such. But on the other side of what you can see is a separate fall with another beautiful pool. I'd like to make that part a refuge for the dryads. Or any creature who wants to use it, really. A place where they'll be safe and those of us aware of them can watch over them to make sure they're okay. That way the land I'm using is not only *not* pushing people out of their homes, but it can also be a place for creatures to return to."

Tears rolled down Calli's as she searched Jordan's expression. "And my work? What I am?"

Jordan took a deeper breath and focused to make sure the words came out right. "I still believe that the system of belief in general is a little broken. But that's okay. I can believe that and still love you. I can know that you're perfect for me in every conceivable way, and even if we don't see eye to eye on things, it only means we might have some fireworks occasionally. I've been stubborn, and I'm not going to let that stubbornness cost me the most amazing woman in the world." She wiped away Calli's tears. "Your turn. Can you deal with me being human? With the eventual end of what we'll have?"

"I've been stubborn too. It was crazy to think we couldn't overcome our differences given how we feel about one another. I will love you every day we have and never take a single second for granted." She cupped Jordan's face in her palm. "And I've decided to leave Afterlife. I'll always be a muse, and I'll always be part of that world. But I lost myself, the essence of who I am. Being in Scotland, around the temple, helped me remember what I was born to do."

"So you're okay with the plans?" Jordan's heart felt like it could burst.

"Thank you for creating something that works so well for both of us. I know it must have cost your business a lot of money, what with having to reapply and your crew waiting around again. It means the world to me."

"Once the council saw the plan revisions and read the letter explaining why I'd made them, they put the permission through within a day. And I'd pay it all again if it meant seeing you smile like this." She leaned in and kissed her. The moment their lips met the world turned right side up once more. Sliding her hands along Calli's arms, she stood and without breaking the kiss, moved them back toward the living room.

"Is something wrong with your bed?" Calli murmured against her lips.

"I want to see you naked in the sunlight with the ocean behind you. My own mythical woman." They undressed quickly and Jordan lay on top of Calli, their skin warm and caresses fevered. After they'd both come once, Jordan slowed down. She kissed and ran her hands over every inch of Calli's body, luxuriating in the sight of her sun-drenched skin under her hands. It was almost painful, how beautiful Calli was, and the desire mixed with love made her dizzy. She rested her forehead between Calli's shoulder blades and took in the moment.

Beyond Calli, the sunlight created a path of diamonds glinting on the water that seemed to lead straight to where they lay. "What are you thinking about?" Jordan asked.

"I'm thinking about all the adventures that lay ahead and all the places where I want to make love to you." Calli shifted onto her side so Jordan could lay beside her. "When we met…no, before we met. The very first time I saw you walk into the bookshop, I knew we were meant to be together. I didn't know why, or what it meant. But the fates have a funny way of bringing people together for a reason. And aside from our love for one another, I think it was so we could make the kind of difference you've already begun."

Jordan tried to keep her attention on Calli's words rather than Calli's curves. "Tell me more?"

"When I took you to see the dryads, I simply knew it was the right thing to do, I didn't know why. When we got in touch with Puck to make sure your land was clear, it was the right thing to do. And because of those meetings, you've created a safe space for them in the long run. Maybe that's part of the bigger plan of us being together. Maybe we're meant to create fun, beautiful places that are also havens."

Jordan threaded her fingers through Calli's. "Combining both our worlds and passions."

She kissed Jordan's hand. "Exactly."

Jordan turned onto her back and Calli curled into her, resting her head on her chest, the sun warming their naked bodies. While she wasn't certain about the destiny part, she was certain that Calli's idea of what they could accomplish together was exciting. From now on she'd have someone to share the adventure with, and there was no question it was going to be the adventure of her life.

Epilogue

One Year Later

Calli cheered her sisters on as they flew past overhead. Competition had been fierce, and the forest was full of laughter, taunts, and even the occasional burst of electricity from some god or another who had lost to another god.

Jordan came over and put her arm around her waist. "I think some of the gods are cheating."

"Would you expect anything different?" She kissed Jordan tenderly. "Thank you for this. It was a wonderful idea." They watched as another group got rigged to the zip lines overhead. The park had opened the previous weekend to a select section of the public that had included Jordan's dad and brother, as well as her best friend, Austin, whom Calli instantly liked when she'd met her. The locals had been invited too, so they could enjoy the experience without a crowd. Duncan and Jacob had been like twelve-year-olds, although they'd given the rock climbing a miss. They spent most every day together, and Calli was so glad they'd have one another right to the end. Jacob had sent her a photo of them drinking whisky beneath the painting she'd bought him from the Bemersyde House auction. He deserved it and was proud of having it in his home, something Duncan teased him about all the time. Sometimes solid companionship was just as wonderful as a romantic relationship.

This weekend, though, would remain in Calli's heart forever. Jordan had suggested an immortals' weekend, and she'd closed it to the public so that whoever wanted to join them from Calli's world could do so. The turnout had been stupendous. Gods in every color, height, and shape rode the forest coaster, flew on the zip lines, rappelled down into the caves, and climbed the cliff faces. The email invitation had included the only caveat: that the gods leave their powers at the door. The day was about fun, baseline competition, not powers or prayers or an audience. The sign at the front gate had reminded them of the one rule.

"This is so bizarre and perfect," Ramona said, coming up beside them with Leith close behind.

"They'll be worn out by tonight." Calli smiled as her sisters Thalia and Erato went running past on their way to the forest coaster, which they'd already been on twice.

"Are any coming tonight?" Jordan asked, scanning the area for potential issues.

"More than would usually come, that's for certain. Your idea to do this today means they'll be here, and they'll be in a good mood, too, which Clio is thrilled about."

Iona ran up, breathless, with a death minion giggling at her side. They held hands and looked like they might be permanently attached. "We're heading into the caves. I thought I'd let you know that a group of dryads have arrived, but I don't think anyone else saw them." She turned to run off again and then stopped. "Oh, and a tiny person named Puck is looking for you." With that, the girls ran off.

"We'd better make sure the dryads are happy." The four of them set off toward the caves, taking the tram that had been set up to take people from one area to another, which reduced the traffic on the roads. They passed the sign for the gardens and temple, and Jordan squeezed her hand. The meditation area around the temple had been a big success, and Calli adored how the temple was such a focal point of the beautifully worked gardens.

The caves were busy, and though a few sky gods hovered around looking uncertain about going underground, others were jumping at the chance to zip line through the caves. The group bypassed the primary entrance and walked to the entrance that was far less noticeable, then made their way down the stairs into the private cave at the end.

Dryads tittered and splashed and played, and when they saw Calli and Jordan they swam over. The one who had been so taken with Jordan before slid up the length of her and pressed her green skin to Jordan's. At a sharp word from the leader, she tittered, her sharp little teeth clacking, and dove back into the pool. Jordan blew out a quiet breath.

The leader spoke, and Calli translated for the group, though she wasn't sure Ramona or Leith heard a word she said, given how wonderstruck they looked. "She thanks you for this place of safety and hopes you'll keep your word, and make sure that any humans who come after you will abide by what you've put in place here."

"I've already made plans for that," Jordan said, pulling Calli close. "As an immortal, Calli has agreed to keep watch and set the right guardians in place throughout time. Although you may need to share. Puck is going to spread the word about this being a safe space, so we may end up with more creatures here at some point."

The leader tilted her head and glanced toward the back, then sprang backward into the water, effectively dismissing them. That was when they noticed Puck sitting on a rock, watching the dryads play. He waved at them, then went back to watching.

"Wow. That was…wow." Leith shook her head. "I always knew my country was magical, but the things I've seen in the last year have been something else." She held Ramona close. "There are actual gods up there, laughing like kids. Have you seen an elephant-headed god fly? Because I have." Her grin was big enough to light the cave.

"Thanks again for staying here while all the work was done." Jordan bumped Leith's shoulder.

"Wasn't exactly a hardship, mate, especially with my lady in charge here," she said, kissing Ramona's head.

"At least you have someone to keep you in line now." Jordan looked at her watch. "We'd better start wrapping things up if we're going to be on time tonight."

Calli led the way out of the cavern and back into the fading sunlight. Dusk turned the hilltop clouds into sherbet puffs and bird song filled the air. "It's Jordan's intention to do this day once a year, to give the immortals time to come together and let off steam. I think it's perfect."

They'd recruited volunteers from the Deadlands to man the rides for the day. That way the gods could truly relax, and the staff didn't have to waver when the gods begged for one more ride or climb. It was nearing closing time and Jordan flipped a switch at the main house that turned lights at every main section to amber. That would let the staff know it was time to turn people away. The staff had also been asked to remind the gods it was time to go freshen up for the event that evening.

Calli pulled Jordan into the shower with her. She never got tired of the feel of Jordan's body against hers or the way Jordan looked at her when they were making love. They still had their ups and downs and blew the roof off with arguments around the issue of religion occasionally, but overall, their life was peace and passion, singing and adventure. After leaving Afterlife, she'd moved in with Jordan at her place in Big Sur. It had been a perfect base for starting their life together. And when they needed a break, they came here, to the cottage.

She wore a long black backless dress that dragged slightly on the floor when she walked, and it perfectly matched Jordan's sexy black tux. "I'm so glad we're sharing this night."

"Me too. Last year's gala was fun, but this one is extra special." She softly kissed Calli's neck. "You look sensational. Maybe we should just stay home…"

Calli danced out of her grasp, laughing. "Later, handsome. For now, we have money to raise."

They left the cottage and drove to the Dryburgh Abbey Hotel, which Jordan had purchased from the absentee owners and had made good changes to. With the help of the recalcitrant staff member she'd spoken to originally, they'd created a welcoming, fun place that catered to Jordan's park, and was also a place for people to relax, get pampered, and have the kind of community she loved during her own adventures. Tonight, though, it looked a zillion times different from the usual.

Clio came rushing out, her black dress floating around her like a cloud. "I'm so glad you're here." She grabbed Leith's arm and dragged her toward the door. "I need you to translate. I can't understand half of what anyone is saying."

Ramona, in a dark red dress that hugged every curve, took Jordan's other arm and she escorted both of them into the building. Black and white curtains were draped artfully from the ceiling, highlighting paintings and sculptures, as well as huge blocks of text from writers. Singers, grouped on a small stage off to the side, provided the background music in beautiful harmony. Teachers from the ACA milled among their students and guests, talking about progress and everything else to do with the school. Duncan came over with Jacob and thumped Jordan hard on the back and gave her a wink before they moved on to chat to the local single widows club.

Calli's pride at being involved made her chest swell, and she looked around for a particular student. When Iona spotted them, she gave an ecstatic wave, and they made their way over to her. Calli hugged her tightly. "Congratulations."

Iona flushed with happiness. "Thank you. I wouldn't be here without you."

"It's been a pleasure to watch you grow into the woman I knew you'd be." Calli had taken a teaching position at the college, working with singers and anyone who wanted to learn to play the harp. She also taught courses on justice, though only one or two a year, as she didn't want it to take away from the more flowing, creative aspects of the school. She and Iona had grown even closer, and she'd loved watching Iona's painting take on the life it had. "You've come such a long way from that timid young woman who tended the temple. The critics are already raving about your work. Your parents would be proud."

Iona brushed away a tear. "Turns out all you need in life is for one person to believe in you enough to help you get where you need to go."

Someone tapped the mic and they turned to face the stage, where Clio stood basking in the limelight. Jordan put her arm around Calli's waist, and she leaned into her.

"Welcome to the annual fundraising gala for the Ancient College of the Arts. As you know, we have this event every year to showcase the wonderful artists who attend the college and to raise funding for scholarships, to make sure that we can reach as many students as possible who want to be artists of all kinds." She scanned the room dramatically. "And now that I know how many gods are here, I'm going to be knocking on your doors personally next year. Whatever offerings you're hoarding from your churches and temples, some of that needs to go back into the community pot to help us fund things beyond your sectors."

There was laughter and a bit of applause, but there was also some uncomfortable shuffling. The gods had come for a weekend of fun and had been caught in Clio's fundraising net. Probably forever.

"I thought my sister Calliope was crazy when she suggested we move the annual gala here this year. For those of you who don't know, we usually hold it at the college in Big Sur, California. But then Jordan was kind enough to open her park to us—"

She was interrupted by cheers and well-wishes that came in many languages and sounds.

"And it made sense to combine the two. We received an incredibly generous donation from the Bemersyde estate auction, which helped us not only provide more scholarships but also helped us build our new cyber center, and it also provided a special grant to our own Scottish scholarship recipient, Iona, who is here with us tonight."

Iona turned bright red as the spotlight landed on her, and she gave a little wave and smile, looking like she wanted to find an easel to hide under.

"And of course, we welcome Amber Scott and Nova Stokes. Nova has become a music mentor at the ACA, and Amber has already embarked on the first steps of her singing career." Both Amber and Nova smiled and waved when the spotlight shifted to them.

She continued talking, but Calli drifted off, thinking of all that had happened in the last year. She'd found love, the kind that would endure. She was living true to herself and her dream of making the world better and had even gotten involved in a political campaign working to end social injustice. Jordan loved her and showed her every day, just as she'd promised to. Jordan tugged on her hand and tilted her head toward the door.

They made their way unobtrusively from the room and out onto the large deck strung with fairy lights. Zeus stood by the railing and straightened a little when he saw them come out. In his traditional white chiton and wreath of olive leaves around his head, he looked every inch the god he was. He didn't say anything, just smiled.

Calli turned to Jordan with a questioning look but understood right away.

Jordan looked up from where she knelt on one knee, a diamond ring wrapped in a Celtic swirl of white gold held in her hand. "Will you?"

She was breathless and shaking in the best way. "I will."

Jordan stood and slid the ring onto her finger. "I hope you don't mind that I asked your father to be here to witness it. Seemed right, somehow, given his position and all."

Zeus drew them together in a crushing hug. "Well done! No fanfare, nice and simple. I like it." He finally released them, and Jordan took in a gasping breath. "I've always liked human women myself—"

"Enough, Zeus." Calli hugged him tightly. "Go inside and keep an eye on the chocolate cake."

He gave a booming laugh and left them alone.

Jordan took her in her arms. "Your song called me, and I'll hear it till I leave this life."

The kiss was a promise of acceptance, understanding, and the depth of love there weren't words for. It was desire, pleasure, and adventure, and they'd make the most of every moment.

About the Author

Brey Willows is a longtime editor and writer. When she's not running a social enterprise working with marginalized communities on writing projects, she's editing other people's writing or doing her own. She lives in the middle of England with her partner and fellow author and spends entirely too much time exploring castles and ancient ruins while bemoaning the rain.

Books Available from Bold Strokes Books

A Fairer Tomorrow by Kathleen Knowles. For Maddie Weeks and Gerry Stern, the Second World War brought them together, but the end of the war might rip them apart. (978-1-63555-874-6)

Holiday Hearts by Diana Day-Admire and Lyn Cole. Opposites attract during Christmastime chaos in Kansas City. (978-1-63679-128-9)

Changing Majors by Ana Hartnett Reichardt. Beyond a love, beyond a coming-out, Bailey Sullivan discovers what lies beyond the shame and self-doubt imposed on her by traditional Southern ideals. (978-1-63679-081-7)

Fresh Grave in Grand Canyon by Lee Patton. The age-old Grand Canyon becomes more and more ominous as a group of volunteers fight to survive alone in nature and uncover a murderer among them. (978-1-63679-047-3)

Highland Whirl by Anna Larner. Opposites attract in the Scottish Highlands, when feisty Alice Campbell falls for city-girl-about-town Roxanne Barns. (978-1-63555-892-0)

Humbug by Amanda Radley. With the corporate Christmas party in jeopardy, CEO Rosalind Caldwell hires Christmas Girl Ellie Pearce as her personal assistant. The only problem is, Ellie isn't a PA, has never planned a party, and develops a ridiculous crush on her totally intimidating new boss. (978-1-63555-965-1)

On the Rocks by Georgia Beers. Schoolteacher Vanessa Martini makes no apologies for her dating checklist, and newly single mom Grace Chapman ticks all Vanessa's Do Not Date boxes. Of course, they're never going to fall in love. (978-1-63555-989-7)

Song of Serenity by Brey Willows. Arguing with the muse of music and justice is complicated, falling in love with her even more so. (978-1-63679-015-2)

The Christmas Proposal by Lisa Moreau. Stranded together in a Christmas village on a snowy mountain, Grace and Bridget face their past and question their dreams for the future. (978-1-63555-648-3)

The Infinite Summer by Morgan Lee Miller. While spending the summer with her dad in a small beach town, Remi Brenner falls for Harper Hebert and accidentally finds herself tangled up in an intense restaurant rivalry between her famous stepmom and her first love. (978-1-63555-969-9)

Wisdom by Jesse J. Thoma. When Sophia and Reggie are chosen for the governor's new community design team and tasked with tackling substance abuse and mental health issues, battle lines are drawn even as sparks fly. (978-1-63555-886-9)

A Convenient Arrangement by Aurora Rey and Jaime Clevenger. Cuffing season has come for lesbians, and for Jess Archer and Cody Dawson, their convenient arrangement becomes anything but. (978-1-63555-818-0)

An Alaskan Wedding by Nance Sparks. The last thing either Andrea or Riley expects is to bump into the one who broke her heart fifteen years ago, but when they meet at the welcome party, their feelings come rushing back. (978-1-63679-053-4)

Beulah Lodge by Cathy Dunnell. It's 1874, and newly engaged Ruth Mallowes is set on marriage and life as a missionary…until she falls in love with the housemaid at Beulah Lodge. (978-1-63679-007-7)

Gia's Gems by Toni Logan. When Lindsey Speyer discovers that popular travel columnist Gia Williams is a complete fake and threatens to expose her, blackmail has never been so sexy. (978-1-63555-917-0)

Holiday Wishes & Mistletoe Kisses by M. Ullrich. Four holidays, four couples, four chances to make their wishes come true. (978-1-63555-760-2)

Love By Proxy by Dena Blake. Tess has a secret crush on her best friend, Sophie, so the last thing she wants is to help Sophie fall in love with someone else, but how can she stand in the way of her happiness? (978-1-63555-973-6)

Loyalty, Love, & Vermouth by Eric Peterson. A comic valentine to a gay man's family of choice, including the ones with cold noses and four paws. (978-1-63555-997-2)

Marry Me by Melissa Brayden. Allison Hale attempts to plan the wedding of the century to a man who could save her family's business, if only she wasn't falling for her wedding planner, Megan Kinkaid. (978-1-63555-932-3)

Pathway to Love by Radclyffe. Courtney Valentine is looking for a woman exactly like Ben—smart, sexy, and not in the market for anything serious. All she has to do is convince Ben that sex-without-strings is the perfect pathway to pleasure. (978-1-63679-110-4)

Sweet Surprise by Jenny Frame. Flora and Mac never thought they'd ever see each other again, but when Mac opens up her barber shop right next to Flora's sweet shop, their connection comes roaring back. (978-1-63679-001-5)

The Edge of Yesterday by CJ Birch. Easton Gray is sent from the future to save humanity from technological disaster. When she's forced to target the woman she's falling in love with, can Easton do what's needed to save humanity? (978-1-63679-025-1)

The Scout and the Scoundrel by Barbara Ann Wright. With unexpected danger surrounding them, Zara and Roni are stuck between duty and survival, with little room for exploring their feelings, especially love. (978-1-63555-978-1)

Bury Me in Shadows by Greg Herren. College student Jake Chapman is forced to spend the summer at his dying grandmother's home and soon finds danger from long-buried family secrets. (978-1-63555-993-4)

Can't Leave Love by Kimberly Cooper Griffin. Sophia and Pru have no intention of falling in love, but sometimes love happens when and where you least expect it. (978-1-636790041-1)

Free Fall at Angel Creek by Julie Tizard. Detective Dee Rawlings and aircraft accident investigator Dr. River Dawson use conflicting methods to find answers when a plane goes missing, while overcoming surprising threats, and discovering an unlikely chance at love. (978-1-63555-884-5)

Love's Compromise by Cass Sellars. For Piper Holthaus and Brook Myers, will professional dreams and past baggage stop two hearts from realizing they are meant for each other? (978-1-63555-942-2)

Not All a Dream by Sophia Kell Hagin. Hester has lost the woman she loved and the world has descended into relentless dark and cold. But giving up will have to wait when she stumbles upon people who help her survive. (978-1-63679-067-1)

Protecting the Lady by Amanda Radley. If Eve Webb had known she'd be protecting royalty, she'd never have taken the job as bodyguard, but as the threat to Lady Katherine's life draws closer, she'll do whatever it takes to save her, and may just lose her heart in the process. (978-1-63679-003-9)

The Secrets of Willowra by Kadyan. A family saga of three women, their homestead called Willowra in the Australian outback, and the secrets that link them all. (978-1-63679-064-0)

Trial by Fire by Carsen Taite. When prosecutor Lennox Roy and public defender Wren Bishop become fierce adversaries in a headline-grabbing arson case, their attraction ignites a passion that leads them both to question their assumptions about the law, the truth, and each other. (978-1-63555-860-9)

Turbulent Waves by Ali Vali. Kai Merlin and Vivien Palmer plan their future together as hostile forces make their own plans to destroy what they have, as well as all those they love. (978-1-63679-011-4)

Unbreakable by Cari Hunter. When Dr. Grace Kendal is forced at gunpoint to help an injured woman, she is dragged into a nightmare where nothing is quite as it seems, and their lives aren't the only ones on the line. (978-1-63555-961-3)

Veterinary Surgeon by Nancy Wheelton. When dangerous drugs are stolen from the veterinary clinic, Mitch investigates and Kay becomes a suspect. As pride and professions clash, love seems impossible. (978-1-63679-043-5)

A Different Man by Andrew L. Huerta. This diverse collection of stories chronicling the challenges of gay life at various ages shines a light on the progress made and the progress still to come. (978-1-63555-977-4)

All That Remains by Sheri Lewis Wohl. Johnnie and Shantel might have to risk their lives—and their love—to stop a werewolf intent on killing. (978-1-63555-949-1)

Beginner's Bet by Fiona Riley. Phenom luxury Realtor Ellison Gamble has everything, except a family to share it with, so when a mix-up brings youthful Katie Crawford into her life, she bets the house on love. (978-1-63555-733-6)

Dangerous Without You by Lexus Grey. Throughout their senior year in high school, Aspen, Remington, Denna, and Raleigh face challenges in life and romance that they never expect. (978-1-63555-947-7)

Desiring More by Raven Sky. In this collection of steamy stories, a rich variety of lovers find themselves desiring more, more from a lover, more from themselves, and more from life. (978-1-63679-037-4)

Jordan's Kiss by Nanisi Barrett D'Arnuck. After losing everything in a fire, Jordan Phelps joins a small lounge band and meets pianist Morgan Sparks, who lights another blaze, this time in Jordan's heart. (978-1-63555-980-4)

Late City Summer by Jeanette Bears. Forced together for her wedding, Emily Stanton and Kate Alessi navigate their lingering passion for one another against the backdrop of New York City and World War II, and a summer romance they left behind. (978-1-63555-968-2)

Love and Lotus Blossoms by Anne Shade. On her path to self-acceptance and true passion, Janesse will risk everything—and possibly everyone—she loves. (978-1-63555-985-9)

Love in the Limelight by Ashley Moore. Marion Hargreaves, the finest actress of her generation, and Jessica Carmichael, the world's biggest pop star, rediscover each other twenty years after an ill-fated affair. (978-1-63679-051-0)

Suspecting Her by Mary P. Burns. Complications ensue when Erin O'Connor falls for top real estate saleswoman Catherine Williams while investigating racism in the real estate industry; the fallout could end their chance at happiness. (978-1-63555-960-6)

Two Winters by Lauren Emily Whalen. A modern YA retelling of Shakespeare's *The Winter's Tale* about birth, death, Catholic school, improv comedy, and the healing nature of time. (978-1-63679-019-0)

Busy Ain't the Half of It by Frederick Smith and Chaz Lamar Cruz. Elijah and Justin seek happily-ever-afters in LA, but are they too busy to notice happiness when it's there? (978-1-63555-944-6)

Calumet by Ali Vali. Jaxon Lavigne and Iris Long had a forbidden small-town romance that didn't last, and the consequences of that love will be uncovered fifteen years later at their high school reunion. (978-1-63555-900-2)

Her Countess to Cherish by Jane Walsh. London Society's material girl realizes there is more to life than diamonds when she falls in love with a non-binary bluestocking. (978-1-63555-902-6)

Hot Days, Heated Nights by Renee Roman. When Cole and Lee meet, instant attraction quickly flares into uncontrollable passion, but their connection might be short lived as Lee's identity is tied to her life in the city. (978-1-63555-888-3)

Never Be the Same by MA Binfield. Casey meets Olivia and sparks fly in this opposites attract romance that proves love can be found in the unlikeliest places. (978-1-63555-938-5)

Quiet Village by Eden Darry. Something not quite human is stalking Collie and her niece, and she'll be forced to work with undercover reporter Emily Lassiter if they want to get out of Hyam alive. (978-1-63555-898-2)

Shaken or Stirred by Georgia Beers. Bar owner Julia Martini and home health aide Savannah McNally attempt to weather the storms brought on by a mysterious blogger trashing the bar, family feuds they knew nothing about, and way too much advice from way too many relatives. (978-1-63555-928-6)

The Fiend in the Fog by Jess Faraday. Can four people on different trajectories work together to save the vulnerable residents of East London from the terrifying fiend in the fog before it's too late? (978-1-63555-514-1)

The Marriage Masquerade by Toni Logan. A no strings attached marriage scheme to inherit a Maui B&B uncovers unexpected attractions and a dark family secret. (978-1-63555-914-9)